E.V. ADAMSON

Murder Grove

HarperCollins*Publishers*

HarperCollins*Publishers*
1 London Bridge Street,
London SE1 9GF

www.harpercollins.co.uk

HarperCollins*Publishers*
1st Floor, Watermarque Building, Ringsend Road
Dublin 4, Ireland

Published by HarperCollins*Publishers* Ltd 2022

1

A catalogue copy of this book is available from the British Library.

ISBN: 9780008439309 (EB)
ISBN: 9780008439293 (PB)

Typeset in Sabon LT Std by Palimpsest Book Production Limited,
Falkirk, Stirlingshire

Printed and Bound in the UK using 100% Renewable
Electricity at CPI Group (UK) Ltd

MIX
Paper from
responsible sources
FSC® C007454

To all my Spanish friends

Prologue

MIA

August

We are standing in the olive grove hoping to find traces of the dead. The light shade of the perfumed trees protects us from the glare of the early morning sun. Blanca, dressed in her customary mourning clothes, her face as wrinkled as a grape left out to dry in the summer heat, grips my hand.

Despite her old age, she is strong. Her watery dark brown eyes show a determination to uncover the truth. She rasps out a sibilant whisper in Spanish, 'Mia, my dear, with the grace of God, we will find her today.'

She doesn't want revenge, she tells me again. All she needs are the remains of her mother so she can gather her bones together and give her the proper burial she deserves. It must have been so lonely for her, Blanca says, her poor mother shot like a dog and left to die in this stretch of dry land near the shadow of Devil's Head.

I look up at the grotesque rock formation that juts out above us and try to make out the supposedly demonic features, but a fragment of memory from the previous night threatens to overwhelm me. I sense Blanca looking at me. She asks if I'm all right and I tell her that she isn't to worry about me. I'm here to support *her*.

Her eyes scan the ground and the two-foot-deep trench dug by a mini JCB yesterday. Her mother has lain here for the past eighty-one years, her grave unmarked apart from the flowers brought by Blanca, blooms that would often be snatched or destroyed by one of the descendants of *los asesinos* – the murderers. Yet Blanca would not allow these small acts of barbarism to interrupt her mourning and, on finding the flowers missing or the petals macerated, she would turn up here on the edge of the once-abandoned village with a fresh supply.

The volunteers, masked and wearing gloves, pour a final cup of coffee from a shared flask, and say something I can't hear. They go to the van and take out the tools they need: a couple of wheelbarrows, mattocks, pickaxes, buckets, shovels, a selection of brushes, large rulers and measuring squares, coloured flags, and various markers for the dead. As the archaeologists begin to work, I help Blanca into a folding chair. She wants to watch every step of the process.

She tells me that she will never forget the look in her mother's eyes as the soldiers dragged her away or the terrible noises that came from her throat. It was worse than any *matanza*, the annual killing and butchery of the family pig. She has not seen her mother since that terrible day when she was five years old. She is, as she told me, alone before God: she has a great-nephew she is close to, her younger brother died years back, and she was never able to have children herself. We sit and listen to the sound of birds and the harsh strike of metal on earth. The soil here is rich in gypsum and the translucent crystals glint in the sunlight. A light breeze plays through the branches of the olive trees, whispering a tale of past horrors.

'*La pobre*,' says Blanca, looking down into the earth. 'For the best part of life you've lain underground. I've been in mourning since the day they took you.'

I grip her hand again as the old woman's jaw works backwards and forwards. We've only known one another for a matter of months, but I feel as protective towards her as if she were my own grandmother.

'We will give her the burial she deserves,' I say in Spanish. 'And you can place flowers on her grave as often as you like.'

'I hope they find her,' she replies. 'Once they find her, I'd be happy to die.'

Before arriving in Spain a few months back with my boyfriend Rich, I'd had an intellectual understanding of the meaning of death in Spanish culture. I'd done a degree in the language, studied the literature and painting, and my dissertation was on the concept of the *duende* in Lorca. 'In Spain the dead are more alive than the dead of any other place in the world,' the poet had written. 'Their profile wounds like the edge of a barber's razor.' Now, as the sharp blade of a pickaxe slams into the earth, I'm reminded of these words, and can feel the reality that here, in this dry corner of Spain, the dead are very much alive.

The men and women from the Association for the Recovery

of Historical Memory (ARMH) believe there could be as many as fifteen bodies here, victims of the Francoist militia during the Spanish Civil War. Blanca's mother, a leftist, was persecuted by the *falangistas* for her political views. In July 1938, her head was shaved and she had been paraded through the village before being shot by the soldiers and, along with a group of other 'troublemakers' and 'communists', pushed into a makeshift trench. Her name was Esperanza – Hope. The irony is almost too much to bear.

With each bucketful of earth emptied into the wheelbarrow I'm convinced that Blanca can sense her mother's spirit rising from the ground. At times her eyes glaze over and it seems she's transported back into the past, enveloped by memories of being held within her mother's embrace and smelling the milky warmth of her skin. She whispers to herself, words she wished her mother could hear: lost dreams, lost causes, lost land, lost peace, lost spirit.

Just then there's a call from one of the archaeologists, Diego. He's standing behind an ancient olive tree, its trunk twisted and split. He says he's found something. But there's something about his voice, its panicked edge, that sounds out of place on an archaeological site, even one that has a mission to dig up the dead.

'Over here – quick!' he shouts.

'Is it my mother?' Blanca cries. She doesn't understand, she says. She was always told that her mother's remains lay in a trench that ran parallel to the road. But perhaps that information was wrong; perhaps she does lie in the shade of the old olive tree. Have they found her mother? '*Madre, ya voy.*'

Blanca tries to push herself out of her chair, but I tell her to stay where she is. I will go and check. The volunteers throw down their tools and gather round the tree. It's then, just as I'm letting go of Blanca's hand, that I hear a scream. It's one of the younger girls in the team. Perhaps she's new, I tell myself, and it's the first time she's seen a skeleton. But she screams again, a high-pitched sound that splits the morning air. I see the girl staggering back, falling down onto the ground, being sick into the dry scrub.

'What is it?' I call out.

I take care not to disturb the trench and rush over to the olive tree. There, in the shade of its enormous branches, the volunteers recoil from what lies there. This is no desiccated skeleton, long buried in the earth, but a fully fleshed body, twisted and bloody.

I can't comprehend what I'm seeing. I try to breathe, but I feel like I'm suffocating. I steady myself by the tree. Another memory from the night before flashes into my consciousness. I'm here in the olive grove. I'm shouting. I feel possessed by something that has been building within me all year. I . . .

Diego interrupts my thoughts as he explains how he realized that the cooler bag full of lunch things and water bottles needed to be in the shade. He went to drop off the bag in a nook behind the olive tree when he saw something strange out of the corner of his eye. It looked as though a clutch of fingers were growing from the ground like strange, etiolated mushrooms. He did a double take, went to have a closer look and was horrified to discover that there was a hand pushing through the earth. He quickly brushed off the thin layer of topsoil and unearthed the corpse.

He crouches down and checks the pulse for the second time. He looks up and shakes his head.

'There's no hope,' he says. 'They're cold, been dead for hours.'

I hear someone talking to me. 'Mia, Mia – are you all right?'

I try to speak, but I can't seem to form the words. I feel cut off from the world. I hear Blanca calling my name, asking to see her mother, and I return to her side, feel the sharp edges of her fingers on my arms. She's crying, demanding to see the body.

'What have you seen?' she cries. 'Did you see her body? Is it Esperanza?'

I kneel down by her chair and take her bony hands in mine.

'It's not – not your mother,' I manage to say. 'It's . . .' But my voice fails me. I can't say the name because that would make the horror, the impossibility of what I've just witnessed, real.

I hear Diego telling one of the other volunteers that they will have to call the police. Also, they will have to close down the dig, at least for the time being. It seems as though the death was quite recent, he says. He's no expert, but it's likely it occurred in the last twelve hours. The body has sustained some significant injuries to the head, he adds. There's dried blood in the hair, brain matter on the ground.

It looks as though this could be murder.

1

MIA

February, six months before

A new country. A new beginning. Just what we need, says Rich again, as we pass over the French border into Spain. I look out of the rain-streaked window and see the Pyrenees obscured by snow clouds. I turn to Rich and watch him concentrating at the wheel. The driving conditions have been awful all day – spray from lorries hitting the wind-screen, reducing visibility to zero for a terrifying second or so – but this does not seem to faze Rich. He directs the Saab like an arrow on course to meet its target.

He's been like this since the day I met him at university. Incredibly focused. Objective. A left-hand side of the brain kind of person. Apart from his obvious physical appeal – with his fine features and slim, athletic build, he's a good-looking guy – some of my friends on my Spanish course thought we were just too different to make the relationship work long-term.

They didn't understand that he was just the kind of man I thought I needed. He had his feet firmly planted in reality – a physicist who believed in evidence, measurements, laws of nature. He would be able to tell me the reason why the tide came in and why the stars didn't drop out of the sky. Matter, its behaviour and motion through time, he would inform me, is the most beautiful thing in the world. Gravity. Electricity. Kinetics. Mechanics. Thermodynamics. His world was the very definition of dependability. He also told me that he'd always protect me. He was a martial arts nut. Black belt. He knew all the techniques to disarm someone. Could he kill someone, I'd asked? He'd nodded confidently, as if it was the easiest thing in the world.

'Are you looking forward to it? Val Verde?' he asks, brushing a strand of his long ginger hair from his face. 'It's a great place, you know.'

'I can't wait,' I reply, not quite feeling the enthusiasm the words suggest. 'It will be like an adventure.'

'I know you had your doubts about it all, but after . . . after everything that went on, I think it will be good for you. Good for us.'

It took courage to give up our jobs in London – I was a Spanish teacher in a big comprehensive in east London, Rich a consultant in solar engineering. But Rich was right, it was the best thing to do after what we'd experienced.

I remember it was a sweltering hot day towards the end of the summer term. There was a playful atmosphere as the school began its preparations to close for the year. I was in a local café on my afternoon off, putting together a light-hearted

8

quiz to test my students' knowledge of Spanish-speaking celebrities when I got a text on my phone. It was from Rich. He'd been looking at Facebook and had come across a post about a girl from my school who had died. At the same moment my phone rang. It was the headmistress, Mrs Beaumann. As soon as I heard her voice I knew there was something wrong.

'Mia, I'm afraid I'm calling with some very bad news,' she said. 'It's concerning one of our students, one of *your* students. It's Emily Thomas. Apparently, she just stepped out in front of a bus at a busy junction.'

The news hit me in the stomach. I had a soft spot for seventeen-year-old Emily and I'd been talking to her – what? – only an hour or so before. I'd bumped into her outside the school gates and I'd walked with her through the streets of Hackney – she was going back to her parents' house and I was heading for the café. Our conversation centred on her plans for the future: she was excited about the possibility of training to be an actress or a dancer.

The headmistress didn't know the circumstances of the death at that moment, but soon rumours started to circulate that it hadn't been an accident. I knew that she was a vegan and that she refused to fly, but Emily's friends talked of her worries about climate change and her anxieties about how we only had twelve years left before the rise in temperatures made the world uninhabitable. She couldn't imagine a future for the planet and some people were thinking that perhaps that's why she had decided to end it all.

Yet I couldn't believe it had been suicide. She was a feisty character, full of life; she had dark hair, dark eyes, and indeed there was something Mediterranean about her spirit. She just wasn't the kind of girl to end it all. Of course, I wracked my

9

brain for any signs of depression or hints of unhappiness during our last conversation. Was it something I'd said to her? Had I responded in a way that she thought was negative or problematic? We hadn't mentioned the environment or climate change. Perhaps not addressing the issue had been the problem? However, no matter how hard I played back that conversation – back and forth, on a never-ending loop – I couldn't come up with anything that could explain Emily's actions. I was left in a kind of limbo, asking myself why.

Rich and I had been talking about leaving London to do something different for years – it was one of those perennial conversations we had whenever we went away – but the shocking news of Emily Thomas's death made the dream more of a necessity. We had to act and we had to act *fast*, Rich had said. We were in our mid-thirties and if we didn't change our lives now, then when would we? It was up to us to do our bit, he added. It might not mean anything in the larger scheme of things – what with carbon emissions rising and all the rest of it – but as everyone kept saying, there's no planet B.

And so the plan to pack in our jobs – and our lives in London – was born. When Rich's mother, Marianne, died in August and he inherited her house, *La Casa de la Luz*, southern Spain seemed like the most natural destination. After all, we could rent out our flat in Hackney and the place in Almería would cost next to nothing to run due to its array of solar panels. The village, Val Verde, was off grid and full of inter-esting people from all around the world. Rich made a few quick trips out there to make sure all the paperwork was in order, and we couldn't wait for our new lives to begin in February, just when England was at its most miserable. Although I never bothered with social media, Rich announced our new adventure with a picture of the spectacularly beautiful valley on Twitter and a quick post, after which he deleted his account. Of course, both of us would have our phones – the house doesn't have a landline – but it would be great for him to step away from social media because the platforms only seemed to make him more angry.

'And if it doesn't work out in Val Verde,' says Rich as we continue to speed along the motorway, 'we can always return to London and pick up our lives where we left them.'

'Yes, you're right. But do you think you'll miss anything about London?'

'What, the pollution? The ridiculously high cost of living? Or the sweaty armpits on the Tube?'

I smile back at him.

'And it will be perfect for you,' he continues. 'You're always complaining that you never got to have a proper conversation in Spanish.'

Again, he's right. Although I loved teaching, my capacity to communicate in a language I adored – sometimes a language I dreamed in – had been limited.

'And it will be good for you,' I reply. 'It might give you the opportunity to . . . well . . . to finally learn Spanish.'

This is a touchy subject for Rich, as it's tied up with his parents' bitter divorce and the conflicted feelings he has towards his mother.

'Perhaps,' he says, running a hand through his hair.

'How will you feel . . . going back there?'

'What? To *Casa de la Luz*? I'll be fine. After all, the thing that held me back – namely, Marianne – has gone now.' He calls her by her first name, rarely Mother. 'She's out of my life.'

'She can't have been that bad.'

As Rich moves the car into the middle lane, his fingers grip the steering wheel and a darkness hardens his grey eyes. 'Let's not talk about her. Not now, not today.'

'Okay,' I say, stretching across to place my hand on his knee.

He smiles, and for a moment the thoughts of the past melt away. From what he's told me of his mother she was a selfish, narcissistic woman. She'd been an actress, a great beauty in her day – ice queen blonde hair, cat-like green eyes, amazing figure – who resented the fact that she'd married young. When she got pregnant – with her only child, Rich – she blamed her husband, James Ellis, a successful architect, for ruining her career and curtailing her freedom. She hated being a mother and had taken to drink. The situation had got so bad that she soon started to neglect him. She went on terrible vodka binges, and one time when his father was out she left a candle burning after collapsing in bed. It had been up to five-year-old Rich – who had been in his bedroom when he smelt smoke – to try to get help. Luckily, no one had been hurt that day, but the incident led to James getting custody of his son. James, who brought Rich up in Wandsworth, wanted to settle the matter in a civilized manner, and so he had paid Marianne a large amount of money to leave, money which she used to travel to Almería, where she'd once made a film. She'd settled in Val Verde, already a village known for its ragbag collection of wild spirits and bohemians, where she restored an old *cortijo*, *La Casa de la Luz*.

'I still can't believe I've never seen it,' I say. 'The house, I mean.'

'Unfortunately, that would have involved a visit to see Marianne, and I didn't want to inflict her on you. Anyway, I don't want to talk about her.'

12

His tone is strained and I don't pursue the subject. We lapse into silence, each of us staring into the gloom of the road, and I think about the sad circumstances surrounding Marianne's death. She had been found in her house after going on what seemed like an epic binge. Empty bottles of gin and vodka were discovered by her corpse. She'd been suffering from cirrhosis of the liver and Rich had told me that her once angelic face had become bloated out of recognition. She knew that if she wanted to have a chance of living she would have to stop drinking, but Rich said that she loved the bottle more than she loved life, certainly more than she'd ever loved him. He'd flown out for the funeral in August, while I'd stayed behind in London – although I'd offered to travel to Spain with him, he told me that it would be better if he went alone.

Rich starts to fiddle with the radio, but there's no reception and a series of jagged noises spits from the sound system.

'For fuck's sake,' he hisses as he repeatedly hits the search button to find a station.

He focuses on the radio and in that split second, just as I'm about to say I think he should concentrate on the road and I'll find something for us to listen to, a lorry – a slow, lumbering thing – pulls out in front of us.

'Rich!' I shout, feeling adrenaline flood through my body like a terrible poison.

The back of the lorry looms so close I can see the traces of rust mottled across its black paintwork like a rush of cancerous cells. Rich hits the brakes, presses hard on the horn. I slam my feet down on the floor of the car in an instinctive but useless reaction. Rich swears again. I don't dare look at him. I don't want to die here. Like this. Just as we are on the cusp of trying to make a new life for ourselves.

I see things from the past flash into my present. No, it can't be like this. I can't have my life end here. I've done so much to win a chance of happiness, I won't allow it. I hear the screech of brakes, the smell of burning. A wave of water from the lorry hits our windscreen. We are so surrounded by water, it feels as though we could be falling into a lake or a river. The windscreen wipers, on top speed, clear the screen, before another wall of water hits us. I feel my jaw clenching, locking, my teeth gritting themselves together.

I ready myself for the impact. I feel like saying something to Rich, but I can't get the words out. My tongue is paralysed. The car continues on its seemingly inevitable path. Only a few minutes ago, I'd been thinking about how Rich controlled the Saab like an arrow on course to meet its target. But I never thought the target would be this.

I close my eyes, expecting the collision, the impact of metal on flesh, the feeling of glass shredding my skin. The noise of the crash. The smell of burning rubber, the rank aroma of blood. Something threatens to rip me back in time. But then, when nothing happens, I dare to open my eyes again. The lorry is still in front of us. We are still behind it, but with what looks like only a couple of inches to spare.

Rich checks his mirrors, indicates and pulls out into the fast lane.

'Fucking idiot could have killed us,' he snarls. He speeds past the lorry, pressing his horn as he does so.

2

RICH

It's almost dusk by the time we reach the village. I would have liked to have arrived in daylight so Mia could have seen the contrast between the dry, almost lunar landscape of the hills, and the slash of green that runs through the bottom of the valley.

I spent the final part of the trip telling her again about the geography of Val Verde: how rainwater percolates through the gypsum rock beds into underground pools before rising to the surface, the source of the small river. Unlike the majority of *ramblas*, or dry riverbeds, which only fill with water during one of the heavy but infrequent bursts of rainfall, this *rio* flows all year round. And although you can't drink it – you have to go to one of the local *fuentes* to collect drinking water – the householders pump water from the stream into tanks, while the gardeners use it to irrigate their strips of land. It seems as though vegetables have been grown here for hundreds of years, and it's thought the irrigation line that runs through Val Verde dates back to Moorish times.

As I relate this to Mia, I get the sense that she's not listening. Perhaps it was the incident with the lorry that upset her – that idiot could have caused a serious accident – but she seems to be in one of her moods again. I've learnt that it's usually best not to try to talk her out of it, otherwise there's a tendency for her to slip back into a black hole. Carry on as normal, that's always been my motto. And it seems to work. After a few hours of silence, when I don't know what the hell has been going through her mind, she'll emerge as if nothing has happened.

'So this is it,' I say as I direct the Saab into the communal car park at the edge of the village. I find a space next to a beaten-up, mustard-coloured camper van. Its back doors are open slightly, through which I can see movement. I turn to Mia. 'Welcome to Val Verde.'

I keep the lights on as we get out of the car and watch as Mia gazes at the jagged cliffs around her. There's an empty quality to her ice-blue eyes.

'I think we'll unpack the bulk of the car in daylight tomorrow,' I say. 'And we can meet some of the neighbours then, too.'

I swing my rucksack over my shoulder and, just as I'm about to start wheeling Mia's suitcase down the track, I smell a whiff of marijuana on the night air. The aroma immediately seduces me, forcing me to relax after the long journey. It also makes me desperate for a smoke.

'*Buenas noches, mis amigos,*' says a male voice. I turn back and see a figure standing by the camper van.

'Hi,' I say.

16

'You're English?' he asks. 'Looking for the eco-charity? Desert Shoots?'

'Yes – and no. I'm Rich, and this is Mia. We're actually going to be living here. In *Casa de la Luz*. Do you know it?'

'Is that the big house where . . .' he trails off. 'Cool, I'm Hans,' he adds, raising a spliff to his lips.

I breathe in the air, greedy for a quick hit. I almost feel like reaching out and grabbing it from his fingers. I sense Mia's eyes on me.

'If you need anything,' he says, stressing the last word, as if he can read my mind, 'just let me know.'

'Will do, thanks,' I reply, turning away from him. I feel a bit embarrassed as I start to wheel Mia's bag, hoping Hans will understand that it doesn't belong to me. 'It's different to Hackney, right?' I say when we're out of earshot of Hans. 'Everyone uses wheelbarrows to fetch and carry stuff here.'

I hear Mia's footsteps behind me as we make our way past the whitewashed houses silhouetted against the darkening sky.

'It's difficult to see at the moment, but this is Payton and Bill's house up here on the left. She's been looking after the house. I told them we didn't want any kind of welcoming party. I knew you wouldn't be keen on that idea. Next on the left is the charity house, where the people from Desert Shoots hang out. They're probably enjoying one of their communal suppers right now. They have a constant flow of new people from all over the world, but they're usually a nice bunch. Oh, and be careful; down to your right is a sheer drop – below are the terraces of vegetables and fruit trees. I'll give you a proper tour tomorrow.'

We walk past another of the charity houses, and outside it

17

stands the figure of a woman I don't recognize. '*Hola, buenas,*' she says, words I echo back to her. We carry on past the crystal path that leads up to the cluster of houses at the top of the village, and continue down the *camino* towards *La Casa de la Luz*. I stop outside a pair of enormous wooden doors and tell Mia that we've arrived. I put down the bags, hook my hand inside a circular hole and slide the doors back. I see the outline of the palm tree in the courtyard, the lion's mouth of the fountain, which is running dry at the moment. A blast of icy February wind cuts its way across the terrace, whipping Mia's scarf into the air.

'Let's go inside, we'll soon warm up,' I say, taking her by the hand. I feel the edge of the key in my pocket, but I'm pretty sure I won't need it as Payton will have left the house open. 'Val Verde is the kind of place where people don't need to lock their homes.' This isn't inner-city London, where we were always vigilant. One of Mia's rituals was the nightly check of the locks on the door and the windows. And who could blame her? London was rife with robberies, rapes, knife attacks. That's one of the reasons it felt so good to leave.

With my free hand I carry her suitcase across the terrace. I open the door for Mia, switch on the light and gesture for her to step inside.

3

MIA

I smell woodsmoke in the air and through a decorative archway I see the flames of a fire licking the glass of a chunky wood-burner. I immediately go and stand by the fire and tell myself I need to relax. The incident with the lorry had obviously put me on edge. But Rich had saved us, saved *me*, and now we're here in our new home. And what a home. Whenever I asked Rich to describe *La Casa de la Luz* he always ended up talking about his mother and making himself angry, so in the end I stopped. I hadn't pictured it as grand as this because he'd always said it was an eco-house, something I imagined being only one or two steps up from a teepee or a yurt.

As I look around I take in the clean, tiled floors, the ceilings made from bamboo canes, the white plaster walls, and the expensive furniture that wouldn't look out of place in a Georgian country pile. The walls are decorated with old Spanish paintings, landscape sketches, portraits of princes and paupers, and a set of still lives of fruit in varying stages of decay. It's clear that Marianne had exquisite – but quite expensive – taste. I walk through some double doors to a library, complete with desk, and then another set of doors which takes me into an enormous space that serves both as a kitchen and a living-dining room. There's a table large enough to seat ten, a couple of squidgy sofas, and a vaulted roof with exposed wooden beams which Rich tells me were hewn from a local eucalyptus tree. At the back of the house is a larder and storeroom and finally an enormous bathroom with marble bath and sink.

'It's amazing, Rich, like a really proper house,' I say, as I wander back into the dining room.

'Of course it is, my mother needed her creature comforts.' There's that familiar note of bitterness in his voice which he uses whenever he talks about Marianne.

Soon after meeting Rich, I'd done my own research on her. Whenever I had the flat to myself I'd watch some of her old films online, something I kept hidden from Rich. In her prime, her beauty was unreal. Her skin was translucent, flawless, and she had that ability to compel you to gaze at her, lose yourself in her. Critics had written about her possessing that almost undefinable trait – star quality – and it was true. Whenever she was in a scene, she really did light up the screen. I'd rather think of her like this than the sad, tragic figure of Rich's recollection.

'Anyway, I love it,' I say. 'And I love you.' I worry the words sound slightly forced. I walk up to him and put my hands around his neck. 'Sorry for being in a mood earlier. It was . . .'

'It's fine, I understand,' he says. 'What do you say we explore upstairs?' He points to a spiral staircase in the middle of the room. He leads me by the hand up the stairs and flicks on a switch to reveal another sitting room, with a floor-to-ceiling window. The view from here is spectacular, he says, something I'll see for myself the next morning. He tells me that there are three bedrooms that lead off either side of this room, but informs me that he doubts I'll want to sleep in the largest one. This is where his mother died. He opens the doors, pushes a light switch and the first thing I see is a wall covered with multiple reproductions of Marianne's face. The effect is dizzying.

'I told you she was a narcissist,' he says.

'She really was amazing looking,' I reply as I walk up to one of the larger black and white photos, an image of Marianne in a short skirt and black boots that looks as though it had been taken somewhere like the King's Road in London.

'I certainly don't want to go to sleep with that face looking down on me, do you? It gives me the creeps.

'In fact, I don't know why she kept these old shots. It must have been bloody painful for her to see herself looking like this, especially towards the end. Maybe she was a masochist too? No wonder she drank herself to death.'

I wish he wouldn't talk about her like this, but I don't tell him what I think. Rich walks over to the bed, an enormous affair covered with highly patterned throws that look as though they're from Morocco, and pillows the colour of the darkest red wine.

'Is that where . . . ?'

'Payton's done a nice job of tidying it all up, but yeah – this is where they found her. Payton and Bill. They told me what happened when I came over for the funeral. Marianne was supposed to drop in on Payton for a cup of coffee and when she didn't turn up, she got worried and came over. The door wasn't locked – as I say, nobody locks their houses here – and she let herself in, calling my mother's name. When she didn't hear anything she ran back to get Bill. They found her here on the bed, surrounded by empty bottles, and thought to begin with that she'd just passed out. They were used to Marianne's drinking binges. Of course, her friends had tried to persuade her to stop – and sometimes Marianne did have a few months off – but I suppose the guilt of what she'd done must have caught up with her.'

'Guilt?'

'Yeah – leaving me like she did. I think she never got over it. I think she realized she'd made a huge mistake. It ate away at her soul like acid.' He turns from the bed and takes me in his arms. 'Anyway, enough of the sob story.'

He leads me past an old-fashioned television console, twinned with an ancient VCR, and a bookcase lined with some of Marianne's old films on videotape. We pass back through the upstairs sitting room and enter a set of rooms in the other part of the house. The guest quarters, which share a bathroom, are more spartan and functional: in one room there's a pair of twin beds, and in the other there's a large double bed covered with a duvet encased in a plain white cover, an old wooden wardrobe and chest of drawers, a bookcase and an old mirror spotted with rust.

'The view isn't nearly so nice – it looks out into the street below – but I thought for now it would be better for us to sleep here,' he says. 'We can always move back into my mother's old room once we've cleared out all the photos and paraphernalia – we can put them into storage in the studio outside. Who knows – perhaps we even need to do an exorcism?'

He makes a woo-ing noise like a cartoon ghost, and tries to tickle me under the ribs in an attempt to laugh me into bed, but jokingly I tell him to cut it out. I wriggle free and go and stand over by the window. Just then I think I see a shadow pass by the entrance to the house. I squint to try to get a clearer view. I'm sure there's someone down there by the archway. I'm about to say something to Rich when it melts away into the night.

4

RICH

I get up early and leave Mia sleeping. As I step outside with a coffee, I let the weak morning sunshine caress my face. My first stop is the studio, which contains the batteries and inverter for the top-of-the-range solar power system; the panels themselves are on the roof. I spend half an hour making sure everything is in good working order before walking through the series of olive terraces that drop down to the river below. I listen to the reeds whisper something unknowable to one another. Across the valley I hear a group of people, most likely volunteers from Desert Shoots, working on a stretch of dry land.

It's odd to be back in Val Verde, strange to be at my mother's house. If someone had said to me a year or so ago that I'd be standing here now, in *La Casa de la Luz*, keen to make a new life in this green paradise, I would have laughed in their face. But a lot had happened in the last nine months

24

or so. Emily, that girl at Mia's school, had died, some said by suicide because she couldn't live with the guilt of existing in a world wrecked by climate change. We'd had a wake-up call about the importance of doing something for the environment. Marianne had died and I'd inherited the house. Lots of life shit. And so, in Mia's words, we decided to make the leap into the unknown.

I knew she was less keen than I was to move. She'd be leaving behind her friends, her job, the London that she loved so much. But when I laid it all out in a logical fashion, she had no choice but to agree that this was the best course of action. The rent on our flat would pay the bills. Living here in Val Verde cost next to nothing, as all the energy was self-generated. Although the garden was a mess, once it was cleared and established again we'd be growing most of our produce ourselves, apart from dry goods like lentils, chick peas, flour and oats. In addition to the olive trees, which meant an endless supply of olive oil, we had almonds, grapes, figs, quinces, pomegranates, loquat, oranges and lemons. Imagine a gin and tonic with a slice of lemon grown by your own fair hand, I'd said to Mia – what could beat that? We'd be living a green life, a good life – for real.

I go back inside to make myself another coffee when I catch a glimpse of a paisley print fabric waft through from the dining room into the library. Marianne's old Liberty dressing gown. A memory of her comes back to me. I don't know how old I am; four years old, maybe. Dad had gone away on a work trip and she was supposed to be looking after me. Instead, she'd left me locked in my bedroom while she went out drinking. I'd banged and banged on the door, made myself sick with fear, until finally I'd fallen asleep. I woke up in the dark to hear loud, drunken voices. It was her with a man, but not Dad. I knocked on the door, told her I needed to go to the loo, but she ignored me. I thought I was going to die in that room. The next morning she opened the door wearing the dressing gown. Her face was all puffy from drink, her mascara smudged giving her panda eyes, her red lipstick smeared around her mouth. She took one look at me and saw what I'd done on the floor and slapped me around the face. She said the room smelt of shit, called me a dirty little bastard and ordered me to clean up my mess. When she returned with a cloth and a bucket filled with hot water I told myself that I would no longer call her Mother. I could no longer allow myself to love her. It was too painful. Whatever reserves of love I'd had for her would now be replaced by hate.

Mia returns to the kitchen. She comes over and drapes herself around me and asks me to come back to bed. The sight of the dressing gown – those repeated patterns shaped like elongated tear drops – disgusts me. I push her away, telling her that I'm too busy.

'Rich – what's wrong?' she asks. She looks like a little girl, the black hair of her pixie cut still messy from bed, framing her innocent face.

'I'm sorry.' I can't begin to tell her about the dressing gown. 'It's coming back here – it's full of memories. Not good ones.'

'Do you want to talk about it?'

'No, it'll be fine.'

She raises her eyebrow slightly, a gesture that serves as a silent question: are you absolutely fucking sure? She knows this makes me laugh and today's no different.

'Sorry – what do you say we go on a tour of the village?'

I suggest. 'Payton and Bill didn't want to bother us last night, but I'm sure they'd love us to drop by this morning.'

Ten minutes later she's in the shower. While she's washing I pick up the dressing gown from where she's left it draped across the edge of the bed. My guess is that, when she unpacks her own clothes from the car and begins to wear her own dressing gown, the one I bought her, she won't miss it. I hear her turn the shower off and so I take the dressing gown outside and put it in the bin. I grab a handful of oranges picked by Payton and squeeze some ready for Mia when she comes down.

'It tastes amazing, like sunlight in a glass,' she says, her face lighting up.

'Let me show you the garden – we can walk down through the olive terraces and then along the river and back up to Payton and Bill's house.'

I watch her face as she sees the garden for the first time. Any trace of darkness disappears as she wonders at the lush abundance of the valley which sits in contrast to the dry, parched cliffs of the surrounding landscape.

'I can see why it's called Val Verde,' she says. 'It's like some kind of miracle.'

'I suppose it is.' I take her by the hand as we enter a gate that leads to the circular pool, full of water pumped from the river, and through to the vegetable garden, strips of land overgrown with weeds. 'Apart from this, I'm afraid, which is going to need some work. I reckon I'll have to get some help. And there's the irrigation line to clear out too.'

'I guess your mother had other priorities towards the end of her life.'

I know what her priorities were – drink and herself – but

I keep my opinion to myself. I don't want to do or say anything that will upset Mia any more today. It's important that she settles in and feels happy here. I breathe in the morning air, perfumed by traces of sage and thyme, as Mia begins to ask me again about the residents of the village and their reasons for moving here. I tell her about Payton, who left her native Boston to travel through Europe.

'I think Bill's her second husband, I'm not quite sure, but they met at some rally or demo in Madrid. He's filthy rich – family money, I think – I don't think he's ever worked. They've lived here more than twenty-five years. She's got some great stories about protesting. Anti-nuclear. Oil in the Arctic. The destruction of the Amazon. Copper mines. Fracking. Endangered species. Population control. Seems like she's done it all.'

'Sounds wonderful,' she responds in a half-hearted fashion.

'Anyway, instead of me talking about them, let's go and meet them.'

We take a path up from the river, through the terraces that belong to Desert Shoots, past a stretch of reed beds and a line of compost loos, and through an arboretum back up to the main track. Walking towards us there's a clutch of volunteers, mostly young, skinny types, some with dreadlocks, carrying mattocks, buckets and lengths of freshly cut bamboo. As we pass we nod and say, '*Hola*' – no doubt in time we'll get to know the ones staying in the village on long-term contracts. Although the charity tries to recruit as widely as possible, the truth of the matter is that because the pay is so low – something like one hundred euros a month – the majority of the volunteers and staff come from families which can afford to support them. They belong to that much-mocked gang of

Trustafarians, a label that's been lobbed at me a few times over the years. And I suppose I can't deny it. One of the reasons I fell in love with Mia was because she came from such a different background to my own. She really had it hard – really suffered – but doesn't like to talk about it, which is understandable.

'Here we are,' I say, placing my hand on the small of her back and guiding her towards the white steps that lead up to Payton and Bill's house. 'And don't look so worried – you'll love them.'

5

MIA

'I hope you don't mind,' says Payton, standing at the front door, 'but I've taken the liberty of inviting a few neighbours over – we're sitting up on the roof. I thought it would be easier if everyone came here, just to show you what a friendly bunch of folk we are.' She's an emaciated woman in her fifties, and speaks with an upper-class Boston drawl. 'Now, come on in. We don't bite.'

We pass through an archway festooned with gaudy purple bougainvillea and enter a cool, dark hallway. Bill appears at the doorway – he's an overweight, late-middle-aged man with a reddened, bloated face. As he lunges to kiss me, his sausage fingers linger just a little too long on my shoulder. His breath smells of brandy and it's only just gone ten in the morning.

'Lovely to see you,' he says, in a ridiculously grand voice. I assume he's putting on the accent as a joke, but he continues to sound like one of those buttoned-up BBC newsreaders from the past. 'How was the drive, Rich? Shit weather on the way down, I expect. You must feel relieved to be here. Sunshine!' He lifts his hands above his balding head and parts them, almost as though he has the power to determine the weather himself.

'Yeah, it's great to be here – and thanks again for making up the fire and getting the house ready,' says Rich.

'It's no problem, no problem at all,' says Payton. 'Now, it's out through here and up the staircase at the back. Bill, could you grab the almond milk from the fridge?'

We follow into an interior so dark I can hardly make out its contents and then out into the blinding light and up a metal staircase. 'Mia, I'll show you the house later if you'd like to see around it,' she whispers, as she steps out onto the terrace.

The sun is so intense up here that I have to shield my eyes with my hands; I realize I should have brought my sunglasses. I can see that there is a small group of people sitting around a table, but I can't make out their sex, never mind their features.

'Here, use these,' says Payton, passing me her sunglasses. 'I've got another pair somewhere.' She calls down the stairs to Bill to bring them up for her and a few moments later arrives with them and the jug of almond milk.

'That's so kind,' I say as I slip on the sunglasses.

'So these are our new neighbours, Mia and Rich, who've just moved into the lovely *Casa de la Luz*,' she says, as she begins to pour the coffee. 'And here we have Anna, who is a brilliant photo-journalist.'

Her beauty hits me like a slap across the face. She has one of those perfectly proportioned faces you see in magazines.

31

She's blonde, about ten years younger than me, with large breasts. As she lifts up her hand and says hello, I notice that she has a big digital camera slung over her shoulder. I try to smile back at her, but I'm conscious it seems forced.

'Anna is staying temporarily in a house belonging to Desert Shoots, where Freya lives,' says Payton, gesturing to a middle-aged woman dressed in yoga pants, with red cheeks, wearing no make-up, her mousy hair a messy bun. 'She gave up a good job in London to come here to be the new gardener at the charity.' She seems familiar; I suppose I've seen so many women of her type – the quintessential 'Bobo', or bourgeois-bohemian – on the streets of Hackney, Stoke Newington and Dalston.

'Next to her is Hans, visiting from Germany,' Payton continues. He's the man who we met last night, living in the camper van. I know I shouldn't judge by appearances, but I suspect he's into drugs. The last thing Rich needs is any more temptation to indulge in illegal substances. Maybe Rich is thinking the same thing, as his face seems strained.

As we start to drink our coffee, there's an awkward silence before Rich begins to ask Anna about her work. There's something slightly artificial about his questions, as if he's rehearsed them or already knows the answers. She has her sparkling brown eyes fixed on him, but he can't meet her gaze. Perhaps it's her beauty that's making him nervous.

Has she published any of her writing and photographs in magazines or newspapers? he asks. She's had a piece and a few photos published in the *Guardian* and a couple of websites have been really supportive; she takes her camera everywhere, she adds. And what is she working on at the moment? She talks about how she's documenting the lives of immigrants in

Spain, particularly the workers in the *invernaderos* of Almería that supply northern Europe with year-round vegetables. She asks him what brought him to this dry part of Spain, at which point he blushes, mumbles something under his breath and changes the subject. She smiles to herself, perhaps finding his discomfort amusing. She shifts in her chair and moves a little closer to him, so close in fact that at one point their legs almost touch. She runs a hand through her glossy blonde locks and turns to look at me. There's something unknowable in her cat-like eyes, as if she possesses some knowledge that gives her an aura of mysterious power.

'And Mia, what did you do – before you left Britain?'

'I'm a Spanish teacher – or I was. In a school in east London.'

'Challenging work. But I'm guessing you'd had enough? Was it burnout?'

'Not so much that,' Rich says, answering for me. 'We just wanted to make a . . . a new start.'

Her eyes move between us, glinting with unspoken amusement.

'So you're here to escape?'

I open my mouth to speak, but she talks over me.

'Well, you've certainly come to the right place. There are plenty of ways of doing that in Val Verde, wouldn't you say, Hans?'

At this, the German man smirks and looks down. A memory of coming home from a difficult parents' evening to find Rich slumped on the sofa comes back to me. His eyes were rolled back into his head. There was a line of dribble down his cheek, as silvery as a slug's trail.

'Don't look so serious, the both of you – I'm only teasing,' she says, before she turns her attention to Hans.

Rich and I sit in silence as Payton, Bill and Freya talk about the maintenance of the irrigation line that runs through the village. I stop listening and instead begin to admire the view. An enormous palm tree sways in the morning breeze. In the distance I can hear the gentle trickle of water as it moves through the rocks down by the river. I spot a terrace full of orange trees, another one laden with lemons. Someone is strumming on a guitar, playing a mournful Spanish tune. The breeze carries the faint aroma of herbs I don't know the names of and the smell of baking bread. It should feel like paradise, but there's something that disturbs me, something I can't articulate.

The sound of my name being repeated brings me to my senses. It's Bill asking me if I can help him make some more coffee. He tells me to go first down the stairs, and as I descend I can feel the ghostly trace of a finger on my shoulders and neck. The feeling is so light that I wonder whether it's real or whether I'm imagining it, but then I remember the way he touched me when I first arrived at the house.

'You should see Anna's photographs – they really are something else,' he says. 'She's so, *so* talented.' He asks if I can go into the pantry and see if there are any biscuits. It's dark in there, he tells me, but there's a switch on the inside of the wall. It's hard to find, but if I reach up high I should be able to flick it on.

As I walk through the kitchen into a dark, cave-like space, I take off Payton's sunglasses. The cool interior seems to stretch far back into the rock face. I'm grappling to find the light, reaching with my right arm, straining my shoulder, when I feel a presence next to me. It's Bill.

'I told you it was a damn nuisance, this light switch,' he

34

says, leaning towards me. 'Here, let me.' He moves a little closer. 'It's just around this corner, in this godforsaken nook and cranny. The way some of these old Spanish houses were built. Charming, yes. Practical, not so much.'

The dark walls of the larder begin to edge towards me. I feel my breathing increase, my heart pulsing in my chest. I close my eyes – *tight shut* – for a moment, just as my mother had once told me.

'Relax now,' says Bill. The smell of brandy is more intense on his breath: does he take it with his coffee? I hear the scrabble of his fingers clawing up the wall. I smell the earthy rankness of this place and feel something else, a cobweb perhaps, brush against my face. I lash out, letting a small scream escape. I hear something smash by my feet. Bill is asking me to calm down. I dare to open my eyes. There are shards of glass and an explosion of red liquid by my feet.

I have to get out of here.

I push my way past him, gasping for air, hitting a lamp that crashes to the tiled floor. Bill is calling out to me, calling up to Payton, calling up to Rich. But I continue to run, dropping the sunglasses as I go. I feel someone's arm on my shoulder again and I wrench it away. It's dark in the hallway, but I think I can see the outline of the door. I hear footsteps crash down the stairs.

'Mia, are you okay?' shouts Rich.

I hear him apologizing for me. I've been having problems, he says. Change is always difficult for some people, says Payton. I turn and see Anna, clever, artistic, beautiful Anna, looking at me with satisfaction in her eyes.

I rasp out some words, incomprehensible to begin with. I try again. 'I – I just need to get, get outside,' I manage to say.

35

'She smashed one of the jars of gazpacho – it was an accident,' explains Bill. 'I was just trying to help her find the light switch in the pantry. To find the biscuits.' His explanation sounds flimsy, and more than a little pathetic.

'Really?' asks Payton, as tension tightens the muscles in her face.

Freya comes to my side and guides me to the door. She tells me to take some deep breaths. She knows what I'm going through – she used to suffer from panic attacks herself. But she smells of the earth too and I step away from her. The door opens and I run outside. The darkness is banished and I drink in the air as if it's my first taste of water after days in the desert.

'You'll be okay now, Mia,' says Rich, enveloping me in his arms. 'I'm here. It's me.'

Hans asks him if I need anything. I want to scream at him to keep the fuck away from my boyfriend. Bill doesn't know where to look and slinks back inside the house, where Payton starts to quiz him about what happened.

'Let's get you back to *La Luz*,' says Rich.

6

RICH

'I shouldn't have let you go down there by yourself,' I say, leading her into the house. 'What about a glass of water?'

'I'm okay – honestly, Rich,' she says, but she doesn't look like it. Her eyes are those of a hunted animal. Her already pale skin is deathly. Her breathing is quick, her words full of panic.

'Maybe you need a lie-down,' I say, putting my hand on her shoulder.

'I don't need a lie-down!' she spits, wrenching my hand off her. 'Sorry,' she adds, as she registers the hurt stinging my face, 'it just got too much for me down there. Claustrophobic . . . you know.'

'Did – did Bill do anything? Try anything on, I mean?'

'No, of course not. I don't think so.'

'If he did, I'll go around there now and have it out with him.'

'No, it's not worth it. It doesn't matter. I don't want to get off to a bad start. Let's just leave it.'

I pass a glass of water to her and we make our way outside. I watch Mia as she sips the water, takes some more deep breaths and, with eyes closed, raises her face to the sun. She gives off an air of unapproachability, as if she's constructed an invisible barrier, sealing herself off from everyone and everything around her. I suppose that's one of the consequences of survival. I'm not an expert, by any means. I've read a few books and talked to a few people about it, but I'm still not quite certain what to say to her when she's like this.

One strategy that sometimes works is distraction and so I ask, 'What did you make of the rest of them? They seem like a nice bunch, don't they?'

She doesn't answer. Her eyes remain closed.

'I can't tell you how kind Payton has been. And it's great to see that we can have an intelligent conversation with people, some of them even our own age – or even younger. I know one of the things we were worried about was missing out on the level of intellectual stimulation you get in London, but I think we should have that covered, don't you? It seems that Anna, Freya and Hans are really interesting.'

There's an emptiness in the air as heavy as death, before Mia sighs and says, 'I thought we were leaving to get away from . . . all of that.'

'All of—?'

'You know what I'm talking about, Rich.'

I swallow, unable to speak.

'I just couldn't bear it if it happened again. You promised me you wouldn't.'

I don't know what to say. Mia is studying me, looking for signs of – what? Guilt? I'm conscious I'm holding my breath.

'You know what happened to your mother, with the booze. I just couldn't bear it if I had to watch you destroy yourself with . . .' Her voice trails off, unable or unwilling to articulate the problems of the past.

Anxiety continues to seep through my system like a poison. I breathe out with such force that I'm certain Mia can hear me exhale.

'Promise me you'll stay away. Stay away from Hans.'

At the mention of his name, I feel suddenly liberated, as if a weight has been lifted from around my neck and shoulders. Mia's only talking about the drugs. It's nothing else. I find myself smiling at her, and I promise that I'll do my best not to pick up my old habits.

'And I'm not sure about that Anna either,' she says, her ice-blue eyes staring into mine.

I take her small frame in my arms; it feels good to hold her, possess her. 'You've got nothing to worry about,' I say. 'Our new start – starts now.'

7

MIA

Sex was often the marker of a new start. Whenever we had a row, it was always solved, and salved, by going to bed. I often wondered whether we had these arguments just so I could get Rich to show me how much he cared about me. And, in truth, the lovemaking that followed a row was the best we ever had. There was an intensity to it that was like dying and then being reborn.

But today, as he says those words, 'Our new start – starts now,' instead of letting him lead me into the bedroom, I turn away from him. I tell him I need to go for a walk, clear my head, get some fresh air. It's something to do with being down there, I add, in that dark, airless larder which was more like a grave than a place to store food. I know he can't argue with this, and so he lets me go. He gives me some instructions about the layout of the village, and he tells me it's impossible to get lost. There's one road in and out: if you choose the left-hand exit it will take you over the hills and eventually to the main road and motorway; the other direction leads past Devil's Head, an enormous rock formation that looks like a demon, past the disused gypsum quarry and the caves and eventually to the local town of San Mateo. He asks how long I'll be, but I reply that I'm not sure. He gives me a bottle of water from the fridge and tells me again that he's sorry.

I leave him standing under the archway and begin a gentle climb up a track he tells me is called the crystal path. It's not hard to see why. With each step I notice sharp edges of the rock glinting in the morning sunshine. The effect is magical, like walking in a dream world. I realize again that I don't have my sunglasses, but it's too late to go back to the house to get them.

Halfway up the track I turn around and look at Val Verde. It's a village of contrasts: the green lushness of the valley enclosed by the arid land of the hills that surround it; the old, traditional Spanish houses now restored and equipped with the latest green technologies; the blindingly bright crystal that catches the sunshine set in the monochromatic desert landscape.

I continue my walk, up onto the road, and past a couple of ruins, their *caña* ceilings collapsed inwards, their walls destroyed by the fatal combination of intense summer heat and infrequent but torrential rain. Just then I hear a voice call out to me in Spanish. I turn and see an old lady dressed in black. She seems unfeasibly old, her face as dry and lined as the desiccated soil up here, far away from the river. Her voice is coarse and her accent is difficult to understand at first – she drops the endings of her words as if swallowing them to help lubricate her voice – but finally I grasp that she's asking me

41

for water. Her friend who dropped her off here only gave her one bottle of *agua*, which she has already finished. I pass the water to her; as she drinks her mouth opens and closes like a turtle. She thanks me and tells me that her name is Blanca Rodríguez García. I introduce myself and tell her that I've just moved into a house in the village.

Out of nowhere she says, in her harsh, rasping voice, 'I'm looking for the bones of my mother.' Her statement is straight and to the point, but it seems so incongruous that I'm sure I must have mistranslated her words. I ask her to repeat herself and she says the same thing again, pointing to a dry patch of land by the road, near an ancient olive tree.

'Her remains are somewhere here, under the ground,' she says. 'She's been here for years, many, many years. All I want is to give her a decent burial, then her spirit can rest in peace.'

I assume she must be suffering from dementia or delusions, but she continues: 'The men took her. First they shaved her head and pushed her through the streets, calling her names. Then she was brought here along with the others and shot. There was no proper grave. No marking.'

She goes to stand by the ground and looks at the earth as if she almost expects to see her mother's spirit. 'Mama, come to me. Mama, where are you? Mama, what did they do to you?' In that moment, the markers of her age – the wrinkles on her face, her stooped back, her paper-thin skin – seem to melt away and she's like a little girl lost looking for her mother. The sight of this is almost too much for me to bear, but I stifle my tears.

'Do you want to tell me what happened?' I ask.

And so there, by the side of the dusty road, the old lady begins to relate how some of Franco's forces, in their purge of the area, persecuted and then executed their political opponents. I'd studied the Civil War in my degree and knew, from books at least, the devastating impact the conflict between the Nationalists (led by Franco) and the Republicans had on the country. Hundreds of thousands of people on both sides had been slaughtered, but the victory by Franco meant that Spain had been forced to live under a dictatorship until the leader's death in 1975. But hearing from a person who had lived through the war and its dreadful aftermath was a different matter entirely.

'The world split into two,' says Blanca. 'Brother fought against brother, sister against sister. It was as if the devil himself came into our lives and possessed us all.' She raises her fist at Devil's Head. 'So many people were slaughtered, butchered like pigs. Blood flowed down the streets, turning the dry riverbeds red. You couldn't trust anyone in case they betrayed you. It was as if the walls were listening to your every word. And if you think it all got better when the war ended, you're a fool. That's when it got even worse. The people who had been the enemies of my mother were rewarded with positions of power. The local mayor, he had been a *falangista*, fighting for his dear Franco. The men who shot my mother and those like her – those who believed in a different system, a fairer system, a more equal society – they paraded around the streets in their uniforms of the *Guardia Civil*, the police. That was a joke. The men who were supposed to oversee law and order had been monsters – monsters and butchers and executioners. Their descendants are just as cruel today.'

Although I'd like to ask her more, particularly about her last observation, Blanca's voice runs dry and she seems unsteady. Her eyes glaze over as if she's being transported

43

back into the past, seized by the ghosts of yesterday. She begins to murmur her mother's name, Esperanza, and sings a kind of lullaby, most of which I can't make out apart from a few words: *el corazon*, the heart; *mis ojos*, my eyes; *la sangre*, the blood; *la tierra*, the earth; and *tus huesos*, your bones.

'Where do you live?' I ask.

She points in the direction of San Mateo, which Rich said was about ten minutes away by car. She tells me her friend will be here to pick her up soon. She will be back again tomorrow, to stand over the grave of her mother. She comes every day, she adds, just to tell her mother that she hasn't forgotten her. She hopes that with the help of an association she will get the permit she needs to dig up the land, find her mother's remains and give her a proper burial. She will not rest until that happens.

'Death will not stop me,' she whispers, her voice faltering. 'Even if I don't manage it in my lifetime I will continue to come here and haunt this place until justice has been done.'

I remember the lines from Lorca – lines I'd quoted in my thesis – about how in every country death is an ending. 'It appears and they close the curtains,' he'd written. 'Not in Spain. In Spain they open them.' This was a country, despite its modern sheen, that still believed in ghosts, the supernatural, spectres. Here the dead lived alongside the living and the barrier between the two worlds was as flimsy as gossamer.

'Where do you live?' she asks, suddenly returning to the land of the living.

'Down there,' I reply. 'In Val Verde. In an old house.'

'Which one?'

'It's the big one that has terraces that lead down to the river. It's lovely. As I say, I've just arrived from London. I'm here with my boyfriend, Rich. It – the house – was owned by his mother, Marianne. Did you know her? It's called *La Casa de la Luz*. The one where—'

But at the mention of the name she turns from me, her face darkening.

'Blanca, what's wrong?'

She begins to move away from me, shaking her fist again at the rock of Devil's Head, cursing under her breath. I follow her, ask what she means, but at that moment a beaten-up old car appears over the brow of the hill and comes to a stop beside her. Another old lady, with dyed auburn hair and a round, chubby face, stretches across the passenger seat and opens the door for her friend.

'Nieves is here, thank the lord,' says Blanca, hurrying for the car. 'I've got to go now. I think you should too. Leave this place. Leave that house.'

I call out her name, ask her to explain a little more. But she eases herself into the car and slams the door, locking it after her. I hope I haven't offended her, I say. What have I said to upset her? She refuses to meet my eye, but I can see that she's crossing herself, grasping the rosary around her neck. I can see that Nieves, her friend, is asking what on earth is the matter, but Blanca is shouting to her, telling her to drive away.

'Who is that girl?' asks Nieves. 'What did she say to you?'

But Blanca doesn't answer and the two friends drive off in a cloud of dust. I'm left standing in the road, looking down at a stretch of dry earth where her mother's bones lie.

8

RICH

I thought the walk would help Mia relax, but when she returns to the house she seems even more anxious and upset. Just as I'm about to reassure her again, she begins to ask me about a patch of land up on the road by Devil's Head. Apparently, she's met an old lady from the town – Blanca – who wants to dig up her mother's body, a victim of the Civil War. Mia doesn't need this kind of shit, she really doesn't.

'And Blanca got all weird when I told her where I lived,' she says. 'In fact, she couldn't get away fast enough from me. Almost as if she was afraid . . . afraid of me or for me.'

'She's obviously got some problems. I wouldn't read too much into it. Look – come and have some lunch.'

When she was gone I explored the store cupboard and found a large jar of red lentils, which I used to make a soup, spiced with chilli flakes and some cumin seeds that I'd ground in a pestle and mortar. I ladle some soup into two bowls from the local pottery and carry them into the dining room. She sits down, but her mind is elsewhere.

'It was so sad to see her standing by the side of the road like that, desperate to find her mother's remains,' she says. 'She said she comes every day and watches over her. I don't know how old she is, but she looks as though she must be ninety or so. You can tell it's the only thing that is keeping her alive – the determination to give her mother a proper burial.'

Mia stands up from the table and walks over to the window, gazing at the terraces beyond. She rests a hand over the thick stone wall and closes her eyes.

'I suppose there were deaths here like everywhere in Spain,' I say, taking a mouthful of soup. 'The Civil War was brutal, we all know that. But it's behind us now. The country had to agree to forget in order to move forwards. How else could Spain make that transition from dictatorship to democracy so quickly? Anyway, you know more about this than I do. What do you think?'

I hope by engaging Mia in an intellectual debate her attention will shift from the macabre, but she doesn't respond. There's a danger she's slipping away from me, melting into the dark recesses of the past. It's not safe for her to go there.

'What was the name of that agreement?' I ask, trying once again to bring her back to the present moment. 'The pact of forgetting?'

Still nothing. 'Mia, why don't you come and have some soup? It's getting cold.'

She returns to the table, but with a strange look in her eyes, as if she's not seeing what's in front of her. She takes a spoon in her hand, but she doesn't eat. Instead, she looks at me and asks me to tell her about the history of the house.

'It's obviously old,' I say. 'You can see the thickness of the wall you were touching just now. I know it was built as one of the original mill houses for – what was his name? Antonio, I think. Anyway, I think he lived here with his family, his children. They lived a simple, self-sufficient life, milling the wheat, growing their vegetables, rearing their animals. I'm told they kept a pig, some donkeys, chickens. Of course, there was a school in Val Verde then, and I think his children went there.'

'What else? What came later?'

'I think my mother bought it in the late Eighties. The whole village had been more or less abandoned until the Seventies. There'd been a terrible drought and the irrigation line had been neglected for years, meaning that lots of the fruit trees perished. All the Spanish people here moved to San Mateo, where they could live in homes with proper sanitation, running water, electricity, heating. After years of hardship, it must have seemed like some kind of miracle to move into a house which had all mod cons, don't you think?'

'But what about during the war? The Civil War, I mean.'

'I don't know anything about that. No one likes to talk much about the atrocities that went on. Like I said, there was an agreement that the past should be forgotten and—'

'But what if you don't want to forget?'

We're stepping onto dangerous ground now, ground that can turn into sinking sand at any moment.

'Mia, come on now. You know that's not good for you.'

'What – remembering?'

'No, just dwelling too much on . . . on the past.' I take another mouthful of soup. 'What do you think? You should try some.'

'Blanca freaked out when I told her where I lived. We'd

48

just been talking about the Civil War. What if this house was used as one of those places you read about, you know, where they tortured people?'

'Mia, I know you've got an active imagination, but—'

'But what? How do you know? As you said yourself, the Civil War was brutal. All sorts of atrocities were committed everywhere, throughout Spain. Why not here – in this house?' She looks around the dining room as if expecting to see the horrors of the past about to reveal themselves.

'Mia, you need to not do this. You know what happens when you get . . . fixated on something like this. We've been through it with your doctors, your therapist.'

The early warning signs are here. Her breathing is quickening, her chest rising and falling as if she's struggling for air. Her pupils are dilating. She realizes what is happening and she looks to me for guidance.

I speak as calmly as possible, the way I've been trained. 'Come on now – try to breathe in slowly. That's right – through your nose. And now breathe out – through your mouth.'

She tries to do as I say, but the breath is still shallow and hurried. I repeat the breathing mantra a couple of times. 'Take a slow breath in and try to count slowly – that's right – one, two, three – you're doing great – three, four, five. And now out. You've been here before and you've got through it. You know you have. That's right – carry on with the breathing.' After a few minutes she manages to get her breathing under control. I reassure her again that all is okay. That I'm here, by her side. I get her a glass of water and lead her upstairs to bed, where she can rest.

I leave the house and walk through the olive terraces, down to the river. I open my mouth to scream, but I can't make a sound.

49

9

MIA

We're having a tour of Desert Shoots and Rich seems like
he's in his element. We're being shown around by a volunteer
called Guy, who looks like he's thrown together his patch-
work of clothes from a dressing-up box but who sounds as
though he went to Eton. Rich has been to the eco-charity
before, but as Guy guides us around the community – with
its makeshift array of solar panels, washing machines
fashioned from the spare parts of old bicycles, and boxes
stuffed with hay which act as slow cookers – his eyes light
up like a little boy opening his birthday presents. It's lovely
to see him like this again. Enthusiastic. Full of life, full of
hope for the world.

'Wow – that's amazing,' he says, as Guy shows us how the
solar cooker works.

To me it just looks like a very shiny satellite dish, but
the two men are obsessed with it. Rich is brimming with

questions. 'So the reflector is axially symmetrical and shaped like a parabola so that . . .'

Guy replies with something I don't understand before he says, 'There's a solar cooker in Auroville, India, which is so large it can make two meals a day for around a thousand people and . . .'

They embark on a discussion about the concept of peak oil, which leads on to talk about the possibility of the sixth mass extinction event, the perils of capitalism, the destructive greed of the one per cent, and the need for mass civil resistance. Although I'm broadly sympathetic to the ideas, I've heard Rich talk about these things so many times before that I excuse myself and ask if I can see inside the actual kitchen. Rich and Guy are so caught up imagining a new, greener future that they hardly turn their heads as I slip away.

I make my way down a series of stone steps, past a couple of feeding bowls placed out for the stray cats that haunt the village, and round to the front of the whitewashed house with its bright blue shutters. I notice that over the top of the door, which is painted the same shade of blue, there's a curious stick figure of a man who looks like he's holding up a rainbow with outstretched arms.

'I see you've found the lucky charm.'

I turn and see Freya, carrying a bucket, her hands dirty, a streak of soil smeared across one cheek.

'Sorry?'

'The indalo man,' she says, gesturing to the wooden figure above the door. 'Apparently, the symbol was discovered in a cave somewhere near here and dates back a few thousand years. It's supposed to ward off evil spirits – not that I believe in nonsense like that.'

'You're not superstitious, then?'

'Me? Not at all. I'm a woman of science – not that you'd know it from looking at me.' As she wipes her sweaty brow she leaves behind another line of dirt. 'Sorry, I need to get out of these clothes. I've been down working on the *acequia*, the irrigation line.' She plunges a muddy hand into the bucket and drags out what looks like a tangle of witches' hair. 'It's the roots of esparto grass – every so often you have to clear them out, otherwise there's a blockage and the line doesn't flow properly and then this—' She stops herself as she studies me. 'How are you settling in?'

'Really well, thanks – it's a beautiful village. Just stunning.' I realize, as I speak, that there's an artificial quality to my words, as if I'm playing a part.

Perhaps Freya senses this because she casts me a look of concern and invites me inside for a cup of herbal tea. 'Just give me five minutes to wash my hands and face and I'll be with you,' she says. She pushes open the door and tells me to make myself at home. 'There's probably no one around at this time of day – most of the volunteers are out working.'

I step inside a space full of shadows and dark corners. My first reaction is to leave, but just as I'm about to make for the door I spot a cork board filled with photographs. I switch on a light, conscious not to leave it on for too long – Rich has already told me that Desert Shoots' solar power system is nowhere near as effective as the one at *La Casa de La Luz*. The faces and names of the charity's staff and volunteers stare down at me. I pick out people I already know: there's Freya Watson, smiling directly into the camera, and Guy Parker, who seems to be looking at something in the distance, and a couple of others who I recognize from my walks around the village.

Accompanying the photos is a flowchart, showing that the organization works on a horizontal rather than a vertical approach, which by my reckoning means that no one person is in charge. Next to this is a potted history of the charity, outlining how it was formed in the early Seventies by a couple of ecologists, Jan Visser from the Netherlands, and Peter Huddlestone from England. When they first arrived in Val Verde, most of the houses had been abandoned; the irrigation line had fallen into disrepair; the terraces were overgrown – in short it was slowly turning into a wilderness. The two men set about recruiting like-minded people to help restore the village, using ecological and sustainable methods. And so Desert Shoots was born.

'I see you're learning about the history,' says Freya, as she returns from washing her hands and face. 'It's an amazing achievement, don't you think? Especially since the whole thing was done on a shoestring. And still is. Once upon a time, I'd never have thought it possible to survive on only a hundred euros a month.'

I have to stop my mouth from dropping open. 'You must be good at budgeting.'

'I get free board and lodging here and, as you can see, there's not much to spend your money on here apart from the occasional blow-out in San Mateo, but even there it's hard.'

Rich had said something along the same lines. I was still accustomed to spending at least forty quid on tapas and wine in London.

'What did you do before you came here?'

'I was an academic, London university. I ran a Masters course in soil science.'

She already knows that I was a Spanish teacher, but she

53

asks me where I lived in London. When I tell her that we lived in Hackney, she says she knows it well – an old boyfriend of hers used to live near London Fields. She asks me what kind of tea I'd like. The charity has a whole range of natural infusions harvested from the land: mint, which grows wild along the banks of the irrigation line, as well as sage, thyme, rosemary, chamomile and, if I like my tea bitter, lemon or olive leaf. I'm in the mood for good old-fashioned builder's, but I sense that if I ask for this I will disappoint her, and so I go for the mint.

I keep waiting for her to refer to the scene at Payton's house, but she's so polite she confines the conversation to safe ground: namely the village and what brought each of us here. I tell her a little about our life in London, our desire to do our bit to make the planet a better place, and Emily Thomas, the pupil who had stepped in front of a bus because of her apparent anxieties surrounding climate change. She looks upset when I tell her this. There've been times in her life when she felt so consumed by panic and anxiety about the state of the world – both the larger picture and her own personal life – that she felt she couldn't go on. I don't ask about the specifics but she tells me she's had more than her own share of shit to deal with. I'm guessing relationship problems. Thank goodness she found gardening, which she says saved her life.

'Trust me – I tried every kind of therapy going, but there's nothing like planting a seed in a patch of bare earth and watching it sprout and then grow,' she says, pouring the tea and handing me a cup. 'I suppose it's something about the nurturing process. That and being forced to wait, to really slow down. Gardening has its own time frame – you just have to accept that some things will take a long time to come to

54

fruition. The other day I was reading about how scientists managed to germinate the seed of a date palm which was about two thousand years old.'

'Amazing.'

'So now I take my time with everything – not just gardening, but everything else too: cooking, reading, walking, thinking. That's another of the reasons why I came here to Val Verde. I want to be able to step back and watch things, really appreciate them.'

I'm reminded of a poem my mother used to read to me, something about what is this life if, full of care, we have no time to stand and stare. How did the rest of it go? In that instant, I'm with my mother again. Holding her hand, looking at a bank ablaze with daffodils.

She looks at me with concern in her eyes. 'Are you okay?'

'Yes – your words struck a chord, that's all.'

She continues to talk about how she plans to improve the soil by the introduction of mycorrhiza, which she tells me is a kind of symbiotic relationship between a fungus and plant. A lot of the scientific terms go over my head, but the gist is that she hopes to be able to improve soil health and therefore productivity. She asks about the land at our house and gives me some tips and advice about clearing terraces and planting. She's going to divide up some herbs for us, some of which have amazing healing properties, and although we've already missed the optimal time for the germination of seeds such as tomatoes, peppers, chillies and aubergines, there are lots of seedlings in the greenhouse going spare too.

'Before you know it, they'll grow and begin to flower and then fruit,' she says, smiling. 'Just give them time.'

10

RICH

After the embarrassing scene at Payton and Bill's house I feel it's only fair to invite them back. Not only to apologize for Mia's behaviour but to thank them for looking after *La Casa de la Luz*. Although it's just going to be the four of us, I still want to make an effort and so, after a morning shop, I spend the afternoon cooking a range of vegan Lebanese and Syrian inspired dishes: hummus, both the traditional kind and one made from beetroot and walnuts; potatoes with chilli, lemon juice and parsley; mixed roasted vegetables with a tahini garlic dressing; and a big tomato and cucumber salad.

'Rich, this looks amazing,' says Payton, as I bring the various dishes to the table.

'And even the flatbreads are his,' adds Mia.

As we take our seats, everyone makes more encouraging noises about the food. Bill has brought what he says is a good bottle – it's French, rather than Spanish – and throughout dinner he makes sure he regularly tops up everyone's glass, especially mine and his own as we're drinking at a faster pace than our partners.

There's a momentary pause in the conversation, a lull that I take advantage of to ask Payton to tell us about her activism. She launches into an account of various marches she's been on as well as a range of what she calls interventionist actions, when she's embedded herself with a group to stop forests being felled, the development of coal and copper mines, airport expansion, and the exploitation of natural resources. I hope Mia will take inspiration from her.

'And then, of course, there's the work I do on optimum population,' says Payton, taking another spoonful of beetroot hummus. 'That seems to take up more and more of my time.'

Shit. I wish she wouldn't talk about this. Not in front of Mia.

'What's that?' asks Mia.

I need to do something to try to change the subject. 'Who'd like another flatbread? Payton? Or some more potatoes?'

Payton, for all her strident political views, is hardly the most sensitive of souls. 'No, I'm fine with this beetroot hummus – absolutely delicious, by the way. What was I saying? Oh yes, Mia, you were asking me about optimum population. Well, I do a lot of work for an organization called Population Matters, which is trying to educate people about the links between sustainability and population growth. Our impact on the Earth can't just be defined by resources – the number of people is also vital to the equation. I mean, how many humans can the planet support?'

Payton continues to talk about the frightening rise in population, the average number of children women have in different parts of the world, and the apocalyptic scenario if we do nothing. I keep trying to distract Payton, but she's fixed on the idea; nothing will prevent her from explaining the issues. And Mia seems transfixed. Luckily, she's not upset. She's brought up the subject of having a child with me in the past, and I've managed to put her off with various excuses: we were too broke, London was not the ideal place to raise a kid, we needed to be more established in our careers, we should wait until we got a flat with a garden. But I've never been brave enough to tell her the truth: that I don't want a child. I never have and it's unlikely I'll change my mind.

'There are some women I know who refuse to have children because of the terrible state we're in,' says Payton. 'Birth Strikers, they're called. Where you do stand on the issue, Mia?'

I can hardly bear to look at her.

'I – I can see your point,' says Mia, softly. 'But it's something I've always assumed I would have in my life – a son, a daughter.'

'But what about the world?' continues Payton. 'Can't you see that if we let things carry on as—'

I can imagine the pain Mia must be feeling. I need this to stop. As I reach out to take a plate, I deliberately knock over my glass. Red wine spills across the surface of the table, cascading down onto Payton.

'Oh my God, I'm so sorry.' I jump up, pick up a napkin and thrust it in her direction.

'Don't worry,' she says, shifting back her chair and dabbing away at her beige trousers. 'Fuck, this is making it worse.'

Bill jumps up to help. 'What about some salt?'

I notice there are only a few flakes left in the small, crystal dish on the table and so I grab the packet from the work surface. 'Here, try this.'

By the time Payton has spread salt across the fabric, gone to the loo to check on her appearance and returned to the table, the conversation has moved on to something more lightweight: the number of fiestas in Spain and their particular features. Mia can join in with this, because she talked about some of these with her students. There's the mass tomato fight in Buñol; the shearing of semi-wild horses' manes in Galicia; and *Los Hombres de Musgo*, in which the men of Béjar cover themselves in moss to re-enact the retaking of the town from Moorish occupiers in the twelfth century.

Payton's face suddenly lights up. 'But how could I forget? The funeral of the sardine! Oh my, it's one of the quirkiest, most charming ones and it's happening in a couple of weeks right here in San Mateo.'

'Oh yes, you're going to love it,' adds Bill.

11

MIA

Rich was against me coming to this. He said it might be too much for me, that it might upset me. But I'm finding it all surprisingly uplifting, amusing even. Payton and Bill were right. *El entierro de la sardina* or the burial of the sardine is one of the oddest of Spanish festivals: held on the night of Ash Wednesday, it marks the start of Lent and centres on the mourning for a dead sardine.

I'm standing in a big crowd, all of us squeezed down a narrow side street in San Mateo, following a wooden coffin that's being paraded around the town by a group of pall-bearers. Two dozen or so sardines have been tacked round the sides of the coffin, their silver skins reflecting the harsh artificial streetlights. Women are dressed in black and wear mantillas, while some of them carry candles, and all of us hold handkerchiefs which we repeatedly use to dab away our non-existent tears. All of this is accompanied by fake wailing, cries interspersed with laughter from some of the children that accompany the ersatz procession, and the sombre, funereal beating of drums.

'Are you sure you're all right?' asks Rich, casting me an anxious look.

'I'm a bit cold,' I say, as I wrap my scarf around my neck and draw my coat closer to me. 'But apart from that, I'm loving it – honestly.'

I suppose he's got every right to be worried. Our arrival in Val Verde two weeks ago had hardly got off to a good start. Despite this, I insisted that it was important for me to offer some support to Blanca, who, true to her word, visited the site of her mother's grave every day. Eventually, she told me the reason why she'd been upset when I informed her that I lived in *La Casa de la Luz*. It had been her grandmother's house and she said that I bore an uncanny resemblance to her *abuela* who had died there. That day she had been convinced that I was a spirit who had come to warn her of something. She realized it sounded silly and she apologized for her foolishness; she was nothing but a stupid old woman. I told her that I understood and from then on, each day, I walked up the crystal path to meet her by the dusty road.

We had become friends of sorts, and with every meeting she told me more about her mother, more about her mission to dig up her remains. Blanca had encountered numerous bureaucratic setbacks, but I promised I'd do everything I could to help give her mother a proper burial. Initially, Rich was cross when he learned that my daily constitutional involved a long conversation with Blanca about her dead mother, but he must have seen that my meetings with her left me stimulated and engaged. And, to be honest, things had improved between Rich and me. He reassured me he wouldn't be tempted to lose himself in drugs again, and helped me realize that I had to let go of the past. I couldn't allow myself to be defined by it. It was the present – the here and now – that mattered. One afternoon, when I'd helped him move his mother's things into the studio so we could use her old bedroom, we had another talk about children. We both decided to wait a little longer before trying. We just needed time to settle into our new lives.

The loud crash of a cymbal and a high-pitched wail from a woman next to me bring me back to the present.

'It's certainly something you wouldn't see in London,' says Rich, taking my hand. 'But promise me that you'll let me know if you want to go home.'

'Don't worry, I will.' I run my fingers through his ginger hair. Any feelings of uncertainty I might have had about him have melted away. 'And thanks for suggesting we take a risk and come here – to Spain, I mean. I know we didn't get off to a great start, but—'

Before I can finish my sentence someone grabs Rich by his shoulders and hugs him. My heart sinks when I realize it's Hans, the German man from the village, who is here with Freya, the gardener.

'This is far out,' says Hans. 'Like I'm having the weirdest fucking trip of my life.'

'Amazing,' says Freya. 'I've never seen anything like it.'

'And the strange thing is I haven't taken anything – not yet, anyway,' says Hans, slapping Rich on the back. 'Shall we meet up in the bar, the large one in the main square? After all, the night, as they say, is young.'

Rich catches me staring at him. '*What?*' he says, looking like a little boy who's just been caught stealing.

'I didn't say anything.'

'You didn't need to,' he counters.

I refuse to let my mood be spoiled by the appearance of Hans and so let this go. We continue to follow the parade, pretending to weep and wail as we do so. The performance of fake grief – all for a dead sardine – is strangely uplifting and I find myself laughing quietly at the absurdity of it all. The town, a cluster of whitewashed houses on a hill, must only have a population of a thousand or so people and it seems most of them are here tonight, all squashed into the narrow streets. At times we pass into alleyways devoid of streetlights, and we shuffle down the cobbles with the aid of a few candles and the glow from an occasional smartphone. I lose all sense of direction as the procession snakes its way around San Mateo and, apart from Rich who stands by my side, it's difficult to make out the faces of those nearby.

Finally, we emerge back into the main square, a handsome space that contains the town hall, a church, a café/bar and a number of benches set under a dozen orange trees. I watch as the pallbearers set the coffin down outside the town hall. There's a building excitement in the air. I haven't got a clue about what's going to happen next and so I turn to the smartly dressed woman in her sixties standing next to me, and ask her.

She tells me that someone is going to come out to deliver a *pregón*, or prosecution, a humorous take-down of some of the town's well-known inhabitants. A moment later a man who looks like he's dressed as a priest, flanked by two teenage boys in military uniform, steps out onto the first-floor balcony of the town hall. The crowd goes wild. The 'priest' begins to talk into a microphone, but I miss great swathes of what he's saying – he's gabbling in old-fashioned rhyming couplets and the jeering crowd are giving him a noisy reception. Rich turns to me for some kind of insight, but I tell him I'm as lost as he is.

Just then I spot Blanca sitting on one of the benches. I leave Rich and push my way through the mass of people, past a small boy wearing a clown mask who makes a grab for my leg. I carry on walking towards Blanca, whose face lights up when she sees me. As I sit down, she points a withered finger into the crowd at a local man, Pedro, who apparently owns the strip of dry land where her mother is buried.

'I've been pleading with him for years to allow me to dig there, but he won't give me permission,' she rasps. 'He maintains that's all in the past. Let bygones be bygones, he says. But he doesn't understand that to me my mother isn't a bygone. She's not dead. She won't rest until I give her a proper burial. He's refusing to talk to me about it now.'

'Well, let me know if you need any more help,' I say, putting my hand on her knee. I notice that there's no flesh on her; she is nothing but skin and bone. I can't bear the fact that she could die without accomplishing her mission to retrieve and bury her mother's body. I say goodbye to her and scan the crowd for signs of Rich, but realize he's gone. Despite my earlier determination to not let the night be ruined by Hans, I feel fear gnawing at my stomach. What if Rich has disappeared down an alley with him? Sure, a quick puff on a spliff might not do much harm, but I know how that scenario ends. And it's not good.

I begin to make my way across the square, full of the noise of the crowd, when I feel something grip my leg again. It's the little boy with the clown mask. I look around the plaza for Rich, but I still can't see him anywhere. The boy in the clown mask tightens his grip around my knee. He's pinching me now, really squeezing the skin beneath my trousers.

'Ouch!' I brush the boy away, perhaps a little too forcefully, and he falls onto the tarmac and begins to scream. He takes off his mask. His black eyes, wet with tears, look at me with primeval fury. His mother, hearing his cries, rushes over to him. He tells her this foreign lady pushed him to the ground.

'What do you think you're doing?' she shouts in Spanish. 'Why do you want to hurt my son?'

Everyone near me turns to look at me. The expressions on their faces all ask the same question: what kind of monster am I?

I manage to say a few words, for some reason in English, 'I – he – I didn't . . .' but I'm drowned out by the tirade of this angry woman, who is soon joined by the child's grandmother. No doubt they assume that I can't understand or speak Spanish. To them I'm just a stupid tourist. I fumble in my bag and offer them a ten-euro note to buy the boy an ice-cream or a fizzy drink, but they tell me not to insult them, they don't need the money of a foreigner. I can't bear to get into an argument and so start to walk away. As I do so, I hear the grandmother say that she bets I don't have any children of my own and it's best if I never have them, that I'll go to my grave a barren woman.

As I make my way through the plaza to the bar, the crowd presses in on me. My head is spinning and I feel a little breathless. Finally, I catch a glimpse of Rich inside the brightly lit café. My stomach fizzes with acid when I see that he's sitting with Hans, along with Freya and Anna. I move a little closer and stand behind a window shutter where I hope they can't see me. I've told him that if I ever found him using the hard stuff again, I'd leave him.

I listen out for clues, but no matter how hard I strain my ears, I still can't hear what they're talking about, due to the din inside the bar. I realize that Rich is not talking to Hans; instead, all his attention is focused on Anna. There's an expression in Anna's eyes that I recognize. It's unmistakable. The Spanish call it *la mirada del amor* – the look of love. And it's directed at Rich.

12

RICH

I look up and see Mia standing outside the bar, but in the few seconds it takes me to leave the table and rush outside, she disappears. Fuck. I look around the square, packed with everyone enjoying the fiesta. I take a brief walk around the plaza before returning to the bar. I ask Hans, Anna and Freya whether they've seen her. They haven't. I gulp down a few mouthfuls of beer, trying to look as though everything is fine, but I feel as though something is eating away at me from the inside. I can't sit here, laughing and joking with my new friends, pushing Mia from my mind, kidding myself she is okay. It's obvious she's not. Not by a long shot.

And I'm not the only one who is worried about her. Ever since the day when Mia freaked out down in that pantry, Payton kept asking me about the state of her 'well-being'. I told her that Mia was just finding it difficult to settle into a new environment and that I was sure she'd be back to her old self soon. And what was that? She asked. I didn't answer her question. Freya wondered whether Mia might be interested in doing some gardening with her. She might benefit from the activity, she said, as sowing, planting and nurturing had been proven to lift the spirits. Hans told me that he often saw Mia with a 'mad old lady'; the two of them would sit and stare at an empty stretch of dry land up by Devil's Head. Initially, I'd suggested to Mia that talking to Blanca was a little morbid, but then I reasoned that at least those conversations got her out of the house.

I finish off my beer and tell Freya, Anna and Hans that I should go and find Mia. Anna glances at me – a 'what, really?' look, which I ignore. Although I'm sure neither Anna nor I have said anything that would give us away, I'm worried about what Mia may have seen. We'd been careful. But I do remember as we sat there that Anna had been giving me what I called her come-on eyes. My God, when she looked at me like that, I wanted to take her outside and push her up against a wall. I wanted to do all sorts of things to her, with her. But I'd made a promise to myself. Nothing in public. Not yet, at any rate. It was all too soon. And so I'd kicked her under the table, my signal that she had to go easy.

I've got myself into one hell of a mess, I know that. But I don't want to hurt Mia. I can't tell her the truth; the news would kill her.

The thing with Anna was only supposed to be a one-off, just a bit of fun. I told myself it was some perverse form of mourning, something I needed, like an appetite that demanded feeding or a bodily function I couldn't control. Perhaps I would have experienced a more straightforward kind of grief if I'd simply loved my mother. I would have been able to purge my feelings by the shedding of tears. I would have been able to relive my life with her by flicking through old photos – all those glorious memories! But the truth was I didn't cry a single tear for Marianne, I had no photographs bound into albums or on my phone, and the memories I had of her were ones I didn't want to revisit.

Everything would have been so different if I'd never flown out to her funeral. I didn't even want to go, but Mia had persuaded me. She said it would be good for 'closure' or some crap like that she'd picked up from one of her therapists. And then there were the practicalities that needed sorting out. Marianne had left her house to me. Certain papers would need to be signed at the notary's office. I considered the trip to be a simple matter of tying up loose ends, a bureaucratic visit rather than a sentimental one.

Stepping off the plane, the heat hit me like a furnace. This was desert country, an expanse of land with some of the lowest rainfall in the whole of Europe. I picked up my hire car, yanked up the air conditioning and drove through a tangle of roads, all lined with ugly greenhouses, their broken plastic blowing in the dry wind, and up the motorway towards Val Verde. I hadn't been back there since a big argument ten years ago when Marianne had called me 'psychologically disturbed', and I had told her that she was an unfit mother. Which is why I was shocked when I'd learnt that Marianne had left me her house; I'd always presumed she would bequeath it to some charity or other. Perhaps it was her way of absolving herself of guilt – after all, she had been the one who had walked out on me when I was a boy.

I drove straight to San Mateo's *tanatorio*, where Marianne's body lay. The place was packed, and I walked into a sea of faces, most of which I didn't recognize. I hardly took any notice of what happened after that. People came up to me to offer me their condolences. There was some kind of service, in Spanish, none of which I understood. Her body was taken to the cemetery to be buried. Payton, together with her husband, Bill, had arranged a wake at their house. I thought I'd just stay for one drink – I had an early morning appointment with the lawyer the next day and then a flight back to London the day after that – and I wanted to return to my hotel. But then I saw *her*. A ray of late afternoon sun enclosed her in a streak of light, but as I watched her drink from a glass of red wine and talk to a female friend, she seemed to radiate a kind of luminescence. I felt I had to talk to her, surmised somehow that she held the secret to my future. Her friend melted away into the crowd and we were left alone, surrounded by a forcefield of electricity of our own making.

'My name's Anna – Anna Fleming – and you must be Richard,' she said. I noticed that she was carrying an expensive-looking digital camera.

I told her to call me Rich. Mia had been the first one to call me that, but I pushed away any thoughts of her. I was in a different place, miles away from home. I'd had a lot of stress recently. I deserved a bit of fun.

'Sorry about your mother – I only met her a couple of times, but she seemed like one hell of a woman.'

'Don't – be sorry, I mean. We didn't get on. In fact, I hadn't seen her for years. She was hardly what you call the mothering type.'

I explained how she'd left my father and me in order to explore her own artistic ambitions. 'She was a product of the Sixties, I suppose. A wild thing. She must have felt emboldened

70

by all that freedom on offer. Sex. Drugs. Travel. Fame. She wanted the lot. What she didn't want was to be tied down by the responsibilities of marriage and motherhood. And so she took off. Bolted.'

'So I guess you're not a feminist, Rich?'

The question took me aback. 'I'm sorry?'

There was a spark in her dark eyes. 'By the sound of it you feel bitter about your mother – this fabulous woman, Marianne Ellis – for wanting to shape a life for herself outside the confines of the patriarchal system.'

I could tell that she was messing with me. There was something supremely erotic about being talked to like this.

'You resent the fact that she had to follow her own destiny, a destiny that didn't involve you, is that it?'

I stepped a little closer to her so I could smell the tang of wine on her breath.

'You know – this place, this valley, can be too much for some people,' she whispered.

'It can?'

'Yes – too wild. I think you need to loosen up.'

'Really?'

'Yes, you need reconditioning. Otherwise, there's a danger you might get stale, old-fashioned. And you wouldn't want that.'

'You're right. I wouldn't.' I stepped even closer to her. I felt a finger lightly brush against the top of my leg. I stifled my gasp in case it could be heard across the room. 'How about . . .'

I didn't – couldn't – finish my sentence. She whispered in my ear, told me to meet her outside in five minutes.

As I stood there, I became blind to the room. I remember

71

that a couple of well-meaning people from the village came up to tell me how much Marianne had meant to them. She'd been a good friend. What a spirit she had. Such a life-force. They would miss her. I could sense them searching my face for any signs of Marianne, physical characteristics she'd passed on to me: the shape of her nose, perhaps, or the curve of her lips. But, after a few minutes in my presence, disappointment clouded their eyes. I hadn't said the things they wanted to hear and my resemblance to Marianne was non-existent, as I knew I looked more like my father. They slowly edged away from me, and as I walked to the door I heard them saying that I must be in shock. I wasn't, of course, I just had no feelings for Marianne and I couldn't wait to get outside to see Anna. Although I'd only just met her, it was as if her presence was slowly infecting me, taking over every cell in my body. There was nothing else I wanted to think about.

I stepped outside and heard the manic chorus of the bull frogs down by the river, their constant croaking mocking my intentions. Surely Anna didn't really find me attractive? She was completely out of my league. What was I thinking? I walked down the steps to the dusty path, but there was no sign of Anna. Of course, she'd slipped away. Who could blame her? It was probably for the best. After all, I had a girlfriend waiting for me back in London. Mia.

I felt the band of sweat that snaked around the collar of my shirt begin to prick my skin. I couldn't wait to cast off my jacket and get back into some comfortable clothes. But I knew that it wasn't just the heat that was making me uncomfortable. How could I have considered going off with Anna knowing what Mia had been through? I was nothing but a shallow, selfish bastard, that cliché of masculinity: a man driven by the needs of his prick. I felt sick at the thought of myself. I'd go back to the hotel in San Mateo, have a cold shower, ring Mia and check she was okay.

But then I saw her again. And everything changed.

13

MIA

I run as fast as I can away from the bar, away from him. From her. Tears sting my eyes, blinding me. As I flee, all I can see are streaks of bright light, women dressed in the costume of widows' weeds, and an empty coffin that seems to float through the streets. I can't bear the noise: the jeering, the laughter, the amplified rhyming couplets that still don't make any sense. I pass a bearded Spanish man in a shadowy doorway who warns me not to venture down to this part of town as it's dangerous. There are immigrants living in some of the rundown houses, men who work in the nearby green-houses. I think about stopping and telling him not to be so goddamned racist, but I can't speak.

As I run, the image of Anna looking at Rich flashes into my mind again. I try to rationalize the situation. Perhaps she's just got a crush on him, I tell myself. He's a good-looking guy. She's just met him. He's been friendly to her. That's understandable. And it's happened to Rich in the past, where his general superficial niceness has been mistaken for something else. Despite my best efforts to convince myself this is what's happening here – there's nothing to it, I've imagined it all – I feel uneasy. I remember other things that have happened in the past too, when he's been off his head on drugs.

I picture Rich and Anna at the table on Payton's terrace that first morning. How their conversation seemed rehearsed. Looking back, they didn't seem like strangers. And then there was the way she looked at me after I'd humiliated myself by smashing that jar of gazpacho in the larder. There was something about her gaze, an amusement, perhaps even a sense of triumph, that had unsettled me.

I carry on down the alley – surely it must curve around to meet the main road at some point? – but I find myself in a tangle of streets that seem to lead nowhere. Now it's so dark that I have to take out my phone and use the torch to guide me. The smell of frying fish and sewage hits me. Welcome to the real Spain, I say to myself. The bearded man's warning, telling me that this area of the town is dangerous, comes back to me. I try to dismiss his words, banish them from my mind. But then I hear footsteps behind me.

14

RICH

I push through the crowds, past the fake funeral cortege and down the main street to where our car is parked. There's no sign of her there. I look around me and call out her name. But all I can hear is the distant noise of the celebrations in the square and the crying of a baby in a nearby house. I take out my phone and dial her number, but the call goes straight to voicemail. I begin to panic. I'll never forgive myself if something happens to her. All this is my fault. If only I'd never met Anna. My mind goes back to that night again. The night of the funeral.

'We can go back to my hotel,' I told her, tasting the red wine on her lips, in her mouth. Even though I'd inherited Marianne's house, I didn't want to stay there.

'No – I can't wait that long,' she said. 'Come with me. I know somewhere.'

She led me down a pathway, through a towering archway

of bamboo and along another track to the river. The sun turned the water to liquid gold and a few moments later both of us were naked. The sex was like nothing I'd ever experienced. Anna led the way, positioning me just how she wanted me. I don't know how long it lasted, but it seemed to go on all night. After each climax we rested in each other's arms, and she told me how much she liked having sex outside. There was a place down on the coast, a wild beach, that she loved. She'd like to take me there. Before she could finish telling me about it, we started again. There was a rawness about it all, as if this was the final night on Earth and we were the last couple in the universe. I felt like I could tell her anything.

It wasn't until the next morning, when the first rays of the sun caressed my skin, that I thought about the implications of what I'd done. It was only a one-night stand, I told myself, nothing meaningful, and I'd soon be back with Mia. After all, Anna had told me she was going to leave Andalucía so she could carry on her travels through Spain, perhaps other European countries, to find some more stories which she hoped she could sell back to British newspapers or magazines.

But now Anna is here. Back in Val Verde.

When I saw her again that day on the terrace at Payton and Bill's house I felt sick to my stomach. I didn't know what to say to Anna and I was certain that Mia could pick up on the fact I was behaving oddly. But thankfully, I think she was more worried about Hans being a potential source of drugs.

What the fuck was Anna playing at? What was she doing here in Val Verde? She told me she'd been up in Valencia when she'd seen a tweet of mine announcing my imminent arrival in the eco-village and so she thought she'd come and pay me a visit. Nothing ventured, etc. She told me she couldn't stop thinking about me and that time down by the river. Of course, I was flattered – who wouldn't be? As soon as she touched me, the anger dissipated and was replaced by lust. I had to have her. Just the once. And the sex was just as good as before. And the once turned to twice, turned to three, five times, every day when Mia's back was turned, seeing that old lady. I told myself that I'd tried my best to resist Anna, but the attraction between us had just been too strong. It was like one of the laws of physics, so real someone should have invented a formula for it.

Tonight Mia had seen us together, but what exactly had she witnessed? Sure, we were sitting at a table together and Anna had been giving me one of her fuck-me looks. But what could Mia prove? That I was friendly with Anna and yes, she fancied me and okay, I fancied her back. So what?

There's no crime in that.

15

MIA

I turn around and see Rich. I immediately try to run from him, but he grasps hold of me. I'm desperate to try to free myself, but he's strong, too strong. He grabs hold of my wrists and pushes me against a wall.

'Mia, Mia, calm down,' he says. 'What's wrong – what's happened?'

I feel as though I'm choking. I can hardly get the words out. 'I – I saw . . .'

'What – what did you see?'

'You and that—'

'Who?'

I don't want to say her name. 'That – that girl.'

'I've been in the bar with Freya, Hans and Anna. I saw that you wanted to speak to your old lady so I headed off for a drink and joined them there. We were waiting for you to join us.'

I suddenly don't trust myself. 'So – nothing happened?'

'What do you mean, "happened"?' Rich's voice is clinical and precise, his words so logical in contrast to my low-level hysteria.

I'm embarrassed to spell it out now. 'Between you and – and Anna?'

As he laughs I can feel his beer-soured breath on my face. 'Of course nothing's happened.'

He's lied to me before, but I can't see his eyes to know if he's telling the truth; the darkness is like a shroud that covers everything.

Suddenly he says something which makes me wonder whether he can read my mind. 'What are you doing down here in this dark alley? You know this isn't good for you.' He releases his grip on me and takes me by the hand. 'No wonder you began to panic.'

He starts to lead me back up the alley and towards a side street that has some streetlights. When we emerge into the artificial glow he grasps hold of my shoulders and studies me, assessing me for signs of, what? Paranoia? Rage? Fear? Knowledge? I still can't get the way Anna looked at him out of my mind. Those brown eyes locked on his face as if she wanted him.

'Now, tell me what all this is about.' His tone is that of a teacher who's just discovered a small child crying in the playground.

I take a deep breath and wipe my eyes. 'It's nothing – I was just being stupid.' I don't entirely believe what I'm saying, but the words trip out of my mouth. 'I must have got confused.'

'You've every right to be suspicious after . . .' He breaks

off from what he's saying, runs his hand through my hair and strokes my face. He leans in and kisses me, a soft caress that begins to erase the vision of Anna and him in the bar. 'But you know you can trust me, right?'

16

RICH

Mia is talking in her sleep, again. I like to watch her like this, as she struggles with her words, her lips quivering like a couple of fat worms, her eyes moving in their sockets as if there's something buried beneath her skull desperate to push its way out.

The scientist in me knows she's just experiencing a normal REM sleep pattern, where her blood pressure rises, her heart rate increases and her breathing quickens. The motor neurons in Mia's body are undergoing a process of hyperpolarization, which results in the almost complete paralysis of the body. She's absolutely helpless, at her most vulnerable. When she's like this she'll most likely be experiencing a vivid dream, which often mutates into a nightmare. These will start with a soft whimper or low moan, which then becomes something more guttural, as if she's got something stuck in her throat or chest.

Sometimes I can hear the words: 'Mummy', 'What's

happening?', 'No – not that', and 'In the woods'. By this point, she can be thrashing around like something possessed, her hands clawing at the sheets and blankets in a frantic bid to brush them from her body. 'No, not on me,' she sometimes says, or, 'Not under – I can't see.' It's the language of a little girl, one trapped in a moment so full of horror that she is forced to play it out over and over again in her sleep. Finally, after she can take it no longer, she wakes with a cry, sometimes a scream.

Tonight, I wonder if she's dreaming about Anna. About what she saw, about what I said to her. I think she believed me when I told her nothing had happened between us. I know I have to be careful, considering everything that's gone on. It's important to show her attention, to show her that I care. And so, as she continues to moan, I switch on the light and reach out for her. I gently wake her and tell her that she's been having one of her nightmares.

I hold her in my strong arms and she, in turn, grips me as if she's fallen into deep water and I'm saving her from drowning. At this moment I know I'm the most important person in the world. Tears spill down her face as she remembers the horrors of her dreams. I whisper to her that I'm here, it's me, Rich. I press into her, reassuring her of my physical presence. I tell her that I will always protect her. No one is going to harm her. And she trusts me. She believes in me. The fear turns into relief and then into something else, something like desire. She whispers that she wants me to make love to her. To make her feel present, *alive*.

And so I do.

17

MIA

I'm walking along the *camino* to collect our post from one of the makeshift letter boxes at the end of the path when I catch a glimpse of her walking towards me. The sight of Anna, with her blonde hair shining in the bright morning sunlight, stops me in my tracks, and I think how best to avoid her. But there's nowhere to hide. And so I continue along towards her, feeling like an animal that is knowingly walking into the sightline of a predator.

My heartbeat is running faster than my walking pace, the hairs on the back of my neck begin to stand on end, and my breathing is quick and shallow. I tell myself there's nothing to worry about. Rich had reassured me that Anna must have a crush on him, nothing more than that. And I'd believed him. He'd made love to me in the middle of the night, and the sex had erased Anna from my mind. But now she's here. The memory of her looking at him with unabashed desire flashes into my mind. It's just a silly infatuation, I tell myself. Nothing more than that.

I try to prepare myself for the encounter – I intend to smile politely, perhaps say hello, and continue along the *camino* – but Anna is slowing down, and she's directing her mega-watt smile at me.

'Wasn't it amazing last night, at the fiesta?' she says. 'I've never seen anything like it. I got some great shots of it all. Want to see?'

Before I get the chance to answer, she frees the camera from her shoulder and cradles it tenderly. She presses a button and it pings to life. The screen lights up and she uses her thumb to move between images. There are shots of the candlelit procession; the women dressed in mourning; the coffin tacked with sardines, and close-ups of mantillas; candle flames; and the dead, unseeing eye of a fish.

'I loved the pagan atmosphere of it all, didn't you?' she gushes, totally insensitive to my obvious lack of interest. 'The way it has all the iconography of a Christian ritual – the funeral procession, the parade, the women in mourning, the wailing – but underneath it was so shockingly transgressive. Who dreamed up this shit, that's what I want to know.' She stops to look at me and blinks, as if a thought has just occurred to her. 'What happened to you last night? We were waiting in the bar for you. Did you get lost?'

'No, I just didn't feel very well, that's all,' I mumble.

'That's a shame – was it the crowd? Did it get too much for you?'

'Just a headache.'

She looks down and continues to flick through her images. 'You missed a wild night. Some guys from Desert Shoots joined us later. They really know how to party, I'll give you that. Here – look at this.'

There's a montage of images taken in what looks to be one of the streets off the main square. A group of young people, some of them with dreads, are playing a drinking game. There's a shot of a handsome, grinning boy in his early twenties, his shirt soaked through with what looks like beer. A Scandinavian-looking woman is dancing on a low wall, her face full of joy. Guy, one of the few I recognize, is pointing at something beyond the frame of the image, his face creased with laughter. And then there's a shot of Hans, smoking something, his eyes rolled back in his head. The photo reminds me of that time I came home from the parents' evening to find Rich like that. Perhaps Anna senses my discomfort because she double-clicks on the image to remove it, but as she does so she leaves her thumb on the button too long or something because she's scrolling through her collection at top speed. A kaleidoscope of digital photographs flashes by: strips of plastic blowing in the wind, the toxic detritus left over after the abandonment of a greenhouse; men on hi-tech metal stilts erecting the supports of an *invernadero*; a close-up of a rivulet of sweat pouring down the spine of a black man's back; and piles of discarded tomatoes, their flesh open and rotting.

'Shit,' she says under her breath. 'I've had this camera a couple of months and I thought I'd mastered every feature, but obviously there's some mysterious button that . . . Sorry.'

'Anyway, I must get to the . . .' But something stops the words from my mouth.

It's a closely cropped image of a man looking directly to camera, smiling at the person taking his photo. Even though

I know every inch of his face, it takes me a while to register that it's Rich.

'Fuck,' she says, pressing down on a button to try to move the image forwards. But the photograph of Rich remains on the screen. 'What's wrong with this stupid camera?'

Although I am fuming inside, I swallow my anger and instead try to make light of it. 'Oh, that's a lovely photo of Rich.'

'Yeah, it's a good one, isn't it?' she says, as Rich's face stares out of the screen at us.

He's wearing an old blue T-shirt that I recognize and his auburn hair is falling around his shoulders and ruffled, almost as if it's dried off in the sun after a swim. I bend down to study the image in more detail. I check the background, but there are no clues other than it was taken against an old stone wall. In the far right-hand corner of the ancient brick-work there is what looks like the remnants of some old graffiti daubed in white paint, but I can't make out what it says. But the backdrop is not the important thing here. My focus returns to Rich. He is smiling and his eyes are on fire.

In fact, his expression is identical to Anna's in the bar last night.

18

RICH

Mia throws a couple of letters and a scientific journal down on the kitchen table. I try to catch her eye, but she turns her head away from me.

'You'd think that they'd make this recyclable, wouldn't you?' I say, as I rip open the plastic envelope and confine the packaging to the bin. 'So much for sustainability, eh?'

But I'm met with a stony silence from Mia. I watch her as she unscrews the base of the stove-top coffee pot and empties the used grains into the compost bin. As she moves towards the sink, I catch a glimpse of her ashen face. Her eyes are as hard as ball bearings.

'Mia? Are you okay?'

She slowly fills the base of the pot with water, but as she begins to spoon the coffee into the filter her hands begin to shake and she spills some grains onto the work surface. She tries to steady herself, but it's no good and after a few more grains fall onto the unit, she bangs everything down in frustration. Water pours out of the pot and seeps its way across the wood, while coffee grains scatter across the unit like hundreds of minute ants.

'Fuck!' she shouts.

'What's wrong?' I try to kid myself I haven't got a clue, but it must be something to do with last night. I'd done my best to reassure her that Anna only had a stupid crush on me, that it was nothing more than that. Now what?

'I can't even make a cup of coffee without fucking up.'

It's rare for Mia to swear once, never mind twice in quick succession. I need to be careful what I say. 'Is this something to do with coming here? To Spain, I mean? I know it hasn't been easy for you, what with—'

As I try to help clear up the mess – dabbing away with cloths and paper towel – she stops to look at me.

'Why did Anna have a photo of you?'

Now it's my turn to swear. But I stop myself from doing so out loud. I carry on mopping up the water and coffee granules, hoping this will buy me a little extra time.

'What do you mean?' I try to make the words sound as guileless as possible, as if I haven't a clue what she's talking about.

'Anna – she has a picture of you on that camera of hers.'

'Does she?' I ask, as I continue to wipe down the surfaces.

'Don't you remember her taking one?'

'I suppose she must have snapped me when I wasn't looking,' I say as I confine the paper towels to the compost and wash my hands under the cold tap to get rid of the last traces of the grains. 'Not surprising considering she carries that camera everywhere she goes.'

'But this wasn't a quick snap.'

What the hell is Mia going to say next? Surely Anna can't have been so stupid as to take a photo of me sleeping or even worse, while we'd just . . .

'No – it was one of you looking straight at the camera. Like you knew you were having your photo taken. Standing in front of an old castle or something?' She raises her eyebrows and crosses her arms as she waits for my explanation.

I need to think fast. I remember Anna taking some photos of me when we'd escaped Val Verde for an afternoon when Mia was seeing her old lady. I'd told Mia that I needed to call in at a solar power stockist down by the coast for some essential pieces of equipment. I knew Mia didn't understand the first thing about our system and she'd be none the wiser if I returned with the remnants of an old car battery. Anna had taken me to her favourite wild beach – a stretch of unspoilt coastline you could only access by a short hike – where we'd had sex, swam, and had sex again. On the way back to the car she'd taken some shots of me standing in front of a derelict look-out tower, but what the hell was she doing showing the photos to Mia?

I wasn't certain exactly what Anna had told her and so I had to keep my answer as vague as possible. 'Oh, yeah, I remember,' I say, trying to make it sound super casual. 'I think it was some-thing to do with a test shot, shutter speeds or was it lighting? It only took a second or so, so I thought nothing of it.'

'Really?' There's an icy tone to her voice.

I try not to let her see me swallow, nervously. 'Is – did – was Anna showing off her camera to you, or—'

'You could say that, yes.'

I sigh in frustration. 'Listen, Mia, if this is about last night,

I've already told you nothing is going on.' I decide the best way to defend is to go on the attack. I begin to raise my voice. 'But if you don't believe me, then there's nothing I can do about it. We've talked about these tendencies of yours before. How you can get things out of proportion – and I know why you do that.'

'But I don't think—'

'I get why you feel you may need to do that, what with your history. What did the therapists say? That you've got a risk of over-attachment, or something? You've lost something – someone – very precious to you in the past, and you don't want that to happen again to you in the future, but in the process you overcompensate and read too much into things. You see things that aren't there. That's the gist of it, isn't it? But you've got to be careful not to drive people away.'

She tries to interrupt, but I raise my hand and carry on talking. 'I know change can be stressful – and I thought coming here might trigger something in you, but you've got to get things into perspective. You can't carry on like this. *I* can't carry on like this.'

She looks down at the tiled floor.

'You believe me, don't you?'

She nods obediently, like an infant accepting its punishment. 'Sorry,' she whispers.

It looks as though the strategy has worked. 'Sorry, I got angry with you,' I say, taking a deep breath and lowering my voice to that of a caring professional, 'but you can't keep jumping to conclusions. It's not healthy for you, and it's certainly not fair on me.' I stroke her hair and pull her towards me. 'Now, how about a nice cup of coffee?' I smile at her as I say, 'I think it's best if I make it though, don't you?'

19

MIA

After coffee, I tell Rich I need to go for a walk to clear my head. Hiking up the steep slope that leads towards the plateau and through the barren, dry landscape, scattered with abandoned, broken houses, I breathe in the heady aroma of wild thyme. As I make my way across the hard ground, covered with shards of crystal, listening to the sound of goat bells in the distance, I replay my recent conversations with Anna and Rich.

She's an intelligent, sharp woman who takes photographs professionally – of course she knows how to use that digital camera. And if that's the case then what's she playing at? Had she scrolled through her images so she could deliberately show me one that she'd taken of Rich? And despite everything that Rich has said to me, about my history, my tendency for – what was it? – over-attachment, I don't believe him. I know something's going on. I've seen that same look of desire – first

Anna in the bar, then Rich in that photo – and I can feel it in my marrow. It can't be my paranoia. Not this time. This feels *real*.

I know there's no point in questioning Rich any more, as he'll just deny it and make me out to be unstable again. I don't want to play the part of the hysterical woman. I've spent my life trying to get myself together, to appear normal, and, for the most part, I've succeeded. What I require is something more substantial than my feelings or my instincts. I need evidence.

I stop on the hillside, suddenly out of breath, and turn to face the valley. It's fascinating to see Val Verde from a different perspective, with the whitewashed houses dotted along the side of the opposite bank, the vibrancy of the strips of vegetable and fruit terraces, the soothing pale green of the olive groves, the tall elegance of the bamboo nearer the river, their tips swaying in the light breeze. I seek out *La Casa de la Luz*, its vast array of solar panels on the roof glinting in the early spring sunshine. I spot Payton and Bill's house, set back from the *camino*, a blaze of bougainvillea framing an archway. I blush as I remember the way I behaved that first day I was there – that embarrassing scene in the pantry – but perhaps it was because I picked up on the odd vibes between Rich and Anna.

As my eyes continue to scan the village, my focus comes to rest on a small white house, with a tiled roof and a blue door. It's one of the houses belonging to Desert Shoots, the one where Freya lives, the one where Anna is staying. What was it Rich had told me that first night we arrived? He'd taken my hand as he led me into the house and said, 'Val Verde is the kind of place where people don't need to lock their homes.'

Suddenly energized, I run along the track that leads down into the village. I cross some stepping stones over the river and take the loop that runs back up through the land belonging to Desert Shoots. As I pass one of the vegetable terraces, I see Freya working with a clutch of volunteers, digging over a patch of bare soil. I walk through the arboretum, the air fresh with the smell of pine trees, and up to the *camino*. A minute or so later, I'm standing outside Anna's house.

I knock on the wooden door, but there's no reply. I knock again. Still nothing. I push and the door opens, and I call out Freya's name. If Anna answers, I can innocently say that I'd hoped to find Freya here so I could ask her about some seedlings that she'd promised me.

'Hello? It's only me – M-Mia.' As I announce myself, my voice breaks. 'Freya?'

It's dark inside the house, as dark as a tomb. I feel a panic begin to crackle and sizzle inside me. For a second, I'm back *there*, in that place I've been running from all my life. But I take a deep breath and count – slowly – to ten and back. By the time I manage to calm myself, I'm convinced no one is at home.

I move slowly around the interior, my eyes now accustomed to the gloom. I don't want to open one of the internal shutters or put on a light in case it draws attention to the fact I'm here. I'm not sure what it is I'm looking for exactly. I'm certain Anna won't have left her precious camera lying around her temporary home as she takes it everywhere she goes, but I still might find something useful. I move slowly, like a cat in unfamiliar territory, making my way around the ground-floor sitting room. There's a wood burner, a two-seater sofa with a patterned blanket thrown across it, a small table, two dining chairs, and a bookshelf. I pass through the small kitchen, at the back of which is a set of stairs, their surface covered with ceramic tiles.

As I climb, I notice that the floor tiles stop halfway up the staircase, as if someone had run out of money or interest and abandoned the job. The stairs open into a small space which contains an old wooden wedding chest, which once would have housed the sheets and bedlinen of a newly married bride. There are two doors that lead off from here. I push open the one nearest to me, and step into the room.

I blink back the morning sunlight that streams in through an open window, but it doesn't take long for me to realize this is Freya's room. Amongst the mess, I spot a clothes rail full of yoga pants and batique-print tops, the air carries a trace of patchouli oil, and on a small bedside table by the unmade futon there's a thick book about the power of herbs. I turn around, close the door and step into the room that must be Anna's. In contrast to the untidiness of next door, this room, with its bamboo ceiling, is neat and tidy, with a double bed complete with clean, bright white bedding, a single wardrobe, and a chest of drawers, on which sits an expensive laptop. I think about turning around, getting out of the house, pretending I'd never set foot here. But then I think of Anna's fuck-me eyes in the bar and the way Rich was looking at her as she took that photo of him. Rich's words – 'You see things that aren't there' – snake through my mind. No, I'm not going to turn around and slink away. I need to find a trace of him, or something that links them together.

Although I'm sure I won't be able to access it, I open the computer. Of course, it's password-protected. I half-heartedly try a few keywords that I pick out at random – AnnaFleming; Annaphotography; FlemingAnna; even AnnaandRich – but of course they're all rejected. I close it and begin to open the drawers of the chest. One contains a mass of leads and cables, another a map of the area, together with a guidebook to Andalucía. Another contains a couple of notebooks, full of handwritten interviews with the men who work in the greenhouses. I find a collection of thongs and underwear, a nest of bras, under which lies a packet of contraceptive pills. So she's having sex, or at least thinking of having sex. This is significant, but it doesn't mean she's having sex with Rich.

I walk over to the bed, and peel back the duvet. As I check the sheet for the stains of lovemaking and find nothing, I feel ashamed. What the hell am I doing? Perhaps Rich is right. Maybe I am unbalanced and my perception really is skewed.

Just as I'm about to leave I stop and look at the wardrobe. It's the one thing I haven't investigated. A quick look and then I'll go. As I ease open the door, I take in a hint of Anna's perfume. It's sexy and sophisticated, just like her. My fingers caress her cool but pricey clothes, labels I could never afford: an Isabel Marant blue denim shirt, a baby pink cardigan by Ganni, black trousers from A.P.C., a red silk Ulla Johnson dress. But there, at the back of the wardrobe, I see something that stands out. It's a man's white shirt by Ralph Lauren.

I feel the blood rush to my face, my hands sweaty as I take it out and examine it. Three years ago I gave Rich a white Ralph Lauren shirt for his birthday. On a night out, one of his friends accidentally brushed past him with a lit cigarette and left a small burn mark on the cotton. Surely it can't be the same one? I peel back the right-hand cuff to reveal a small hole, surrounded by a halo of darkness.

The walls of the room begin to close in on me. I'm back there, back in the earth again.

I try to open my mouth to scream, but I can't breathe. The soil is in my nostrils, in my throat. I blink and the grit hurts my eyes. I try to move my arms, but it's too heavy. The same with my feet, my legs. I can just about wiggle a couple of my fingers, a sign that I'm still alive. Just.

The memory has played itself out so many times over the years that I'm uncertain how much is true. With each remembering comes another reconstruction, another slight edit, another reimagining. I know the facts, of course, and they don't change. It's just that each time the events of that day – 6 May 1990 – come back to me, I visualize them in a slightly different way. Of course, I know what happened from the newspapers and what various people – the police, counsellors, Mum's relatives – told me over the years. How, one Sunday afternoon, my mother and I had been out walking with Peter, our Fox Terrier, near the woods close to our house in Forest Row, East Sussex.

It was a beautiful spring day. Bluebells bloomed all around me. Mum said that the air smelt fresh, like a new beginning. Peter was off the lead and suddenly he took off, perhaps captivated by the trail of some distant rabbit. Mum called after him, but he was gone, disappearing into the trees. Mum started to run – the last time this had happened Peter had been gone for hours – and she told me to stay where I was. She'd only be a minute. I remember I sat down on a damp rock and started to pick some bluebells to make into a bouquet for Mummy. Sometimes she'd be sad. I saw her crying at the kitchen table. Sometimes she'd shout at someone on the telephone. A man I think was my daddy. But he'd been gone for such a long time that I only had a faint memory of what he looked like. He was more a silhouette, just the outline of a man, than an actual living being.

Just as I was interlacing the stems of the bluebells together, wrapping them around one another into a plait, I heard a scream.

'Mia!' Her voice was like I'd never heard it before. It was high-pitched, cracked with fright. Like something from one of the films that she watched late at night when I was supposed to be asleep.

I dropped my little bouquet and started to run towards her voice. The trees all looked the same. Row after row of closely knitted pines like some kind of sinister maze. I called out for her and heard nothing. I ran in what I thought was the right direction, past an enormous pile of rotting wood. The sound of my own breathing scared me. Where was she? Where was Peter? I scoured the forest for signs of another person, a grown-up who would know what to do, who would be able to put everything right. What had happened? Had Peter gone down some rabbit hole? Had Mum fallen over and hurt her ankle?

Then her voice split the air again. 'Don't look. Eyes shut, tight shut.' Was she talking to herself or to me?

Another scream. 'Mia – run! Get help. Please, please, don't—'

Her words mutated into a howl. I didn't know what to do. I couldn't move. Tears poured down my face. The world outside seemed to melt away. I looked at the bluebells and remembered the flowers I had picked to give to Mum. Normally, I did everything she said. She got mad when I didn't. Sometimes she shouted, her eyes got all hard, her forehead became knotted with lines. Sometimes she opened the door of the fridge and poured herself some of the clear, sour-smelling liquid that made her go all sleepy.

But something told me not to do as she said. Not that day. I needed to see what was wrong. I had to go to her. I wiped my tears with the sleeves of my cardigan and ran as fast as I could towards the source of her voice. Ravens seemed to mock my efforts, calling to each other in a cruel commentary, or was it some terrible warning? But I carried on. At one point, I tripped, crashing to the ground with a thud, grazing my knee, cutting the palms of my hands. But despite the stinging pain, I pushed myself upwards. I had to see my mum. I carried on, through the pines, towards what looked like a clearing. As I approached, I heard something, not my mother's voice, but something that sounded like muffled cries, a kind of gasping, a quick intake of breath, that I'd last heard when Mum had burnt herself on the oven. But I knew it didn't come from her. It was much deeper. It was the sound of a man.

I moved slowly, like the neighbour's cat that snaked its way past our house without Peter seeing. Instinct told me to be quiet, to make myself invisible. I hid behind a tree and gradually shifted my head to one side to see. The spectacle forced me to emit an involuntary cry. I moved my head back behind the tree and clamped a hand over my mouth. I couldn't move. I thought about shouting for help, but then the man – the man who was doing something to my mother – would come for me. Perhaps this was some kind of game? Like the time I'd come downstairs to see her with someone. I thought the cries I'd heard then were ones of pain, but she told me she was having fun and that I should go back upstairs.

I shifted my position and looked out from the other side of the tree. That's when I saw the blood. There was a knife on the ground, covered in it. And a pool of redness by Mum. The man was heaving himself up and down on her. Mum lay still, not moving. Perhaps she was playing dumb, like I did sometimes when my friend Sally came round for hide and seek. I'd hold my breath and not move, close my eyes, thinking that if I stayed silent and blind to the world she wouldn't find me. The man was red in the face, not just from what he was doing to Mum. There was a splatter of blood across his forehead, on his cheeks and chin. His palms were covered with it too.

I had to do something, I knew that. If only I could stop him. I looked around at the ground. There was a rock, a good-size one. I bent down, but my hands looked tiny compared to the moss-covered stone. I tried to prise it out of the ground, but it wouldn't budge. There were some sticks, old, rotten things, but they wouldn't be much good against the big man.

Just then I heard something. A rustling. Then a loud bark. I looked up. It was Peter. He'd seen something – Mum? – and had started to run towards her. He must have thought it was some kind of game, I think, one that he hoped he could join in. Peter bounded towards the man, who turned his head and swore under his breath. He'd been interrupted. It was obvious he wanted to finish something. As Peter – the most loving, kind, innocent creature you'd ever meet – bounced towards him, the man picked up a rock and threw it at him. The stone hit him on his side, and Peter winced in shock and pain.

I couldn't bear it any longer. I knew he'd already hurt Mum, but I couldn't let him hurt my dog too. I moved quickly, out from behind the tree, and called for Peter. He recognized me, pricked up his ears and started in my direction.

But the dog wasn't the only thing that saw me.

The slam of a door wrenches me out of the past. I hear footsteps below and the vague sound of someone humming. Shit. Is it Anna? I stand up and look for a way out. There's no escape apart from the front door, back down on the ground floor. I bend down and check under the bed, but the space has been taken up by a couple of suitcases. I scan the rest of the bedroom for a place to hide, but there's nowhere apart from inside the single wardrobe and that would be a tight squeeze. Perhaps there's somewhere amongst the mess of Freya's room. As quietly as I can, I edge my way out of Anna's room, but just as I'm about to step across the landing, I hear the scuffle of a person coming through the kitchen, around the corner and up the stairs towards me. It's too late to do anything, and so I freeze.

'Mia – what are you doing here?'

It's Freya.

'I – I . . .' I can hardly speak. I feel paralysed, the pull of the earth near.

'My God, are you all right?'

She runs up the stairs. She tries to make sense of the situation, glancing towards the door to her room and back at me, before she takes me by the shoulders.

'Tell me, what's wrong? What—?'

'I'm sorry.' My words come out as a series of disjointed fragments. 'It's just that – Rich – and Anna. I saw – in the bar. He said it was – nothing. But on her – her camera. A photo. Him. And then – in her room – a shirt – a cigarette burn – a present – his.'

She pieces together the words and somehow makes sense of what I'm saying. 'Oh fuck, you poor thing. They've been having an affair?'

I nod as the tears begin to form in my eyes and run down my cheeks.

'The bastard,' she says. 'How long has it been going on? Sorry, you probably don't want to talk about it. Look at you – you're shaking all over. Come downstairs and I'll make you a cup of herbal tea. I've got just the thing to calm your nerves.'

20

RICH

Mia's hardly said a word to me since arriving back at the house. And so I suggest a trip to the beach to try to cheer her up. It's probably too early in the year for her to swim, but I know Mia loves the sea. Just looking at it seems to do her the world of good.

I could do with a change of scene too. I keep telling myself it's probably best to keep my distance from Anna. I've even told myself that it would be better if I cooled it for good. Each time we meet – usually when Mia goes off to see Blanca, and Freya is out – I prime myself to break it off with her. But with one flash of those dark eyes, one whiff of her musky smell, one touch of her skin, those resolutions fall away and I find myself in her bed. Afterwards, I lie there, looking up at her bamboo ceiling, and lose myself by smoking a joint.

I hide my stash in a tin behind a stone down on one of the terraces, as I'd promised Mia I'd kicked the habit. My mind goes back to that awful work trip to a posh hotel in the home counties, when I'd got wasted the night before I was due to give a presentation. During my PowerPoint talk about the new technology of a certain range of solar panels, I'd started to talk gibberish. Really mental stuff that didn't make any sense. I knew I was doing it, but I couldn't stop myself. Initially, my bosses were sympathetic – they assumed I was having some kind of fit or breakdown – until the hotel management complained that one of the chambermaids had found drugs in my room. It's not surprising that they sacked me and I'd had to find another job.

With the car windows wide open, we drive out of the village, along the road that winds over the mountain and down to the motorway. We pass abandoned old houses, terraces of olive trees bounded by walls of prickly pear, a couple of goat farms. After twenty minutes on the motorway, driving south, the greenhouses begin to crowd the edges of the road. It's impossible to see into them as they are constructed with opaque plastic sheeting. A toxic smell fills the car, something so rancid it catches the back of the throat.

'God, what's that awful stench?' asks Mia. Her voice is sharp, tinged with anger.

'I guess it's from the greenhouses, the chemicals,' I reply. 'And all in the search for the perfect tomato.'

My attempt at trying to lighten the conversation fails, as she falls silent once more, her face a picture of misery.

'You okay?' I ask, as we take the turning for Campohermoso that leads towards the Cabo de Gata, the natural park.

She nods, but turns away from me.

'I don't know about you, but I'm looking forward to a

good lunch by the beach,' I say, smiling and placing a hand on her knee. 'I think we deserve it, don't you?'

'What do you mean?'

'I know it hasn't been easy for you – all of this, moving to a new country. Even though you're the linguist and can speak the language, I realize it's been hard.'

She doesn't answer. What's she thinking about? The dreams, the nightmares, have been getting worse. She calls out in the night and the shadows under her eyes are more pronounced.

'Anyway, I thought you deserved a bit of a break and so I'm taking you to . . . well, let's just say a very special place. It's not fancy or stuffy, don't worry about that, but I think you'll like it. I came here with Marianne – on one of the rare days when we could still have a civilized conversation.'

Her face darkens as we drive through the land decimated by hundreds of *plásticos*. She's probably questioning whether there's any place worth visiting in the midst of all this ugliness. It looks like a shanty town. Makeshift washing lines are strung up between broken-down shacks. People sit on their doorsteps, their faces dirty, their eyes empty. We pass men on bicycles, swinging wildly along the road as if this is the first time they've been on two wheels. Occasionally we glimpse inside an old greenhouse, the plastic sheeting ripped away to reveal the hollow interior: a framework of metal, a covering of rotting crops, an expanse of dead ground. To lift the mood I put on one of the CDs that Mia chose to help pass the time on the drive from England. Camarón de la Isla, a flamenco singer – not my choice of music, but I know she likes it. But even this does nothing to improve her spirits.

As we drive towards the coast, the number of greenhouses

lessens and in the distance we spot an old windmill. The road becomes a series of twists and soon we're dropping into a landscape that looks like the inside of an extinct volcano. Stone walls stretch up precipitous cliffs, a sign that this was once farmland.

After Las Hortichuelas, a green oasis surrounded by barrenness, we turn right, along another bendy road with steep drops either side, and into a valley occupied by the former gold mining town of Rodalquilar. We climb higher, up to a point where we cannot see anything in front of us – as though we're about to drop off the edge of a cliff – until the view opens up to reveal a coastal road and an expanse of shimmering blue sea. I'd hoped that the sight of the coastline would help cheer her up, but she still looks unmoved.

I pull into a patch of rough ground, deserted apart from a couple of camper vans, that looks out over the bay. As we get out of the car, the midday sun warms our faces. We stand in silence and watch the waves gently caress the shoreline below. In the near distance, there's a line of palm trees that lead down towards what almost looks like an island clustered with little white houses. I tell her that's where we're going for lunch – La Isleta del Moro.

After parking, we walk through the town to the jetty and gaze out to sea. A cluster of small fishing boats rise and fall with the currents and the gentle breeze. In the distance there are the twin peaks of an extinct volcano. We've got a bit of time before lunch and so we climb to the top of the headland that sticks out into the water like the back of an enormous whale.

'This was one of Marianne's favourite places,' I say, desperate to make conversation. 'She drove out here when she was making a film. I suppose when Marianne came here the whole area was different. No greenhouses. No tourists to speak of. She told me it represented a taste of freedom for her.'

Finally, Mia breaks her silence. 'What's it like being back in that house? I bet it's hard for you, isn't it?'

'It's easier now we've cleared away all her stuff and ripped down those posters and photographs. At least it doesn't feel as if she's haunting the place. Anyway, let's not talk about her. Today is all about us – and having fun.'

I take her clammy hand and lead her back towards the village and the restaurant which is situated right next to the sea. The head waiter, a man with rotting teeth but a friendly disposition and an understanding of rudimentary English, ushers us to a table covered by a crisp white cloth and the obligatory wicker basket filled with bread. I order some sparkling water and a bottle of chilled white wine, and ask him what's on the menu. Although Mia is vegetarian – and I'm vegan – I know that she sometimes has a craving for fish.

'Go on, have some sea bream or whatever, I won't mind,' I say.

'No, honestly, I'm sure there's something else.'

Her voice is flat, lifeless as one of the fish I spot on the plate of a fellow diner.

'It's a special occasion. Honestly, I won't think you're a bad person.'

The waiter continues to hover by our table.

'Well, now there's no way I'm going to have fish.' She says it lightly, as if it's a joke, but the way she turns down her mouth at one corner suggests to me she's irritated.

'Look, Mia, if you want fish, please have it – that's why we're here.'

She tells the waiter that we'll need a little more time and he bows his head and retreats inside. The terrace is beginning to fill up with more people: a few middle-aged tourists with big hats, three-quarter-length trousers and open-toed sandals; a couple of Spanish people from the city; a Scandinavian family, all bleached blond hair and blue eyes, who look as though they could be in an advert for a holiday company or a mail order catalogue.

Mia runs her finger down the menu. 'I'll have the broad beans to start and then an omelette with a big salad – that will do me.' She looks up with a strained smile. 'And what about you?' She passes the menu to me, but I don't open it.

'No fish?' I ask.

'No, I'm happy with just that, thanks.'

I can feel my temper begin to bubble and rise within me. 'But – but that's why I brought you here, so you could have something special, something different.'

'Rich – honestly, I'm not in the mood. It's okay.'

I slam the menu down on my plate. Mia looks startled, her eyes fluttering like the wings of an insect that's about to be killed. The sudden crash attracts the attention of the Scandinavians next to us. The waiter glides over and asks if we are ready to order.

'I'll have the broad beans – we'll both have the broad beans, without the ham – and a big mixed salad, one to share,' I say. 'For me, I'll have the vegetarian paella, and she will have . . . what's the best fresh fish you have?'

'Rich—'

108

'Today we have the *rape* . . . the monkfish. Or there's the *lenguado*, the sole, or then there's the—'

'Really, I'm happy to share the—'

'She'll have monkfish.'

'Very good, sir,' he says and disappears.

There's an awkward moment when neither of us says anything. We stare out to sea, at the beauty of the bay, the glint of the Mediterranean sun on the water, the fishing boats bobbing on the surface, the volcano in the distance. I take a sip of wine and then another. We're supposed to be having fun, but a cloud of misery hangs over our table, turning the sunshine black.

'There's no point sulking,' I hiss.

'I'm not sulking. I'm just a bit surprised by your behaviour, that's all.'

'This was all done for your benefit, you know.'

'I said I was happy not having fish. I don't care about the bloody fish.'

'It was all supposed to be perfect. Bringing you here. Having something special. A bit of a treat, you know. I just don't understand why you'd want to spoil it.'

'*Me* spoil it?'

The waiter appears with our starters. We fork the broad beans cooked in olive oil, sea salt and garlic into our mouths in silence, occasionally ripping off a chunk of bread to wipe our plates.

'It's delicious,' says Mia, as if she's got a mouthful of sawdust. 'Really nice.'

Her icy politeness infuriates me, but I don't say anything. I gulp back some more wine, and Mia looks at me as if to say, *Steady on – you've got to drive back.* That only makes me want to drink more. I reach for the bottle swimming in its bucket of melting ice, and pour myself another glass. I offer some to her, but she shakes her head.

She clears her throat and smiles stiffly. She's finally going to talk to me. 'So . . . the villagers seem like an interesting lot.'

'They are. All a bit odd in their own way, but I like that.'

'Who do you like the best?'

'What do you mean?'

'I just wondered if you feel you've made friends with anyone in particular?'

Is she trying to hint at something? About my relationship with Anna? I feel a line of sweat break out behind my collar. The waiter takes away our plates. The fish and the omelette, he says, are on their way.

'I like Payton – as I said, she's been really supportive.'

'She certainly seems passionate about her causes, which of course has to be admired. The other day she was telling me again about population and how it's getting out of control. She's a member of some group, a charity I think, that is campaigning to achieve a sustainable human population.'

'Sounds sensible – it's at the heart of the green movement. After all, we only have a limited amount of resources. What with reaching peak oil, the depletion of fossil fuels, limited food supplies and the overfishing of the oceans . . .'

Just then the waiter appears brandishing a bowl of salad, a plate of fish, which he places in front of Mia, and the vegetarian paella for me. I don't feel I can complete the sentence and Mia looks at what's in front of her as if she's just been served a platter of vomit.

'God, I'm sorry,' I say, gulping down more wine. 'Listen to me droning on like a jerk.'

110

She uses her fork to cut into the monkfish, flaking away the white flesh. She moves it around her plate, before scraping it off her fork with her knife, and instead starts to eat the salad. 'And what about . . . the rest of the people we've met? Hans, for instance.'

'He's a fun guy, harmless in his own way.'

'You haven't . . . ?'

'What? Bought from him? Jesus, no.'

She studies me for signs that I'm lying. 'And what about . . . what about Anna?'

I sigh as I throw my fork down onto my plate. 'For fuck's sake, Mia. We've been through this.' I grab the bottle to fill up my glass, but realize it's nearly all gone. I know I can't order any more. As I return the bottle to the bucket the rattle of the ice seems to me the loneliest sound in the world. I look over at Mia's plate. She still hasn't eaten any of the fish.

'Is there something wrong with it?'

'Rich, please.'

'I suppose it must be off – is that it?'

'No, it's fine – I just . . . I just don't have much of an appetite.'

'There's obviously a problem – waiter! Waiter!' I click my fingers, knowing how much Mia hates such vulgar displays. He scuttles over, all smiles. 'I think – I think this fish must be off or something.'

'Off?'

'Yes, off – rotten.'

'Rich, *please*. Please can we not do this.'

'But – it's fresh from the boat this morning.'

'But you see my girlfriend here ordered it and she hasn't

111

touched it. Can you see her plate? Look at it. Not one mouthful.'

Mia stands up, pushes her chair back from the table, but, as she does so, she knocks over her knife which clatters onto the terrace. The Scandinavians swivel in their chairs to look at us. I stare back, rudely, and raise my hands as if they're the ones causing a scene.

'I'm sure we can send it back to the chef,' says the waiter, keen to restore calm to his terrace. 'What else would you like? Would you prefer to see the menu again?'

But Mia looks at me with – what? Disgust? Disappointment? Regret? Then turns and storms off.

'Mia, Mia!' I shout, but she ignores me. I grab her glass of wine and drain it.

Normally, in situations like these, I'd run after her, try to make it up to her, whisper sweet things into her ears, kiss away her tears. But not now. Instead I take out my phone and make a call.

To Anna.

21

MIA

I walk along the beach, feeling the soft sand between my toes, listening to the sound of the waves licking the shoreline, and wish I was back in dirty old Hackney. Rich had promised me that we'd be living some kind of 'green dream'. But this is nothing short of a living nightmare, as if both of us are slowly losing our minds. What's happening to us?

I think back to the first time we met, at a drunken student party, in my final year. He seemed so sweet then, so funny and laid-back, not the unfaithful, angry man that I'm living with now. My best friend from my course, Sophie, who knew practically everything about me, invited me to a house party with an Eighties theme, hosted by a mate of her boyfriend, Joe. It was a messy affair – too many Jägerbombs and terrible music. We spent the night doing silly moves on the dance floor, mixing our drinks, flirting with boys.

Towards the end of the night we were just thinking about

going home when into the house walked one of Joe's friends dressed in ripped denim and a funny, curly wig, his skin smeared with fake tan. I've never heard such laughter as when he stepped into the sitting room. It was like the speakers were playing the sound of hysterical guffawing at top volume. I suppose we were all drunk and some of the lads had probably taken something. Apparently, Joe had originally said that the party was going to be fancy dress but, when he changed his mind, he'd forgotten to pass this on to his friend Richard, who had come as George Michael.

As he removed his wig, I felt so sorry for him that I took him a drink.

'I think you might need this,' I said, passing him a glass of cider.

'Thanks,' he replied, gulping down the amber-coloured liquid. 'I can't believe I was the only one who didn't get the message.'

'I don't know, I think you rather suited that wig.'

'You could always keep it – as your pet, I mean,' he said, lifting up the frightful thing. 'I think it actually might have a life of its own.'

I'd seen him hanging out with Joe, but I'd never bothered to speak to him before. But the more I talked to him, the more I realized I felt at ease with him, comfortable; a sense that he already knew me. We were getting on so well that Sophie came over to see what was going on. She prised me away from him and took me off to the kitchen to ask what I thought about him. I told her I really liked him. Did she know anything about him? She said that Richard was a year younger than me – he was in his third year, while I was in my fourth. Joe had told her that he was a decent bloke from his physics course. I suppose that was enough of a recommendation in those days. Sophie said that, if it was okay with me, she'd head home with Joe now. I told her that I'd be fine, that I'd see her tomorrow. And so I went back to Richard. We had a few more drinks and, when the party was over, he walked me to my flat. He told me all about his crazy actress mother, Marianne Ellis, who'd abandoned him as a child. But his stories weren't full of self-pity. Rather, he made her out to be some wild, exotic creature who was just too bohemian for the banalities of motherhood. I didn't talk about my own mother, of course; that conversation came much later.

We kissed that night, but we didn't go any further. We took it slowly, and he respected that, believing that I was just one of those girls who preferred romance to sex. There was a certain truth to that, but again the real reason lay in my past. We moved in with one another after our finals. I enrolled on a post-grad teaching course and Richard – or Rich, as I called him – started a job with a solar power company. Our whole future looked so bright it was almost blinding.

I knew I should tell Rich about what had happened to me when I was a girl. I told myself that if we were going to be serious, then it was his right to know. But every time that I readied myself to sit him down and tell him about that nightmare day in the Ashdown Forest in 1990, I always found an excuse. I needed to do some work for my course. He'd had a bad day and was in a bit of a crap mood. He'd had too much to drink. But eventually, one night after dinner, and feeling so nervous my whole body felt like it was twitching, I sat him down with a glass of wine.

'You see, when I was small, only six years old, something

115

happened to me, something bad . . .' I began. I could feel the tears prick my eyes, but Rich just held my hand and listened. He knew exactly what to do and, after I'd told him all about my mother, and Iain Hastings, and how I'd survived, he hugged me close and whispered in my ear. He said he would always protect me. That he'd never let anyone else hurt me. That I could always depend on him. I felt his strong arms around me, and I felt safe. Safer than I had for years.

That night, I dug out a bundle of yellowing newspaper cuttings, a mix of national and local papers, news reports, features and comment pieces, that had been left to me by my aunt, Sheila. After my mother's murder I had gone to live with her, together with my dog Peter, and I had taken her surname. She had been the one who had talked me through it all and who had given me the kind of love and support I needed. She had been the one who had told me that my mother had been pregnant at the time of her murder. My mum had never mentioned it to her sister, neither had she told me. There were no records of her visiting the doctor for a pregnancy test. I like to think that perhaps she never even knew that she was pregnant. It makes it a little easier to bear.

The edges of the parcel, tied in red ribbon, were fraying with age, and the musty smell of the package transported me back into the past. I passed the papers over to Rich who did not say a word as he scanned the awful headlines.

HORROR IN THE FOREST – MOTHER BUTCHERED

MOTHER AND DAUGHTER BURIED IN SHALLOW GRAVE

JO GIBSON MURDER DAUGHTER – HOSPITAL SAYS SHE WILL LIVE

116

JO GIBSON LATEST – SUSSEX MAN, 18, ARRESTED FOR BRUTAL MURDER OF MOTHER AND ATTEMPTED MURDER OF DAUGHTER

JO GIBSON WAS PREGNANT POST-MORTEM REVEALS

HONEY TRAP – THE INSIDE STORY OF HOW AN UNNAMED UNDERCOVER POLICEWOMAN SECURED THE CONFESSION OF FOREST ROW KILLER

PRISON SUICIDE OF FOREST ROW KILLER

IAIN HASTINGS' FAMILY STILL MAINTAIN KILLER'S INNOCENCE

When Rich finished reading the cuttings, he looked shaken and pale. 'So this man, I don't even want to say his name, this monster . . . he died in prison?'

'Hastings killed himself, yes. I only learned about it later, but he hanged himself while awaiting trial. He was arrested after some kind of undercover sting operation – a female police officer got him on tape confessing to the killing. There was a big fuss about whether it was legal or not. Before Hastings died, he changed his story and said that he was innocent.'

'Well, he would say that, wouldn't he?'

I'm wrenched back to the present by the sound of Rich's voice. He's on the beach and he's calling my name. He runs towards me and drops down onto the sand before me. He's full of contrition, telling me he knows he's been a prick, that he shouldn't have said those things to me, that he's begging for my forgiveness. He just wanted to make the day

117

nice for me. He wanted it to be special. He lifts up his hands in supplication, then gets up and tries to take me in his arms.

But I've had enough. I tell him I don't want to talk to him.

'Mia – come on, I know I was a shit back there, but it was only about a bit of fish.'

'It's more than that, and you know it.'

'What's that supposed to mean?'

I look around at the beach, one of the most beautiful I've ever seen, and yet I feel like I don't want to be here. 'I just want to go back.'

'Okay, I'll drive us to the house now.'

'No – I mean to London. I've had enough. I can't—'

'But it's only been a matter of weeks. We knew it would be hard, settling in, starting afresh in a new country. And what with your—'

'Don't give me that. The fact that I survived – the fact that I'm still here – means that I'm a damn sight stronger than you give me credit for.'

'Of course you are, and I didn't mean to suggest anything else. Just that, with your history—'

'Can't you hear yourself, Rich? You just don't get it, do you? Yes, something horrific happened to me when I was a child. But that doesn't define me, I've never let it define me. My reason for wanting to leave has nothing to do with that.'

'Well, what's it to do with? Is it the house? The village?'

I take a deep breath and tell him the truth. 'It's because of you, Rich.'

Although I whisper the words, they function like quiet bullets fired across the beach which penetrate deep into his heart. Life seems to seep out of his eyes. His upper lip

118

begins to tremble. He tries to reach out to steady himself, but there's nothing here to hold onto. He looks at me as if I'm going to change my mind, that I'm going to say something nice, something to make up for the hurt I've caused him, but I remain silent.

'I don't understand what I've done wrong.'

I can't begin to explain. Dozens of tiny thoughts snake their way through my mind, but the more I try to untangle them, the more I find myself being unable to utter a word.

'Tell me, what is it? Is it the drinking? If it is, I'll cut down – I'll stop.' He panics as he runs through a list of his supposed faults. 'I know I've taken a bit of weed – you've probably smelt it – and I know I promised you I wouldn't take anything since, since what happened before . . . so if it's that, then I'll quit. I'll throw my stash away.'

I continue to stare at him as he falls apart, tears forming in his eyes.

'I realize I shouldn't try to control you – I know I've a tendency to do that – but it's only because I want the best for you, that's all. I realize I need to give you more space. I can do that. You can show me how to do that. Mia – I promise, I'll do anything for you.'

I think back to that night in the square, the night of the funeral of the sardine. I remember the way Anna was looking at Rich. That photo of Rich on Anna's camera. The memory of his shirt with the cigarette burn hanging in her room. I don't believe him when he says Anna's only got a crush on him. That it's all one-sided. In retrospect, I'm convinced I've smelt her when I've returned from my talks with Blanca. He carries around a musky aroma that clings to him like sex on dirty bedsheets.

I *know*.

'I realize my temper is a problem, but I've always had a passionate nature,' he says. 'I thought that's what you liked about me. That I *believed* in things. Believed in you. That I wanted to make the world a better place – for us, for our . . .'

He's always resisted the idea of having kids, so why is he bringing it up now? At this moment, the prospect of having a child together makes me feel sick. I cut him off.

'Don't, please don't, Rich. All I want is for you to tell me the truth. The truth about you – and Anna.'

22

RICH

'Why does she have your shirt – the one I bought you – in her room?' Mia's face is full of pain, like a painting I once saw of a tortured medieval saint.

Shit. How does she know about the shirt? I try to buy myself an extra second of time. 'Which shirt?'

'You know which fucking shirt, Rich,' she snaps. 'The one I got you for your birthday. With the cigarette burn.'

It's difficult to begin with, the truth sticking inside me like a half-digested thing, but eventually I vomit some of it up. She tells me that if I don't, she will leave me. My only chance, she says, will be if I'm open about everything that's happened. That is the only way to save what we have together.

'It was stupid of me. It meant nothing, it was just . . .'

'Just what?'

'Sex – nothing else. I suppose I must have left the shirt there – in her room – after . . . but like I said, it was just a

121

stupid, mindless animal thing. Something – I don't know – primitive. It was wrong – I was wrong – but it's over now.'

Shock, disgust, disappointment, anger show in her face. Is there something like relief too?

'And you're certain about that?' she asks, her eyes searching out my every pore, as if by looking she'll be able to spot signs of my deceit. 'It's over – you're sure?'

'Completely. God, Mia, I've been such a jerk. I should never have got involved with her, there's no excuse. But yes, it's all finished. I don't know why . . . why I did it.'

'When did it start? How soon after we moved here?'

I can't bring myself to tell her about the real birthplace of the relationship – that it originated in the rank aftermath of Marianne's death, blooming in the hours after her funeral – and so I say that it began in the days after that first meeting at Payton's house. She makes me tell her every detail. Who made the first move? It was Anna, I tell her, which is more or less the truth. What was the sex like? It was . . . amazing, I say. How could I lie? How many times had we done it – had sex? I grapple for an answer. Five? Six? What did Anna give me that I couldn't get from her? I don't know how to answer this.

'She was . . . forbidden.' It's the best I can manage. 'There was something, I don't know, something wild about her.'

Mia nods, tears spilling down her cheeks.

'I love you, Mia, you know I do. Please forgive me. I'll do anything you want. Just don't abandon me. Not here, not like this.'

She stares off into the distance, at the paradise beach, the stretch of aquamarine sea, the far horizon.

'Look, if you want to go back to London, let's go back to

London. We can give the tenant notice on the flat, pick up where we left off. We can close up the house, pack up the car and drive back. We could be there by the end of next week or the week after. What do you say?'

There's always been something enigmatic about Mia, a part of her that she keeps secret. I suppose it goes back to her childhood. She wants to keep what happened in the past private. But now, as I look at her, waiting for her answer, that mysterious quality seems to have deepened. She's like a dark pool that stretches far underground – no matter how long you stare into it you'll never see what lies beneath.

'I don't know, Rich,' she says, wiping the tears from her cheeks. 'How do I know you'll not hurt me again? How do I know I can trust you?'

She lets me take her in my arms. She's shaking despite the heat of the afternoon sun.

'This was the first time I've ever done anything like this – and it will be the last, I promise you. It was – I don't know – some kind of madness on my part. Losing Marianne, moving here. Escaping from London, escaping from reality. None of it makes any sense, I know.'

'How can we carry on living in the same village as her? As Anna?'

'Perhaps now it's all over she'll move on. She won't want to hang around here. There's nothing left for her. I think her work, photographing the greenhouses, interviewing the workers, is nearly done. And even if it isn't, she can find somewhere else to rent. Another house somewhere, far away from Val Verde. Why should we be the ones to leave when . . . I was going to say we've done nothing wrong, when clearly I have.' Shit. My heart is thudding. Sweat burns on my skin. My mouth is dry. 'But why should *you* have to leave here? I know you'll like it if you give it another chance. You said yourself how much you've enjoyed talking to Blanca, getting to know her. You're helping her, right? You want to do the best for her?'

'Don't bring my work with Blanca into this. This is about you – what *you've* done. What you've done with . . . with Anna.' She spits out her name like she's tasted poison. 'So . . . you'll tell her. You'll tell her to leave?'

I can't believe what I'm hearing. 'If that's what it takes to keep you, then yes. Yes, I will.'

'Okay – and I want to see her gone by the end of the week.'

I swallow hard. What the fuck am I going to do?

23

MIA

My mother lay on the ground, covered in blood. I stood beside the tree and Peter ran towards me, his big tongue lolling out of his mouth, his tail wagging behind him like a crazy snake.

And the man was walking towards me, a determined gleam in his eye.

I called for Peter again, and the dog increased his pace, reaching my side.

I felt his soft fur and the quick lick of his hot tongue. But there was something odd about him, a harsh, metallic smell. I brought up my fingers and saw they were covered in a sticky redness. I ran my hands through his fur again, but there was no sign of injury. It must be my mother's blood. I held my hands in front of me, feeling as though my legs couldn't move, feeling as though something, some root or clump of earth, had grabbed my ankle. I looked up, through my bloodied fingers, and saw him. He was blond, a dirty sort of blond, with workman's clothes on, a checked shirt, and muddied wellington boots. I wanted to ask him what he'd done to my mum, but I couldn't speak. My mouth felt numb like that time I staggered out of the dentist's after having a tooth out.

The world was melting in front of me, like it was slipping off its axis. The trees started to bend, the grass shimmered. I thought I was about to faint, but then I felt a hand touch me, ever so lightly, on my shoulder.

'I don't want to hurt you,' he said. 'You haven't seen anything, have you?'

I shook my head, but I was certain that it was already trembling, along with the rest of me. I felt sick. I reached out to hold onto a tree and brought up my breakfast, the toast and Marmite Mum had made for me. Who would make my breakfast now? But then I realized the awful truth. The man who had killed my mother was here, standing over me. I wouldn't be having any breakfast. Not any more. This was it. This was how it would end. I knew about death, of course. Charlie, our guinea pig, had died and we had buried him in the garden. Mum told me all four of my grandparents were dead. And I'd seen bad things on the TV when I wasn't supposed to be watching. But this was different. This was real. First Mum, in that horrible way, and now it would be me.

The man grabbed me under the shoulder. Peter started to bark. He jumped up at the man.

'Fuck off, you stupid dog,' said the man, kicking him.

I somehow managed to find the courage to speak, but my voice was just a whisper. 'Don't – don't you hurt Peter. Please.'

The man kicked him again and I heard Peter whimper. I had to do something. I let my body go all loose, like a rag doll, and dropped to the ground. At the same time Peter bit

126

into his ankle. I wriggled free and started to run. Peter was by my side. He was barking as if in triumph. We were free. We ran towards the clearing. I forced myself not to look at my mother on the ground, but still I registered flashes of red. Her clothes were all wrong too, her skirt rucked up around her waist, her top pulled down displaying her white skin. I wanted to stop and straighten them, make her decent again. But I knew I couldn't. I had to keep running. I began to call for help, but my voice was weak, as if the man had somehow cut my vocal cords. I could hear him behind me, breathing. With each step the forest floor of twigs and rotten branches cracked and snapped. I didn't know where I was going. My eyes were full of tears and the smell of my sick mixed with the raw stench of the blood on my hands.

'Help!' I called out, the noise disturbing a group of wood pigeons. As they flew away the birds clapped as if they had just enjoyed something at the theatre, as though all of this had been staged for some kind of sick entertainment.

'Help!' I cried again, my voice breaking. 'Help me . . . please.'

But there was no one there.

Any sense of triumph and freedom died as soon as I felt his hands on me again. He hit me around the head with a rock, I think, because I remember falling to the ground and everything going dark. My last thought was for Peter: please don't hurt him, not my Peter.

I awoke with a pain splitting my head. I ran my hands over my scalp, and my fingers came back with more fresh blood on them. My blood was mixed with my mother's blood now. The image of her lying on the ground flashed through my brain again. Her body distorted, her limbs at unnatural angles, her clothes torn off her. I tried to get up, but staggered and fell back onto a carpet of leaves. I heard something nearby. It was him. He was still here.

Digging.

I opened my mouth to scream, but my voice was just a rasp. I tried again. I called for Peter, but he was nowhere to be seen. If he'd touched Peter I would . . . what? What could I do? I realized I had no one to tell. Not Mum. Not a teacher. Not Sally or any of my other friends. And I couldn't hurt him. I was powerless to do anything about it.

I began to panic. My breath seemed to get out of control, like that time I fell into the deep end of the swimming pool and I thought my lungs were going to fill up with water. When I emerged from underwater, the noise of my rapid breathing scared me.

I knew I had to try to calm down. I think about what Mum would want me to do. Eyes shut, tight shut, she had said. I closed them, blanking out the world. The darkness frightened me. I could still hear the man nearby. Uncovering the ground. What was he doing? With my eyes shut I remembered walking with my mother through the churchyard, past rows and rows of graves. I'd asked her about them and she'd told me that that's what they did with the bodies of those who were no longer with us.

My eyes stretched wide open at the certain knowledge of what was happening. He was digging a grave with the end of a large branch. A cloying sensation filled my throat at the thought of it. I looked over at the man. He was sweating. There was a panicked look about him and he kept glancing over his shoulder.

I had to do something before it was too late. But what? I could try running again but I was sure he'd just grab me like he'd done last time. And the smash around the head would likely be even harder.

It was then I thought about Mum's phone. It would be in her pocket.

This time I managed to get to my feet, and I tried to move as slowly, as stealthily as possible, like I did in those games I'd played with Sally. My feet were small and luckily as I shuffled along the ground I didn't make much noise. I was careful, despite the tears that still stung and clouded my vision, to avoid stepping on twigs or branches. I moved through a clump of trees until I saw her. She was still lying there, in the clearing. The blood had spread out around her now, staining the earth. I wanted to turn my head away, not look, like she'd told me. But I had no choice.

Her skin was losing its colour, taking on the hue of a ghost. I reached out and touched her arm. She was already getting cold. I wanted to lift her limbs, put them straight, clean her up a little, but I had no time. I looked over at the man, now consumed by his task. My tears were hot on my face and I used the wet sleeve of my cardigan again to wipe them away. I took a deep breath and told myself to just do it. And so I did. My hands moved over her body until I found the bulge of her phone in a pocket.

I brought out the mobile, opened the lid, waiting for the gentle glow of its screen. But something wasn't right. There was no light. Mum hadn't switched it on. I pressed hard on the start button, and a moment later the screen lit up. I was nearly there. But then it emitted its jaunty wake-up call, a noise that carried across the forest floor. I tried to muzzle it, shove it inside my cardie, but it was too late.

The man looked up. I heard the sound of leaves swishing on the ground. He was coming towards me.

'What the fuck—' he said. His voice was deep, angry.

He wrenched the phone from my hands and stamped on it. As I saw it being smashed to pieces, its shiny casing trampled into the earth, I realized my hopes were dying with it.

'I've had enough,' he said, grabbing me again. 'It's time for this to end.'

He dragged me across the forest floor, my arms flailing out, my voice calling, screaming, tearing the air apart. The last thing I saw was a shallow grave.

I don't know how long I'd been there. It could have been minutes, it could have been hours. I remember waking up, seeing black, panicking, thinking that the blow I'd received had not only knocked me out but blinded me too. I tried to wiggle my fingers so I could rub my eyes, but I realized I couldn't move my hands. I did the same thing with my feet, but everything felt numb, pinned down. Had the man killed me? Was I dead? Was this what it felt like? Was I in some kind of hell reserved for children who couldn't save their mothers from murder? I thought about Mum lying there, surrounded by that misshapen dress of blood. I recalled him seeing me with Mum's phone as I tried to call for help, how he'd smashed it before my eyes. The feel of his hands on me. The sight of that shallow grave.

I knew then what had happened. I was in the ground. I was in that grave. I opened my mouth to scream, but tasted the earth oozing into me. It felt as though the soil was crowding in on me, pushing into every orifice. Soon I would be nothing but dirt.

I panicked, gasped for air, took in another mouthful of soil. I tried to spit some of it out, but a small clod worked its way to the back of my mouth and slipped down my throat. I started to choke. I tried to breathe through my nostrils, but again the earth manoeuvred its way up inside me. I was being consumed by the blackness. Soon the insects came for me. I felt something scuttling inside my left ear. The hard back of a beetle on my lips. A worm curling its way up my nose. I must have lost consciousness then, and started the slow process towards death and nothingness.

The next thing I sensed was the sound of a dog barking, coming closer. Peter? I heard myself groan in an effort to scream, to tell him that I was here. I tried to kick out with my legs. Every ounce of strength I had left I used to push my way up and out of the earth. But I don't think I moved an inch. What happened then seemed so quick. The barking came nearer. My ears hurt, sensitive because I'd heard nothing but the rustle of the leaves in the wind, the beating of my own heart, the sound of fear in my throat. Then I heard a voice, a man's voice. Please let it not be him. Please say he hasn't come back to finish me off. Let me just rot in the soil.

But then I heard the sound of digging. The barking got louder. I tried to move my head, my fingers, my toes. The soil seemed to press down onto me. I felt more of it shunt its way up my nose, down my throat. Was he piling more earth on top of me? But suddenly, there was a rush of air. Something, someone, was touching me. I saw a light, a flashlight. Then a splash of water on my face. A wipe of a handkerchief. I could see. There was Peter, barking. Although I wanted to say *something – I didn't know what – I still couldn't talk. But I knew I was alive.*

'Fuck, sorry,' said the man. He was breathing quickly, like he was upset. 'What's your name, love? Look at the state of you. Take it easy. You're going to be fine.'

He touched my hands, my face. He had lovely, soft fingers, and he was holding a half-empty bottle of water. 'You're frozen. I'm going to call the police. Don't worry – you're going to be okay. Shit. Shit.' He dialled the number and could hardly get the words out. The murder of a woman. Yes, that's right. She's dead, in a shallow grave. Looks like – it looks like she's been stabbed to death. And what looks like the attempted murder of a little girl. He had to repeat the words – yes, that's right, she was buried alive next to the woman. No, there's no sign of the perpetrator. At least not that I can see.

So it was true. My mum had been murdered. It wasn't just a horrible nightmare. It was real. And I had been left for dead. As I sat there, blinking away the soil, I felt the lick of Peter's tongue on my cheek. 'Is this your dog? I was out walking and he was barking like crazy. I tried to ignore him, but he wouldn't have any of it and kept running, turning back to make sure I followed him. Lucky for you, I did. He saved your life. What's he called?'

The man took off his jacket and wrapped it around me. I felt his strong hands on me. He'd pulled me out of the ground. He'd rescued me. I was safe.

24

RICH

I'm sitting in the bar in San Mateo, waiting for Anna. I have a beer and a small plate of salted almonds in front of me. Music is blaring out of the sound system, competing with the jabber of a Spanish talk show on the wall-mounted television. All around me people are talking, talking, talking, but all I can think about is what I'm going to say to Anna. How am I going to explain what I need her to do? Of course, she may decide to finish it, and that might very well be for the best. At least then it would get me off the hook with Mia. But the truth is I don't want to end it with Anna. I can't imagine giving up the feel of her, the taste of her. I do, however, need to get her out of Val Verde.

On the way back to the car in La Isleta the other day, after that horrible little scene with Mia on the beach, we passed a block of flats. It was not too fancy, although some of them did have a view of the sea. I noticed that on one of the flats, on the ground floor, there was a sign that said, 'SE ALQUILA' and in English underneath, 'TO RENT'. The image had branded itself on my consciousness – it might offer, I surmised, a neat way out of a tricky situation. If I could just install her there for a few weeks, or months, I could pretend to Mia that she was out of our lives for good. But I'd still be able to see her, nipping down to the beach for a little afternoon siesta or whatever while Mia was seeing the old lady, Blanca.

As I try to untangle the knotted mess of my fuck-up of a situation, I see Anna enter the bar. She's looking even more gorgeous today, wearing a pair of tight denim shorts and a cutaway blouse, her blonde hair tied back, and her face free of make-up. As she sees me, she waves and comes over to my table.

'You okay?' she whispers. She reaches out across the table to take my hand, but stops herself when she remembers that she's not allowed to do that.

'Yeah, fine, why do you ask?'

'Just that you sounded weird on the phone when you rang me from the beach.'

'I just wanted to hear your voice.'

A waitress appears by our side and Anna orders a black coffee. I take a sip of my beer to steady my nerves, even though I could do with something a lot stronger. Like a glass of whisky or some kind of pill.

'Listen, Anna—'

'This doesn't sound good. What is it?'

'Mia knows all about us and—'

'But that's good, isn't it? You said that you wanted to tell her, that if you could only tell her then it would all be out in the open and you could leave her.'

The waitress returns with Anna's coffee. I look around me, making sure no one from Val Verde is in the bar, before I continue, keeping my voice low. 'It's proving more complicated than I thought.'

'So, you don't want to leave her, is that it?'

'No, it's not that at all. It's hard, you must see that. Mia and I share a long history. We've been together years. We've just moved here, to a new country—'

'So you just wanted to fuck me and now you've had your fill you're going to throw me over? Is that it?'

'No, it's not like that. I care for you. I want us to be together. But you're going to have to give me a bit more time.'

'But if Mia knows everything, why wait? I don't see the problem. Sure, you're going to have a shitty, horrible row with her, but that's to be expected. Breaking up isn't for the faint-hearted, Rich. Perhaps you haven't got it in you.'

Anna pushes her untouched coffee aside and stands up to go.

'Let me explain. Please, Anna.' I realize that only the other day I was using similar words to beg Mia to listen to me.

She stares at me, assessing whether to turn away and never see me again, or to listen to what I have to say. It's one of those moments you read about in novels or see in films, an instant when a future can be decided. I think time freezes. That, or I seem to have stopped breathing. I don't know how long it lasts, but as I stare at Anna's face her features melt away.

I blink away the weird time lag and finally her face forms itself into a vision of beauty once more. God, she is stunning. I feel an overwhelming urge to run my fingers over her full lips, push a little bit of my hand into her mouth. I shift in my seat, uncomfortable in my jeans. I can't let her go. I have to keep her, despite everything.

'I've got a plan – if you'll just sit down.'

I think she's about to do as I say, that she's about to tell me she'll go along with whatever it is because she loves me. Instead, she says, 'You know what, Rich – I think you should fuck off.' She turns away and heads for the door.

I scrabble around for some money, leaving a scrunched-up five-euro note on the table, and rush after her. I don't care if anyone sees me now. I need to do something to bring her back to me.

'Anna! Anna!'

She bolts across the square, towards the church. But I'm quick. I grab her hand and pull her down a side alley, where no one can see us. I know I'm strong – all those years of martial arts – and I pin her against the wall. She seems to be excited, aroused. This is what she wants, this is what she's always wanted. For me to show my passion for her. Not in words, but in actions. I move in to kiss her, but she pushes me away.

'What the fuck do you think you're doing?' she hisses, spraying my face with spittle. 'Didn't you just hear what I said?'

'Anna, just calm down. Let me explain.'

'Why should I listen to you? I've heard this crap before from men who don't want to leave their girlfriends. It's fine, Rich, really, I don't mind – but I wish you'd told me from the beginning.'

'Don't give me that. You knew I had a girlfriend, you knew that—'

'Yes, one you said you were going to leave, don't you

remember? What I don't understand is why you haven't broken up with her. I thought you didn't fancy her.'

'I couldn't – you just don't understand.'

'What I do understand is that it looks as though you love her more than me.' She pushes me away, disgust in her face. This is it. This is the way she'll leave me. These will be her last words to me. This will be the last time I'll see her face. I won't be able to touch her, hold her, kiss her, feel her. I can't let it happen. I grab her again, but I'm careful not to hurt her. I don't want her to think that I'm violent.

'It's not as simple as that. You don't know about the—'

'About what, Rich?'

'About the past. The fact that—'

'What?'

The words spill out of me. 'That when she was a little girl her mum was murdered by some fucking maniac and that Mia was left for dead.'

I immediately regret what I've just said. Mia had made me promise never to talk about it. I know I should never have told anyone, especially not Anna. I feel as though the wind has been punched out of me, like when one of the more experienced karate guys lands a blow to my guts.

I drop to my knees, breathless, but when I look up, back at Anna, she is gazing at me with a slight smile on her face, as if she's the one in control.

25

MIA

The thought of them – kissing, in bed, their skin touching, their flesh melting, melding – is nearly driving me insane, threatening to transport me back into the past, back into that dark place.

They're together now, I know that. He told me that he was going to meet Anna at the plaza bar to end it all, and inform her that she had to leave Val Verde. But how could he manage to resist her? How did I know she wouldn't try to seduce him? That they wouldn't sneak back to her house and have sex?

As I walk with Freya through the streets of San Mateo, avoiding the central square in case I catch a glimpse of Rich and Anna together, I try to concentrate on her chatter about life on the project. The sense of community. The delicious vegetarian and vegan cuisine. The medicinal properties of the herbs found growing wild in Val Verde. How we should all live more in tune with nature. But I realize I'm only half-listening. My mind keeps going back to them. How many times have Rich and Anna had sex? It can't have been only five or six occasions, like Rich says. I picture them together. The peeling back of skin, the opening of their bodies. The rank stench of them.

Rich and I have been together thirteen years, ever since uni, and after that length of time I suppose he must have become bored with me. I get that. But what I can't understand is why he chose to hook up with Anna so soon after arriving here. Was it something to do with the excitement of moving into this wild landscape? Was it the drugs again? I knew that he'd started smoking cannabis when he was at school – and not just the odd puff. He'd been a heavy user. I'd read a lot about how this particular strain of cannabis was bad for the development of the teenage brain. Had that warped his mind? He'd also told me that at one point his mother had been into drugs too: had Marianne taken something while Rich was in her womb? Or was it more to do with the fact that she had neglected him as a boy? Or is it all my fault? Maybe he isn't in love with me any more. Is it as simple as that?

'Mia, are you okay?'

'Sorry – just a bit . . . off today. I didn't sleep well.'

Freya looks at me with genuine concern in her eyes, like she wants to help. 'Is it Rich?'

'Yeah – we had a big argument about Anna.'

'Shit.'

'But at least it's all out in the open now. He promised me

he's not going to see her again. That it's over. He's going to tell her that she's got to leave the village.'

'Well, I for one won't miss her. Even though we share a house, we've never had much in common.'

I'm about to tell Freya more about the row with Rich when I spot Blanca coming out of the vegetable shop. The old lady is having trouble holding her string bag and we rush over to help just as a couple of potatoes drop through the netting. After picking them up, I introduce her to Freya and she invites both of us to her house. She's got something to tell me. As we follow her, I fill Freya in on the background, and tell her that although I've been helping Blanca deal with the bureaucracy of retrieving her mother's remains, this is the first time she's welcomed me into her home; normally, our meetings have taken place either in a café or at one of her friends' in the more modern part of town.

Walking into Blanca's house in the oldest section of town, tucked down one of the side streets, is like stepping back in time. I'm relieved that I'm being forced out of the present – it's a welcome distraction from my thoughts about Rich and Anna. She gestures for us to sit and asks if we'd like anything. She's going to make herself a Cola Cao and I say yes, that would be lovely, even though I'm not that keen on the overly sweet, instant hot chocolate drink. Freya has told me before that her Spanish is next to non-existent, and so I tell her I'll translate as we go along.

As Blanca busies about her small kitchen at the back of the house I take a few moments to look around, my eyes gradually adjusting to the gloom. The small, cramped sitting room is dominated by a *mesa camilla*, a round table covered with numerous lace mats and a patterned blanket, under which sits a *brasero*; in the days before central heating this was one of the few ways to keep warm during the cold winter months. The floor is made from old, cracked tiles and the limewashed walls are stained nicotine yellow and flaking: as I brush past the *mesa camilla,* I notice a ghostly trail of white dust on my coat.

The walls are covered with objects that seem to have little place in the modern world: a pair of tiny shoes, made from esparto grass; a dirt-ingrained reproduction print of the Virgin holding the baby Jesus; and an old, gilt-framed mirror which is too mottled to see yourself in. The chairs, bent and twisted, low to the ground, their seats fashioned from woven reeds, look like something only fit for small children. A side table holds a cluster of black and white photographs in cheap frames: a group of little girls, brides of Christ, at their first communion; a man on a donkey, riding through the dry landscape; and a prematurely aged woman holding a bunch of grapes standing outside what looks like *La Casa de la Luz*. As I bend down to get a closer look, Blanca returns to the rooms with our hot drinks.

'That's my grandmother,' she says, passing the cups of Cola Cao to us. 'It was the day of the grape harvest. But I think the vines are dead now.' She picks up the photograph and brings it up to my face. 'Don't you think she looks like you? She's got your eyes.'

She gives me the photo to study and I have to admit there's something about the woman's face that looks familiar. She can't be that old, only in her forties, but she looks like she could be two or even three decades older.

'Yes, old before her time,' she says, as if she's reading my thoughts. 'She had a sad life, *la pobre*.'

141

She gives a deep sigh, crosses herself and then points to a pile of papers tied with a black ribbon on a low stool. It's all her correspondence with not only the Association for the Recovery of Historical Memory (ARMH) but with Pedro and his lawyers too. With bright eyes and a crooked smile, Blanca begins to tell us that she's had news from the ARMH that they've agreed to investigate her case. She talks quickly about her mother, articulating fragments of memory that float through her mind. The way her mother whispered to her as she carried her in her arms to bed. The soft touch of her lips as she kissed her goodnight. The feel of her mother's tears on her skin as she was dragged away from her daughter by the men who would kill her.

'I got the news this morning, look.' Her frail hand picks up a letter from the top of the papers, which she shows to me. It's been written by the ARMH, based in León, and says that the organization has won its legal battle to force Pedro to give permission to dig up the section of land by the road near Val Verde where they believe Blanca's mother, and a group of other individuals, have been buried since 1938. They hope the dig will be scheduled at some point this summer. They will organize everything – a team of volunteers will treat Blanca's mother's remains with respect and they hope that soon they will be in possession of her body, or what is left of it, which she can then rebury in consecrated ground.

'I'm so pleased for you, but it's about time. How long have you been waiting for this?'

'Since the moment my mother was shot by those bastards and she was kicked into the ground. Her spirit was never peaceful, you know. At times, as I stood by that grave, I thought I could hear her whispering to me from the earth,

142

"Why have you deserted me, Blanca?" And it wasn't only when I was there, by that olive grove, that I could hear her. At night, I'd come down to get a glass of water and I thought, on a couple of occasions, I saw her standing here, where you are now.'

She holds her hands together in front of her heart and looks towards the Virgin. 'At times I felt Our Lady had deserted me. I would often kneel there, in front of her, and beg her to help me. I didn't understand why she had abandoned me. But now I see that it was a test. My prayers have been answered.'

She steps a little closer to me and I smell the trace of something floral, violets perhaps. 'I'm so grateful to you, my dear Mia, for all your help.'

'I didn't do much – just filled in a few forms, made sure they went off to the right people, that's all.'

'You've been the whole world to me, like a fresh flower on a grave.'

It's a strange expression, one I've never heard before. I wonder whether it's an idiom local to the area or whether it's just Blanca's poetic touch. As I'm about to ask her about it, she reaches out and clutches my hand.

'But what about you, my dear? I know there's something wrong.'

'I'm just a bit tired, that's all.'

She presses down – hard – on my wrist. 'No, I can sense it's something else. I've always had the second sight – I inherited it from her' – she points to the image of her grandmother, standing in front of our house. 'Not that it did her much good. To her it was a curse, passed down from the devil.' Her old, tired eyes seem to see deep within me. 'What is it, my child?'

I hesitate, hoping that I won't have to tell her. But she continues to stare at me. I try to move my arm, but she squeezes it tighter. Freya looks over, concerned, as I've stopped translating and she doesn't know what the old lady is saying to me.

'I've just had an argument with my boyfriend, Rich. I told you about him.'

'I see – I thought as much.'

'It's nothing much, and we'll get over it. Just a silly misunderstanding.'

'I don't think so, I see it's more than that.'

What does she mean – 'see'? She's looking past me now, over my shoulder as if there's someone there, standing behind me. Her eyelids begin to flutter a little and she starts to sway. There's a gobbet of spit in the corner of her thin, dry lips. Is she about to have some kind of fit?

'Let's get you into this chair.' Freya jumps up to help and we support her together. As I take hold of Blanca's frame I'm conscious yet again of how little of her there is. She must weigh – what? – something like seven or eight stone. We guide her backwards and down onto the chair. 'Do you need some medication? Blanca, is there something wrong?'

The frothy spit has turned into a steady stream of saliva that leaks from her mouth down onto her chin. I spot a box of tissues on a small table, next to which are a few bottles of pills. I don't know what the medication is for and I don't want to make it worse. I use a tissue to gently wipe her face.

'Is she all right?' asks Freya. 'Do you think we should call a doctor?'

Blanca must understand that word because she tells me she

144

doesn't want to see a doctor. They will just take her to hospital, where she'll die. She whispers that she needs to stay alive for the sake of her mother.

I monitor the quick rise and fall of her chest. I take her pulse, which does seem to be racing. But then she opens her eyes and looks directly at me.

When she begins to talk her voice is low. 'Don't trust him.'

'Blanca?'

'He's betraying you.' She reaches out and takes hold of the photograph of her grandmother. She speaks directly to the image. 'You know what's happening, but you don't want to face up to it. He is seeing the other woman behind your back.'

'Is this about your grandmother? Your *abuela*?'

'He says he is going to end it and you believe him. Don't.'

'Blanca?'

'You go out one day and you come back and find them together. They are sinners. Dirty sinners.'

'Do you want some water?'

'He promises you, but they are empty promises. He doesn't love you. He never did.'

'Mia, what's she saying?' asks Freya, but I ignore her. I can't repeat this to her.

'What about a tablet? Which one of these?' I hold up the bottles for Blanca to see, but she is blind to what is before her. 'Will they help?'

'Finally, you can't take it any more. You wait for him to go out – he's going to see her – and then you take one of your sheets, the best sheets given to you on your wedding day. You wrap it around the beam and then use the other end to make a noose. That's how you end your life.'

Then her eyes focus on mine and she looks like she's back with me, back in the here and now. Fully conscious again.

'Thank goodness, Blanca. You had me scared then. I thought you were having a bit of a turn.'

'I know what I'm saying,' she snaps. 'There's nothing wrong with me.'

'I was about to call the doctor.'

She grips my hand again and whispers, 'My grandmother hanged herself in that house. It was a choice between that or jumping off Devil's Head, and she couldn't face that – she had a fear of heights. And so she chose to die at home. Mia, make sure you don't make the same mistake.' There's a frightening intensity in her eyes now. 'Watch out for him – and for her. They're dangerous.'

26

RICH

I'm lying in bed with Anna by my side, both of us still covered in a sheen of post-sex sweat. The heat from the afternoon sun oozes through the window. I can hear the gentle whisper of the waves in the distance and low-level chatter from a nearby bar. I know I'll have to be heading back to Val Verde and Mia soon, but I just want to savour these last few moments of bliss in the flat by the sea.

Mia seems much happier since Anna moved away from Val Verde three months ago – she believes our relationship is back on track, that I'm fully committed just to her, that I've given Anna up – but there's still something bothering her. She continues to have those awful nightmares. And she's obsessed not only with the case of Blanca – apparently, the date for the exhumation of her mother's bones has been set – but with the old woman's grandmother too, who she believes committed suicide in our house.

At night, spooked by the cry of a scops owl or a bullfrog, she walks to the doors that look out onto the terrace and peers into the dark. Sometimes, when everything is still and the only sound is the trickle of the river below the house, she looks up at the beams, a darkness clouding her eyes. When I ask what's wrong she mumbles something about the ghosts of the past. She quotes Lorca at me, something about how the dead in Spain are more alive than the dead of any other place in the world. Any normal boyfriend would tell her to stop seeing Blanca. To put the dead to rest. To leave the ghosts alone. But I know that her visits to the old lady are the only time I'm able to slip away and see Anna.

Now Anna shifts onto her side and uses a hand to support her head. I can feel the heavy presence of her gaze on me.

'Rich?'

'Yeah?'

Her fingers begin to run up and down my chest. 'I've been thinking.'

'Mmm?'

'About Mia – about what she went through as a child.'

I push myself up and face her. 'What do you mean?' I'm conscious of a note of panic in my voice. 'What about Mia?'

'You know you told me about what happened with Iain Hastings, well, I've been doing a bit of research and—'

'Research? What kind of research?'

'There's a lot about the case on the internet. Not just old newspaper cuttings, but forums, blogs, true crime nuts.'

Her words make me so uncomfortable I get out of bed and begin to dress quickly. 'Why would you go to the trouble of looking up stuff like that?' I don't want to hear the answer and turn my back on her as I pull on my shorts.

'There's so much about it that's fascinating, and a lot of detailed discussion about Iain Hastings' innocence.'

'What?'

'I've read all about it and I think there are grounds to say that what happened to Hastings was a miscarriage of justice.'

The anger begins to burn inside me. 'You've got to be fucking kidding, right?'

She gets up from the bed and faces me. There's a certain aggression in her nakedness. 'There's one blog in particular, full of legal and medical documents that have been uploaded to the site. It seems to suggest that Iain had some kind of condition, a type of autism, I think. He was easily suggestible. There's an account of a kind of honey trap operation, where a female undercover officer got him to confess to the crime. It was completely inadmissible, of course, but by that point the damage had been done. Iain must have—'

'So you're on first-name terms with a murderer now?'

'Rich, just listen,' she says, finally covering herself with a light linen dressing gown. 'If Hastings was a vulnerable individual then that means his confession wasn't a valid one. He killed himself while he was awaiting trial. The police really messed up. I think it would make a great story.'

I can hardly get the words out. 'A *story*?'

'Yeah, especially if I get Mia's cooperation.'

'Are you out of your fucking mind?'

'It would be great for me – a real boost to my career.'

'Really?'

She comes up to me and presses herself – hard – against me. I feel the curve of her breasts against my chest, the touch of her hand on my crotch.

'I know it's a tricky subject – for Mia, especially. But surely you can see the bigger picture. If that poor man, Hastings, was innocent, then his family deserve to know. Imagine what it must have been like for them – what it's still like for them – thinking that their son or brother or uncle died a murderer.'

'But you know Mia's not going to give you the time of day – especially after everything that's gone on. You do realize that, right?'

The pressure of her fingers makes me hard again. Fuck.

'I thought you might be able to talk her into it.'

'Sorry, there's no way,' I say, breaking away from her. 'I wouldn't even dream of asking her. She'd kill me if she knew I'd ever talked to you about it. Sorry, Anna.'

'Why don't you just think about it?' There's an edge of desperation in her voice. 'I know it's a lot to take in, and of course I don't expect her to say yes straight away. It must have been really awful for her. But I promise to handle the material sensitively and . . . I don't know, if Mia were to give me an interview then—'

'An interview? Of course she's not going to give you an interview.' I need to get away from her, before I say or do something I regret. I take a deep breath. 'Look, Anna, just drop it. I thought you were busy doing the thing about the greenhouses and the migrant workers. What happened to that?'

'It's more or less finished, apart from a few tweaks and additions. The editor likes it and—'

'So that's great, isn't it?'

'Yeah, but I need to find the next story. I've got bills to pay.'

I grab the car keys and kiss her on the cheek. 'Sorry, Anna, but I'm sure you understand. I get that you need to generate work, that you need to find a new story. But it can't be this one.'

27

MIA

I'm sitting on the edge of the bath, looking at a strip of plastic. The digital reader counts down to the results. Any second now I will know. I've been unusually tired, and my breasts feel quite tender. We agreed that the pill wasn't a viable option, while condoms are terrible for the environment. So after a great deal of thought we settled on me using a diaphragm, which has worked well in the past. I think back to that night – was it about six weeks ago? – when we drank a few glasses of cava, followed by a bottle of red. The details are hazy, but I have a vague feeling that I neglected to use the spermicide.

As I wait, my heart racing, various scenarios flash through my mind. If I am pregnant, what will I say to Rich? I know we agreed to wait a little longer before trying for a child. Will he think this is my way of trying to trap him? And, after everything that has happened between us – after Anna – do I still want to have a baby with him? Or perhaps a child will bring us together, help heal our broken relationship. Or is this nothing more than a pathetic pipe dream?

But then the word flashes up on the screen: 'Pregnant'. I should feel elated – this is what I've wanted for a long time – but I'm flooded with panic. Instead of celebrating the joy of a potential new life, all that consumes me is the thought of my mother in that grave, her baby left to die inside her. My breathing quickens. My heart seems like it's going to explode. As I stand up, the bathroom floor swirls before me. I grip the side of the sink and splash some cold water onto my forehead. I need to take some long, deep breaths but my lungs feel like they're already full. I catch a glimpse of myself in the mirror. A pale face, haunted eyes. I look like a ghost. I think of my mother in that wood, dying before her time. Despite the fact that I keep telling myself that I can't keep going back there, down into the earth, I often wonder whether a piece of me, some fragment of my psyche, remains there in that damp ground.

I remember what Freya said to me once about the healing power of nature. Perhaps if I get some air, feel the texture of leaves, breathe in the aroma of wild herbs, then I'll feel better, calmer. I walk through the house and out onto the terrace. The evening sun is blindingly bright. I steady myself by an olive tree and allow my eyes to adjust to the light. I make my way down the vegetable terraces and stop by a line of tomato plants. I run my fingers through the aromatic leaves, and as I breathe in the musky smell, I begin to relax.

The only sound I can hear is the twilight chorus of the bull-frogs and the animated chatter of the bee-eaters which roost in the reed beds. But then, down on the river bank, I see a figure, standing there, looking directly at me. I'm certain – by the silhouette, the shape of the body – that it's a woman. I move a few paces forwards, shield my eyes with my hand to block out the intense rays of the sun. It's then that I see her. I know who it is. She's back.

Anna.

She spies me and, instead of turning away, she walks down to the stepping stones and starts to cross the river. There's an air of determination about her, as if she's on a kind of mission. What the hell is she doing here? I compose several derogatory comments in my head, but before I get a chance to speak to her, she holds up her right hand as if in a gesture of surrender.

'I know what you think of me – and you've every right to hate me – but—'

'Rich isn't in – he's out getting the water from the *fuente*.'

'I know – I waited until I saw him leave the village,' she says, securing her camera over her shoulder. 'It's you I want to talk to, Mia.'

'Why . . . why do you want to talk to me?'

'If we can just go inside – I can explain.'

'What are you doing here – back in the village?'

'It's nothing to do with Rich – don't worry. I mean, I'm not here to cause any more trouble.' Her eyes look desperate, pleading. 'If you can give me a few minutes, I can explain.'

I don't say anything, and the silence must unnerve her, as she starts to speak again. 'Look – I've got something to ask you.'

'I think you've done enough damage, don't you?'

'I get why you think that – and if I was in your shoes, I'd say the same thing. But what I'd like to talk to you about has nothing to do with what happened with Rich. It's about what—'

153

I cut her off. 'I've got nothing to say to you, Anna. And if I were you, I'd stay away from here. No one wants you in Val Verde, least of all Rich.'

She arches a perfectly shaped eyebrow and just as she's about to speak, she changes her mind and nods her head. She studies me for a moment and looks at me with sympathy, as if she knows something about me that saddens her. Is it pity she feels for me? What – because Rich betrayed me? Because, at one point, he was infatuated with her? That he found her much more attractive than me? I allow my fingers to drop to my stomach and for an instant, my hand rests over my midriff. I think of what is inside me, just the size of a pinprick, but still, it's there. I have something of Rich's that she will never have. Her eyes follow them down and it's then that I allow myself to smile. Does she pick up the trace of contentedness in my face? The hint of triumph in my eyes? Whatever it is, she turns from me, makes her way back down to the river, crosses the stepping stones and disappears into the reeds.

I'm just about to go back to the house when I spot her again, emerging from a stretch of bamboo. She's got her gaze directed straight towards me. She shifts her position and brings up her camera in front of her face. Before I can move she points the camera at me. I can't see her finger pressing down on the shutter, but I'm sure that's exactly what she's doing.

She's taking a photograph of me. And it feels as though she's caught me in a trap.

28

RICH

'I don't understand – she came here . . . to the house?'

'Yes, she came up from the river, over the stepping stones. She said she wanted to talk to me.'

As I heave a five-litre bottle of water off the floor and onto the work surface, I can feel the panic rising within me. 'What about?'

'I don't know – she said it wasn't anything to do with you. In fact, she told me that she'd waited for you to leave the village. She must have watched you drive off in the car to get the water.'

'What?'

'I know – I thought that was weird too.'

'And what did you say to her?'

'Nothing. She seemed pretty insistent, even wanted to come inside the house, but I told her to leave.' Her hand drops down to her stomach and rests there for a moment. 'I said I wasn't interested.'

Anxiety grips me, tightening the muscles in the back of my neck, my shoulders. 'And she just left – just like that? She didn't say anything . . . else?'

'No – but just as I thought she'd gone, back across the stepping stones and into the bamboo and reeds, she emerged and stopped to look at me again. I'm sure she took a photo of me – or quite a few—'

'She did *what*?'

'She stood there and pointed that big digital camera at me. It was weird; I felt as though I was . . . I don't know, that she was trying to . . . Sorry, I'm not making sense.'

I encircle Mia in my arms. 'Oh my God, you're shaking. She really freaked you out, didn't she?' I take hold of her shoulders and ease her back a little so I can look into her face. 'You're sure . . . she didn't say anything else about me?'

'No – should she have done?'

The worry that Anna has told Mia everything – about our continued affair and the flat by the sea – worms its way through my brain. 'I told her to stay away from here, never to come back – what the fuck was she thinking?' But if she's been here once, she may come again. And she could say anything. She could blow everything apart. 'Don't worry about her – if she comes here again, she'll have me to deal with.'

'What do you mean?'

'Just what I say. I can't have you being bothered by her.'

'I just don't understand why she'd want to take my photograph.'

I think of that last conversation I had with Anna about Iain Hastings and her theory he might be innocent. I can't begin to mention it to Mia. If she knew that I'd discussed her past with anyone – let alone Anna – our relationship would turn to dust in an instant.

'She must be trying to fuck with you, I suppose, best not to think about it.' Anna's fucking with me too. I told her to drop the Hastings story. And the next thing I know she's turning up here, unannounced. Or worse, waiting for me to leave before she approached Mia.

'There's something else,' Mia whispers.

I flex my fingers and try to shake the tension out of my wrist, but it just doesn't shift. I picture Anna here, stalking Mia, pointing that great big camera at her. I see her talking to her, asking her questions about her past, about her mother, about that shallow grave. My fist clenches and I hit out, first a strike to the plastic water bottle and then a quick punch on the worktop. The noise of the impact startles Mia, who emits a little cry. The pain that comes serves as something of a relief, a throbbing intensity which moves from my hand up my arm and to my shoulders.

'Are . . . are you okay?' Mia asks, an unsettled look in her eyes.

'I'm fine – I just . . . I just wish Anna would disappear . . . disappear off the face of the earth.' I feel a pressure in my lungs, like I can't breathe. 'I'm just going to get some air.'

I open the door to the terrace and step into the garden. As I pass the flower beds, the summer air fills with the aromas of lavender, rosemary, jasmine and the heady, sweet smell of the devil's trumpets. I remember someone once telling me that the plant was poisonous if ingested. Tropane alkaloids, I suppose: hyoscine, hyoscyamine, norhyoscine, which would bring about hallucinations, dilated pupils, blurred vision, rapid heart rate, respiratory failure and, finally, death.

Dread spreads through me like its poison.

29

MIA

I'm leading up to telling him about my positive pregnancy test, but then his temper possesses him and he strikes out. As he hits the water bottle, I'm worried that the force will split the plastic and the liquid will pour out all over the floor. Then as he slams his fist down on the worktop, his face creases in pain. I'm relieved when he says he needs some air and steps outside. By the time he returns to the kitchen, I've changed my mind.

'What were you saying?' he asks through gritted teeth.

'N-nothing.' I take a breath to steady my nerves. 'You don't think Anna will come back again, do you?'

'I'll make sure she doesn't.' There's something about his tone that disturbs me. His eyes look hard, almost possessed.

'What do you mean?'

'Just that – you won't have to worry about her.' He picks up another large water bottle and carries it into the larder. From there he shouts, 'I need a drink – do you fancy one?'

'No – I'm fine, thanks.' I think of what's growing inside of me, the thing that is only – what? – about six weeks old. I read once that at this age it's the size of a baked bean.

Rich returns with a bottle of red, which he proceeds to open and pour into a large glass. 'That's better,' he says, as he takes a swig. He turns to look at me and smiles. 'Sorry about that,' he says, referring to his recent flare-up of temper. 'It's just that . . . she's got no business coming here, harassing you like that. Anyway – enough of that.' He changes the subject and asks me about Blanca, the irrigation rota, what we might have for supper, but my mind can't move on from what I just witnessed.

'Mia, is something bothering you?' he asks, finally. 'You look – I don't know, different somehow.'

This is not the right moment to tell him. 'I'm . . . I'm fine. It's just that thing with Anna. It spooked me, that's all.' I take a deep breath. 'You – you wouldn't do anything stupid, would you?'

'What do you mean?'

'I don't know – to hurt Anna?'

'What gives you that idea?'

'I don't know – just something you said about how you'd like her to disappear off the face of the earth.'

'That's just a figure of speech. You don't think that I'd – that I could . . .' He laughs and puts his arm around me, drawing me closer. 'Mia, you've got one hell of an imagination.' He passes his glass of wine to me. 'Take a sip of this – relax. It will make you feel better.'

'No thanks. Just a glass of water.'

'You stay there – I'll get it.' He walks across the kitchen, cuts up a lemon into thin slivers and adds them to a jug of water. 'And I'll get on with making something to eat,' he says, as he passes me a glass. He looks into the fridge, assesses its contents. 'What about pasta – there's some fresh pesto I made the other day.'

'Yeah, that would be great.'

I study him as he prepares the simple supper, tipping the strands of spaghetti into the boiling water, adding a drop of olive oil to the pan and a pinch of sea salt. He strips a lettuce, washes it and tears it into shreds into a large ceramic bowl, makes a mustard and honey dressing and tosses it. He takes out a sharp knife and slices a couple of large, over-ripe tomatoes, their juice seeping out. He sets the table and cuts up some bread which he places in a bowl. He drains the pasta – his face momentarily disappearing in a cloud of steam – mixes it in with a few generous dollops of fresh pesto and serves it. Each of these simple actions should be relaxing for me to watch – it's the kind of banal normality that has provided me with such comfort in the past – but as I watch him the tension builds inside me until I reach a point where I think I can't stand it any more. I spoon a few swirls of spaghetti into my mouth, but I realize I'm not going to be able to swallow them down.

'Sorry, I—'

'Mia, are you all right? Can I—?'

'Just – give me a minute.' I push myself up from the table and make it outside just in time before I bring up the contents of my stomach onto the terrace.

I wipe my mouth as I finish, and as I look into the darkness of the night, I think back to the sound of Rich's fist hitting the plastic bottle, followed by the thwack on the work surface, and the terrifying violence in his eyes. He'd

160

once told me that he could kill someone, which at that time had made me feel safe, secure. But now that thought fills me with fear.

30

RICH

'I can't believe you came to the fucking house – what were you thinking, Anna?'

Her eyes are full of fire, blazing. 'What did you expect me to do – let the story go? Just because you're a man and you're used to getting what you want?'

'Don't give me that bullshit.'

'I just wanted to talk to her, woman to woman. I—'

'You didn't think Mia would actually listen to you, did you?'

'I – I'm not sure. I thought she might be able to see – I don't know – see beyond all of what happened between you and me and—'

'And what? Give you an interview? Some kind of fucking exclusive?'

'No, of course not. It wasn't like that.'

'Well, I can tell you now, that's not going to happen. There's no way Mia will talk to you – or talk to anyone about what happened. She said you took her picture. Did you?'

'Yes, but—'

'Jesus Christ, Anna.'

'I was just testing the light.'

'Yeah, right. Well, you can delete the images right away. And do it now.'

'Fuck off.'

'Where's your camera?' I scan the room for any sign of it. I walk over to the table by the window, but it's not there. I pull open a couple of drawers and toss out some of Anna's underwear onto the floor.

'What do you think you're doing?'

'Where've you hidden it?' I bend down and peer under the bed. 'Tell me, where's the fucking camera?'

Her eyes take on a shifty quality. 'It's not here. It's – it's gone in for a repair.'

'Don't lie to me, Anna.'

As we fall into silence, I can feel hostility emanating out of my every pore. The aftermath of a recent storm has left the sea angry and noisy, and through the open window I can hear the crash of the waves on the shore, the drag of the pebbles back into the sea. She takes a step towards me, places a hand on my chest and starts to tell me she's sorry. Her camera really has gone in for repair, she says. She licks her lips in a way I used to find a turn-on. Now the touch – and the sight of her tongue – means nothing to me, as if she's been leached of all traces of eroticism. I realize in that moment I want nothing more to do with her.

'I can't do this any more, Anna.' My voice is weary, almost a whisper.

'What do you mean?'

'I think it's time we called it a day.' I realize the words are a cliché, but I can't be bothered to explain myself fully.

'Are you joking? But you were saying how you couldn't get enough of me. That you were going to leave her – you said you wanted me. We were—'

I put up a hand to stop her. 'You told me, when we first met, this was only going to be a casual thing. We had a great time, I'm not denying that. And you're . . . well, you're something else . . . you're great. But you said you were going to travel around Spain, looking for . . .' I'm about to say 'other stories', before I stop myself, as I don't want to remind her of the story that she discovered under her nose. A story I led her towards. 'You weren't supposed to come back here, to Almería.'

'I thought we had something special, Rich. You certainly said as much.'

'I know – but it's run its course. Surely you can see that.'

'Look, if this is about . . . about Mia and Iain Hastings, then I can drop that. The story means nothing to me, compared to you.'

I don't know what to say. The waves sound so loud now they could crash through the windows. The air smells of salt and something else, something fetid.

'I'm not prone to begging, but I'll . . . I'll do anything you want.'

'You know what Mia's been through – what hell she's suffered—'

'Yes, but you can't always be tied to someone because you pity them.'

'It's more than that. I feel I need to . . . I need to protect her somehow.'

Her cheeks are tinged with the colour of anger now. 'What – you think she can't survive without you, is that it?'

'No, I don't mean it like that, but—'

'That's always been your problem, Rich – you've got a vastly inflated sense of your own masculinity. I blame it on your mother.'

'Don't bring my m— Marianne into this.'

'Have I hit a raw nerve?'

'Don't be so bloody—'

'You and your abandonment issues.' There's an edge of cruelty in her voice now. 'I'm no psychologist, but it seems so obvious. Rejected by your mother, you're desperate to find someone to replace her.'

'I don't know what the hell you're talking about.'

'You don't?'

'No, just shut the fuck up.'

'Or what – you'll kill me?'

'Don't be so melodramatic.'

'But you can't deal with a real woman, with opinions and desires. You have to seek out a husk of a person, someone so damaged you know they're grateful for you, someone so hurt and traumatized there's no risk they'll ever reject you or walk away from you. Someone just like Mia.'

The sound of the name triggers something deep within me. My hand whips up to strike her. Instead of shrinking away, she seems to turn her cheek towards me, almost inviting me to hit her. I stop myself just in time, but the damage has been done. Both of us know it's over.

'I can't stay here. I'm going.' I grab some things, hastily throw them into a holdall and make my way to the door.

As I'm about to leave she calls my name. 'Rich, I'm going to make sure you regret this. I'm going to make your life a living hell.'

31

MIA

It's the day of the village fiesta and the hot August air is heavy with the sound of sadness. One of the young volunteers from Desert Shoots is strumming on a guitar and singing 'Gracias a la Vida'. Her voice is sweet and pure and as I stand there in our garden listening to the plaintive lyrics, I feel the sting of tears in my eyes. '*Gracias a la vida que me ha dado tanto.*' 'Thanks to life, which has given me so much.'

I'd first heard the version recorded by Mercedes Sosa, but later preferred the original written and performed by the Chilean singer-songwriter Violeta Parra. I knew she'd taken her own life back in 1967, and some have interpreted the song as her suicide note. The lyrics make me think of Emily Thomas, that girl I'd taught who one day stepped out into the road and died under the wheels of a bus. She had so much to live for – she was so full of vitality – and yet she ended her life in that way. I still don't understand it.

'It's a beautiful song, isn't it?' It's Freya, who has just arrived bearing an enormous platter of griddled vegetables. 'I used to listen to it myself, the Joan Baez version.' She looks momentarily distracted, as if a once-distant memory has suddenly invaded her consciousness. 'Anyway, what should I do with this?' she asks, looking down at the burnt red and green peppers, aubergines, red onions, fennel and courgettes.

'That looks amazing – thanks so much, Freya. If you could put it with the other food on that trestle table over there, in the shade, that would be wonderful.'

'Quite a good turn-out,' she says, looking over at the several groups of people gathered in the garden.

There's a crowd of young people from the eco-charity, their tanned bodies visions of lithe youthfulness. There's Blanca with her friends, who cluck around her like little birds; the date for her mother's exhumation is set for tomorrow. In the far corner of the garden, under the shade of an olive tree, I spy Bill and Payton, engaged in what looks like a heated argument. Rich is standing behind the bar, serving drinks. It looks as though he's had more than a few himself: he seems more ebullient and vocal than normal. I still haven't found the right moment to tell him the news about my pregnancy, and I'm beginning to wonder whether the hesitancy I feel is significant.

'Are you okay?' asks Freya.

'Sorry?'

'It's just that . . . I don't know, you look a bit anxious. Is it – is it about Rich?'

For a moment, I consider telling Freya about my pregnancy. But it's still early days and anything could happen. 'No – just a bit tired after getting everything ready for today.' I take her arm. 'Thank you again for this, I really appreciate it. The vegetable platter looks amazing. Let's go and put it on the table – it's nearly time to eat, I think.'

We walk together through the groups of people, through clouds of laughter and light conversation, and stop by a trestle table laden with food, a dish supplied by every guest or household. There's a fennel and orange salad, a big bowl of lettuce leaves garnished with marigold petals, mountains of couscous and bulgur wheat, an enormous cheese board full of manchego and the local goat's cheese, a couple of vegetable tarts, a homity pie, a vegetable lasagne and a tray bake with cauliflower, chickpeas and pomegranate seeds. Freya adds her platter to the mix, and I encourage people to start helping themselves. As everyone begins to eat, the level of conversation drops a little, the only sound the continued arguing of Payton and Bill, who are still ensconced in the far corner of the garden. I move a little closer to them, hoping that I can encourage them to have some food, and begin to hear snatches of their conversation.

'She was only in her early twenties, for God's sake,' hisses Payton.

'If you weren't so goddamned . . .' I miss a few words here, '. . . then I wouldn't have to . . . go elsewhere.'

'Don't fucking blame me, Bill. You know how—'

I'm about to turn away – I don't want to get involved – but Payton looks over in my direction and sees me. Her face strains into a rictus smile. 'Mia . . . what a lovely party, thank you so much.'

'Sorry . . . I just wanted to let you know there's some food, if you'd like it. I didn't mean to—'

'Excellent, excellent,' mumbles a red-faced Bill, knocking back the last of his red wine.

As he stumbles off towards the buffet, Payton looks at him with disgust. 'It's the same old story – just with a different girl,' she says. 'And they're always so young.'

'I'm – I'm sorry.' I feel my words are inadequate but it's the best I can do. I remember the way Bill touched me when I went into the pantry, just before the incident with the jar of gazpacho. 'Has it . . . happened a lot?'

'Like all the time.'

'Why do you stay with him?'

'It's complicated,' she sighs.

I think Rich once told me that Bill was stinking rich and I'm about to ask her more about this when I spot Hans moving across the terrace. He's grinning at everyone, obviously stoned. He spots Rich by the bar and comes to stand by his side. Rich passes him a bottle of beer which he pretends to open with his teeth and the two laugh and joke together.

'Let me get you a drink,' I say to Payton. 'A glass of cava?'

'Thanks.'

As I approach the bar, the music from the guitar – now something from the Spanish classical repertoire – makes it difficult for me to hear what they're saying, but there's a glint in Hans' eye that unsettles me. What does he have planned? When Rich sees me I'm certain he nudges Hans and both try to adopt innocent expressions.

'Hey, Mia – great party,' says Hans.

'Yeah, it's going really well,' adds Rich, in a slightly stiff manner.

'Payton would like a glass of cava.'

'Coming right up,' says Rich. 'And the same for you?'

'No . . . I'm fine at the moment.'

'You need to chill out, Mia,' says Hans. 'Enjoy your own party.'

I can't be bothered to argue or explain, but I cast Rich a sideways look which I hope he'll understand as a gentle warning not to get carried away with Hans. I turn from them, ready to take the glass of fizz back to Payton, but as I begin to walk across the terrace, feeling the heat from the early evening sun on the back of my head, I notice something out of the corner of my eye. No, it can't be. I do a double take. It is. It's Anna.

She's standing in the corner of the garden and she's got her camera pointed at me again. She's taking my fucking photograph. This has got to stop.

Instead of taking the cava to Payton, I gulp it down. The alcohol goes straight to my head. As I stride towards Anna, I feel immediately emboldened, ready to go into battle.

'You've got one hell of a nerve, coming here.'

She doesn't respond but carries on clicking away. She's wearing a pair of indecently cut denim shorts and a white skin-tight top that accentuates her large breasts and shows off her slim, tanned stomach.

'Stop it. Anna. Listen to me – put that camera down.'

I watch as the index finger of her right hand moves up and down with a terrible efficiency. How many images has she captured of me? Why is she doing this?

'What the hell are you doing? I said that's enough!' I reach out to try to knock the camera away from her face, but she steps to one side and continues to snap away.

I feel like an animal that's being hunted, trapped. The old panic begins to burn through me. I need to end this. I strike out again, and this time I manage to grab hold of the black strap of the camera, and as I wrench it towards me it slithers out of her hands like a long, slippery eel. I have the camera in my hands now.

'Hey!' she cries.

'I told you to stop it – stop taking photos of me.'

'Give it b-back,' she says, slurring her words. She's clearly drunk.

'Not until you tell me what you're doing here. Is this some kind of sick revenge – because you can't have Rich?'

'What?'

'Because he left you?'

'He left *me*?' There's a taunting quality to her words and her eyes look dazed and glassy. 'Is that what he told you?'

I'm conscious that the genial hubbub of the party has quietened. People are watching, staring in horror at the scene that's unfolding before them. I look down at the digital screen of the camera, but it remains as black and empty as the view from my shallow grave. Then I hold down a button and the display lights up. A moment later I see image after image of myself: standing talking with Payton; with Rich and Hans at the bar; the panic in my eyes as I turn my head and see Anna; knocking back the glass of cava; then tearing across the terrace with fury in my eyes; my arm reaching out to grab the camera; and finally my face contorted with murderous rage. As I try to delete the photos, my fingers turn to jelly and the camera emits a series of high-pitched bleeps.

'What the fuck do you think you're playing at?'

'Just taking a few test shots.' There's something mocking in the way she addresses me, as if she knows that I know she's lying and she's challenging me to confront her.

'You've got to erase these photos.'

'Do you need some help? What about asking Rich – he's always been there for you, hasn't he?'

'What do you mean?'

'Shall we call him over – your protector?' She shouts across the terrace, 'Rich!' She addresses me again, and again a taunting quality poisons her voice. 'He always comes to your rescue, doesn't he? Your real-life knight in shining armour. Poor little Mia, always the victim.'

The comment unnerves me. I feel dizzy, and I see a blackness around the edge of my peripheral vision. I'm being sucked back down into the earth. I reach out to try to steady myself, but there's nothing to hold onto. In that moment, Anna takes advantage of my weakness and reaches out and snatches back the camera. She looks down and checks that all the photographs are still there.

'Luckily, you don't seem to have done much damage.'

'I need to sit . . .'

Just as I'm about to faint, I feel someone by my side. It's Rich.

'Mia, are you okay?' he asks as he guides me to a nearby chair.

But before I can answer he turns on Anna in a fury.

'What the fuck are you doing here, Anna?' he hisses. 'Come on, I think it's time for you to leave.'

He goes to take her arm, but as she pushes him off she loses her footing. Just as she stumbles, he grabs hold of her again and prevents her from falling over. As he holds her, his strong fingers dig deep into her skin.

'Hey, you're hurting me. Let go of me.'

'Come on – the show's over,' he says. 'You've got to leave now. You're fucking embarrassing yourself. You're sick, Anna. You need help.'

173

Anna stops in her tracks, like an animal that's just realized it's heading to the slaughterhouse. There's desperation in her eyes now.

'Come on.' Rich tries to pull her towards the house, but she continues to resist him.

I catch sight of Freya, Payton, Bill, Hans, and Blanca and her friends, all looking appalled by the scene.

'*I* need help – that's a joke!' says Anna, turning back towards me. She looks at me as if I'm some kind of freak, like one of those medical specimens in a jar, a deformed baby floating in formaldehyde.

'That's enough, Anna.' Rich's voice is stern now. 'If you don't—'

'If I don't what? You're in no position to threaten me, Rich.' She flicks back her hair and squares her shoulders as if she's a female warrior about to go into battle. 'It wasn't that long ago you were begging me to fuck you again.'

'For God's sake, Anna. Don't do this – not here.'

'I told you you'd regret dumping me. No one does that to me.'

She wrenches her arm free of Rich and comes to stand before me. Her eyes are bright with something – drink, drugs, or the heady thrill of confrontation?

'Oh, didn't you know, Mia, about our little pad down by the sea?'

I feel my throat tightening. What's she talking about?

'Lovely little fishing village – La Isleta del Moro. Wonderful view of the extinct volcano. Great restaurant overlooking the water. I'd really recommend it.'

'Anna, I warned you,' snarls Rich.

'What've I got to lose?' she replies. Anna seems determined

174

to finish what she started: the final stage in her plan to destroy my relationship with Rich. She turns to me. 'We never stopped seeing one another. Rich just told you that I'd moved away. Well, only so far as La Isleta, where we fucked every afternoon in the flat Rich paid for, while you went to see your sad old lady.'

The words slice into me, deep cuts to the heart.

'Anna, I said enough!' shouts Rich.

'Rich – is it true?'

He can't meet my gaze. The fact that he doesn't reply gives me my answer.

'Well, you'll be pleased to hear it's over between us now, so you're welcome to him.' She slings her camera back over her shoulder and, with a spirit of bold defiance, walks away.

I can hardly believe it when Rich follows her. After everything she's just said.

'That's right – fucking go after her.'

He looks appalled. 'Of course I'm not going after her. I can't stand the sight of her.' He takes a deep breath, as if he's preparing to endure something unpleasant like an operation without anaesthetic. 'Look – I'll try to explain everything when I get back,' he says, touching me on the shoulder.

'What are you going to do?'

'I'm going to make her delete those photos she took of you. She's not going to get away with this.'

32

RICH

I'm standing outside the house, scanning the *camino* for Anna, but it looks as though she's given me the slip. My blood feels as though it's boiling. I can feel my heart pumping in my chest. Cortisol is coursing through my veins. My body – my mind – is primed for action, for attack. I run down the path to the car park. Her car – a beaten-up white Fiat – is still here, but there's no sign of her. Where the hell has she gone? I think about shouting out her name, but instead I just whisper 'Fuck you' under my breath.

It's probably just as well Anna made a quick exit. God only knows what I'd do to her if I found her. I walk back down the *camino*, trying to work out what to say to Mia. I pace up and down the path outside the house, wondering whether to go back inside. How am I going to talk my way out of this? If only Anna hadn't turned up at the fiesta, if only she hadn't told Mia about the flat by the sea.

The memory of Mia sitting in that chair comes back to me. It looked as though she was almost physically wounded by Anna's cruel words. I want to go back inside the house and tell her that Anna means nothing. That I would do anything to win her love back. If Mia asked me to kill for her, I'd do it – that's how much she means to me. I see my strong hands circling Anna's neck, pressing down – hard. Her eyes begin to bulge out of their sockets. Her face flushes red with blood. Her arms begin to flail out, her fingers try to scratch me, but I hold her firm and begin to squeeze the life out of her.

A slap on my back jolts me back into the moment.

'Man, that was heavy stuff.' It's Hans.

'I just needed some air and to get away from . . . well, you know.' I squeeze my fist tight, to stop me from punching the wall. 'What a fucking shit storm.'

'Looks like you could do with this.' He takes out a pre-rolled spliff, lights it and then passes it to me. The sweet, sweaty smell of the cannabis in the air immediately makes me relax. 'Here.'

A couple of drags won't hurt me. And he's right: I desperately need something to help me calm down.

I inhale – it's good, powerful stuff – and lean back against the thick outside wall of the house. We don't talk as we continue to smoke, each of us trapped in the prison of our selves, until I break the silence.

'I should probably go back in there – and apologize to Mia.'

'I wouldn't if I were you – I'd give her some time. She looked fucking furious the last time I looked. Like she could, I don't know, kill you or something.'

Shit. I take another drag on the spliff.

'I didn't realize that . . . about you and Anna.'

'Well, I suppose everyone must know now after that horrible little scene.'

He nudges me as if to congratulate me. 'You're a dark horse, Rich.' He laughs as he tries to lighten the mood, cheer me up. 'But I've got to say, she's a looker, that Anna.'

'I suppose she is.'

'So it's over between you now?'

'Yep – it probably should never have started.'

'And what about Mia? Do you think . . .'

'I don't know. I don't want to talk about it. I just want to forget it – forget everything.' I inhale deeply again, feeling the tension slip away.

Hans suggests we go for a walk and we begin to climb up the crystal path. We stop halfway up the hill and sit on a broken wall where we enjoy the rest of the spliff. We're high above the irrigation line where the land hasn't been watered for decades. The only thing that seems to survive up here is the prickly pear: the ground around us is full of rotten fruits, their red, decaying insides spewing out onto the dry soil like something obscene. The sun has set now and yet the valley is still alight, illuminated by the brightness of a full moon. Shards of crystal sparkle in the ground. Everything is quiet apart from the slow trickle of the water in the riverbed and, in the distance, what seems like the faint sound of chanting or wailing.

Hans sucks on the spliff and blows a few smoke rings into the night air. 'That's the sound of the ceremony you can hear. I know when I talked to you earlier you said that you weren't interested . . . in the after party. But perhaps you've changed your mind?' he asks, with a dark glint in his eyes.

'I'm not sure.'

'You've got nothing to be nervous about.'

'Nervous? Who said I was nervous?'

'No one, just that . . . well, it can be pretty daunting, taking ayahuasca for the first time. But we've got a great *ayahuasquero* – he's Peruvian but speaks English – who'll take you through every step of the process. It's like ten years of therapy in one trip. Just keep your heart open and you'll be fine.'

His words make me feel uncomfortable. Despite all the trappings of my alternative lifestyle – my decision to come and live here, off grid in an eco-village, my green credentials, my veganism, my desire to make the world a better place – I don't like the idea of my heart being open. I never have. If I talked to a therapist, I guess they'd say that was because of the abandonment I'd experienced when my mother ran off to pursue her own happiness. I was stunted. I had issues with trust. I liked to control. I knew I had a problem with anger. I wasn't easy to live with. And I'm sure they would be right about all of those things. But perhaps this would help me.

'And where will it be again?'

'In the clearing, the *era*, the old threshing circle, down below Devil's Head. I spent the last couple of days weeding it, making it look cool. I've got cushions, a couple of tents people can lie in, a few hammocks under some trees.' He takes another drag on the spliff. 'It's like a big reset. Like when your computer is fucked and needs an overhaul. Your circuits will get rewired so you can see the world clearly again. You're going to be reborn.'

It sounds exactly what I need. 'Okay – count me in.'

33

MIA

I'm standing in the kitchen playing the argument over and over in my mind. Tears sting my eyes and my breathing is shallow and fast. A flat – together – in La Isleta? Fucking in that place by the sea while I was busy trying to help Blanca with the paperwork for the exhumation of her mother. I picture their bodies clammy with the sweat from sex, the pair of them clinging together in a moment of mutual orgasm. The image sickens me and I have to steady myself by the sink. And what did Anna mean when she said that I was a victim? My hand rests on my stomach in an attempt to quieten the butterflies that feel like they're trying to escape from my abdomen. Thank goodness I never told Rich about the fact I'm pregnant. Perhaps now I never will.

'My dear, that was awful for you.' It's Blanca, who has materialized by my side. 'Most of the guests have gone now, me and my friends are the last to leave. But let us help you clear up.'

'Oh no, honestly, you don't need to do—'

Before I finish my sentence, the women – all in their sixties or seventies – get to work, clearing plates, washing dishes and glasses, sweeping up, moving chairs and furniture. She leads me into the sitting room where I apologize for what she was forced to witness. She takes my hands in hers as I talk, but she doesn't seem to be listening. Instead, she's staring up at the vaulted ceiling, her eyes fixed on the exposed wooden beams.

'Blanca, what's wrong?'

Her friends break off from the cleaning and begin to fuss around her, asking her if she's having one of her odd turns, whether she needs a glass of water or a pill. The party was too much for her, says one of them. She should never have witnessed that horrible scene, it's upset her, another adds. And then there's her mother's exhumation tomorrow, a third one observes – she's had too much sadness in her life, she can't take any more.

But Blanca continues to fix her gaze on a particular spot. 'It was here that she did it – my grandmother,' she whispers.

I think back to what Blanca told me that day in her house. About her grandmother's suicide by hanging. Although I know it's still hot outside, the temperature seems to drop and I feel a shiver on the back of my neck as if a ghost has touched my skin with a ribbon.

Her friends fall silent as they listen to what sounds like an incantation. 'She knew the solid weight of the eucalyptus beam would hold her,' she continues. 'And using one of her best sheets, given to her on her wedding day, she fashioned the last garment for herself – a noose that would end her life.'

She shifts the focus of her watery eyes from the ceiling to

181

me. She asks her friends to wait outside for her, a request that does not please them. Finally, after a great deal of complaining, they relent. Once they're gone, she tightens her grip on my hands. 'I may not know English, but I could still understand. I've warned you already, and that was before what I've seen today, my dear child. It's happening again. A dangerous triangle. An unfaithful man – I saw so much anger in him. A flirt who has used her charms to attract him – she is no good. And an unhappy woman who cannot bear the pain any longer – that is you.'

She looks at my stomach and nods. She mutters something under her breath, but I catch the idiomatic phrase, 'Dar a luz', which translates literally as 'to give light' and means 'to give birth'. How does she know I'm pregnant? I've told no one of my news. Then she looks up at the ceiling again and wrinkles her nose as if smelling something unpleasant.

'You need to be careful,' she says. 'The stench of death – it's here.'

34

RICH

I'm sitting in a semi-circle of a dozen people; apart from Hans, most of them are strangers. By each of us there's a metal bucket and loo roll, and a few hammocks have been tied up to the olive trees that sit on the edge of the old threshing circle. Devil's Head looms above us, its rocky promontories jutting out into the night sky like enormous horns, a cave inset into the cliff forming a jagged mouth, and two deep crevices staring out like all-seeing black eyes.

The shaman is a flat-faced Peruvian called Jesús, of all things. He looks like he's in his late fifties, has straggly black hair and dark eyes. He's wearing a traditional multi-coloured hat with long ear straps, a series of beaded necklaces in yellow, blue, white and pink, and a bright orange tunic. From within his body comes a tuneless, repetitive chant, its vibrations seemingly so powerful they echo through me like the deep bass of a drum. We all drank the ayahuasca – a bitter-tasting sludge as dark as molasses – about forty minutes ago, but I'm still waiting for something to happen.

I look at the others in the semi-circle, their faces illuminated by the light of the moon, and wonder whether the drug has taken hold of them yet, but it's impossible to know. A woman sitting next to me – dressed in hippy pants, and old enough to be the grandmother of one of my friends – is tapping her hand on her knee, as if she can discern some hidden rhythm in the seemingly irregular, dissonant chanting. A man in his early twenties, wearing shorts but no top, has his eyes closed and is slowly letting his head drop forwards before completing a neck circle. A shaven-headed woman is looking up at the sky, perhaps at the moon, with a desperate, hopeful expression, as if to pray that the experience will answer some of her deepest concerns.

Before we began, Jesús gave a little pep talk, where he told us about the history of the drug – the 'vine of the soul' – and its possible benefits, how 'mother ayahuasca' raised consciousness, how it helped deal with trauma, how it had the power to heal and transform. But tonight all I want is to feel nothing. I'm hoping that the drug will just wipe me out. I'd like to erase myself.

Jesús insisted that no matter what we experienced we should try to stay within the designated area. We might feel like purging – manifested by sickness or an emptying of the bowels – but this was perfectly natural and nothing to worry about. It was the body, the mind, and the soul ridding themselves of unnecessary toxins, memories and spiritual blocks. The main thing was to trust in him.

I still can't feel anything and I'm about to write the whole thing off as a massive fraud, when I see something in front of me.

A couple of beetles.

I can see in microscopic detail the raised ridges on their backs, and I can hear the brush of the hairs on their legs as they scuttle towards me. I feel my mouth drop open with astonishment, surprised by my own superpowers. But then the two beetles turn into a colony, a horrible swarming mass surging towards me. I close my mouth, afraid that they'll scuttle into me and rattle their way down my throat. I try closing my eyes, but this makes no difference.

But then suddenly the beetles are replaced by a clat of earthworms, squirming their way towards me. I feel them on my head, in my ears, up my nostrils, at the corner of my mouth. I try to brush them off, and for a moment I feel relief that they've disappeared. But then I feel something rising within me. I'm going to be sick. The sudden rush within me is so powerful I don't have time to reach for the bucket.

After a while, I begin to enjoy the sense of relief that comes with the purging, the kind of release Jesús must have been talking about. I look around me to check on the others in the semi-circle, but their figures have disappeared now and all I can see is what looks like a black velvet curtain. It's shimmering in the light with a beauty and a majesty, and also a sense of promise. Behind it lies the secret of life, I feel. This is what I've been expecting. The answer to all my questions. The enigma that has been eluding me will be revealed. There's a hush, an impossible silence. The curtain twitches, only for it to close again. But then suddenly it's pulled back. I see a figure on a bare stage. They have their back to me. I try to open my mouth to ask them to turn around, but I can't talk. I want it to be Mia. I need her to tell me that she loves me. I realize that's all I want.

A foot pivots, a hip swings and then, with a whoosh, I see who it is.

It's Marianne. She's beautiful and young, like in one of the films from her heyday. But she's even more stunning than she was in real life. Her skin is porcelain white, flawless. Her eyes are bright with life. She's going to tell me something important, something that will change me forever. I can sense she's holding some secret knowledge that she wants to share.

She opens her mouth to speak. No words come out, but her eyes turn dark with hatred.

'No one could ever love you,' she whispers as she turns her back on me. 'Not Mia. Not Anna.' She pauses. 'Not me.'

The black velvet curtains close and the floor of the stage turns to earth. The curtains become trees. I'm in a forest. I can hear the wind in the trees. I feel the dapple of spring sunlight on my cheek. I see a woman walking a dog. A small girl is playing by the bluebells. I'm watching from behind a tree. I know what I want to do.

I want to kill.

35

MIA

After seeing off Blanca and her friends, I make my way back down the dusty *camino*. As I walk, I have the sensation that someone is watching me. I stop on the path and listen. In addition to the distant sound of what seems like South American chanting and the flow of water down by the river, I hear only the rise and fall of my own breath. I inhale and turn my head slightly and catch something else. Is that the sibilant whisper of someone breathing or is it just the noise of the warm evening breeze in the trees? I look around me, deep into the shadows, but see nothing.

The singing seems louder now, most likely coming from up by Devil's Head. Some of the villagers had told me that there was going to be an ayahuasca ceremony tonight. Over the years, I'd heard some far-out things about the drug: although I'm sure many people find that it helps free them of certain mental and emotional blocks, I've read of others who blame it for pushing them over the edge. I just hope Rich hasn't been tempted to join in; he has a history, after all.

Just as I'm about to enter the courtyard I hear footsteps behind me. I spin around and see a figure.

It's Anna. Her blonde hair looks almost ghostly in the moonlight.

'What the hell are you doing – coming here like this?'

She doesn't respond. Instead, she turns away from me and starts to walk towards the crystal path. I think about letting her disappear into the night, but why should I? She's stolen my boyfriend, wrecked my life, fucked with my head. It's time to tell her a few home truths.

'Don't walk away from me!' As I say the words, I realize how pathetic they sound, as if I'm an exasperated parent talking to a badly behaved child. I'm so furious with Anna that I begin to follow her, up the crystal path. As we climb, she sometimes twists her head to look at me. I wonder if she's a little scared of me. I hope so.

'You were the one that was following me just now,' I call out to her. 'How do you like it?'

She pushes on with an extra burst of energy and it seems she's sobered up a little since earlier. But then, as she passes through a tunnel of prickly pears – their monstrous forms stretching out into the moonlit sky like a series of swollen, deformed hands – she loses her balance. She stretches out to right herself and brushes past one of the cacti.

'Fuck,' she says to herself. She stops as she tries to clear her arm of the invisible spikes, but this only intensifies the pain. 'Shit.'

She turns to see me behind her and, as she tries to twist back, she loses her step. She stretches out to hold onto something, but unfortunately the only thing she can grasp is the fat pad of a prickly pear. The noise she makes is a mix of pain, frustration and fear and she falls to the ground.

'What the fuck do you want?' she says, slurring her words a little and fighting back the tears.

I can't deny that I get a little jolt of pleasure from seeing her on the earth, her denim shorts riding up the tops of her legs, her face creasing in agony. But then I see her for what she is: not a 'love rival' or a 'seductress' or any other label, but a woman in pain who needs my help.

'Here,' I say, stretching out my hand.

She looks as though she doesn't trust me. I see that her eyes are glassy and it's clear that she hasn't sobered up after all.

'I'm okay, thanks. Just fuck off, Mia.'

'I was only trying to help.'

Her tone is sarcastic and biting. 'Yeah, right.'

'Do you have any idea what pain you've caused me?'

'Oh yes – it always has to be you, doesn't it? The p-perpetual victim,' she says as she pushes herself upwards.

Her words echo her earlier ones at the party. 'What do you mean?'

'Nothing.'

'No, come on, if you've got something to say, I'd suggest that you—' Again, I feel as if I'm talking like a cross teacher or someone much older than I really am.

She turns to carry on up the crystal path, but I hear her saying, almost under her breath, 'I know what happened.'

The words don't so much chill my blood as turn it to poison in my veins. I feel as though I'm going to be sick. I know in that moment exactly what she's talking about.

I grab her arm. It feels hot and sweaty. My fingers slide down her wet skin and I notice, even in the moonlight, that she's bleeding. The tips of my fingers are covered in her blood.

As I start to speak I can hear the tremble in my voice. 'W-what are you talking about?'

She addresses me coolly, almost without emotion. 'I know why you're so damaged. I know how your mother was murdered.'

The words sound like something I might hear in a dream. In fact, the whole scenario – the pale light of the moon, the distant chanting and the drumming, the monstrous forms of the prickly pears rising out of the ground, the feel of the blood on my skin – is like something from one of those night terrors that continue to haunt me. I try to swallow, but my throat is dry and my tongue feels paralysed.

'How do I know?' she asks. 'Oh, Rich told me everything about you. About your poor mother murdered in that wood. About how you witnessed it all. About how the killer tried . . . tried to bury you alive.'

I can't believe what I'm hearing. Rich would never have spoken about the details of my past. It was our secret. It wasn't that I was ashamed, rather that my mother's memory was so precious I felt I didn't want to share it with outsiders. I always tried to resist being defined by those experiences. The last thing I wanted to be was a victim. And here she was – Anna, the woman who had taken Rich from me – telling me about it all.

'God only knows how that must have fucked you up,' she continues. 'I know Rich told me how difficult it's been for him, always trying to support you, being by your side. Trust is a problem for you, I suppose. I can understand that. Rich says it makes you unbalanced at times, not in your right mind . . . *needy*.'

She pronounces the last word with the knowledge that it has the power to damage me, like the tip of a sharp knife plunging straight into the heart.

'And then being left in the ground like that, next to your mother, that must have been awful. What a monstrous thing to do to a small child. And the consequences will be felt for a lifetime, of course they will. I suppose a little piece of you died that day; part of you will always remain there in that ground. No wonder Rich felt trapped for such a long time.'

I want to ask her why she's being so cruel to me. But when I move my lips nothing happens. I can make no sound. I feel as though I'm having some kind of stroke. How could Rich have betrayed me like this? The sexual infidelity is nothing compared to the breaking of his promise not to talk to others about my past.

She falls silent then and smiles, the smile of accomplishment that comes with the knowledge that she has won. She has humiliated me and reduced me to dust. She's right: I am nothing. A part of me did die that day in 1990. I was foolish to think that I could live a normal life. I've had a career, a nice flat, a boyfriend, but I was just going through the motions. I was playing at life, getting through each day, each week, each month, by the miracle of learned behaviour. I was nothing but a reflection, as empty and shallow as the image cast by a mirror.

'I was thinking of doing a story about you – that's why I took those photographs. And about Iain Hastings' innocence. If the evidence I've seen checks out, it's one hell of a miscarriage of justice.'

191

I'm conscious of something happening inside my head. It's not exactly a snapping or something breaking, more of a slipping away, like I'm stepping outside my body so that I'm able to witness the scene unfolding before me. I can see Anna, a streak of blood smeared down her arm, her blonde hair glinting in the violet and silver night, her full lips curving to form that triumphant smile. I see myself, dumbstruck, a hand slowly reaching out for one of the large rocks. It's a heavy thing and the quartz digs into my fingers. The whole thing seems to move in slow motion, as if I'm watching a silent film that has been decelerated frame by terrifying frame. I know what is going to happen, of course I do, but it seems as though I'm blind to the consequences of my actions. I'm vaguely aware of a sharp sensation in the palm of my hand, and perhaps it's the feel of the rock cutting into my skin that rouses me from the waking dream.

I'm back in my body again. What the fuck am I doing? Anna's eyes travel to my hand and she too realizes what is happening.

The smile has been wiped off her face. 'Jesus, you're even more fucked up than Rich said,' she whispers.

I look at the rock in my hand. I see the look of fear in her eyes. 'I wasn't – I didn't . . .' But the words don't seem right. 'Of course, I wouldn't do . . .' The rest of the sentence dies on my lips. I wouldn't do what? I can't bear to think what was going through my brain.

I drop the rock onto the ground, and, as it crashes down, a few crystals splinter off its hard surface onto the dry earth. The noise serves as a concrete marker of the reality of what nearly happened.

'You're insane,' says Anna. 'You're properly insane.' She

starts to climb the path again, with a more determined pace. 'I think Rich should know what you nearly did, don't you?'

'No, but listen, it wasn't—'

'Stop following me!'

She continues upwards, occasionally slipping away into pockets of darkness unlit by the moon.

I continue to shadow her, up the hill, past a couple of abandoned houses, and towards the old threshing circle, the spot where the ceremony is being held. I have to stop her speaking to Rich. She's got the wrong idea about what happened back there, with the rock.

As I quicken my pace and push forwards, I get out of breath. Anna is ten years younger, ten years fitter than me. But as she reaches the top of the crystal path, she slows down. She stops and stares at something, her form swaying back and forth as if she's in a kind of trance. I'm certain that she's been drinking, and suspect she's also taken something.

I approach, silently, stealthily. I'm about to call her name when I see what she's looking at: a semi-circle of people, all sitting on the ground, their eyes closed. A South American-looking man, who I suppose is the shaman, is sitting cross-legged on the earth and chanting, but his song has quietened now, and at times his voice drops almost to a whisper. The words are obscure, a mix of Spanish and some ancient language that I've never heard before.

I follow Anna's eyes, directed towards Rich. He too has his eyes closed, but his hands are outstretched in front of his face, batting away some invisible enemy. He looks like he's in some kind of distress – God only knows what hallucinations he's having and whether this drug will leave any lasting damage.

It's obvious that now would be an inappropriate time to interrupt – even a novice like me knows this could be dangerous – but Anna takes a step towards the circle. I retreat into the shadows, behind a large carob tree, in case I need to run; I couldn't bear a public humiliation in front of these people, these strangers.

The shaman spots Anna and quietly, without alarm, stands up. He moves swiftly, darkly, almost like a shadow himself, holds up a palm and shakes his head. There's a majesty to him, an authority that cannot be challenged, and Anna turns away. As she looks back and steps into a spot of moonlight, I see panic in her eyes, as if she's scared to encounter me again.

I skirt around the edge of the threshing circle, hiding myself as best as I can, and follow her onto the path that leads towards Devil's Head. I just want to explain myself. Despite everything she's done – the affair, the deception, the flat in La Isleta, even the fact that she knows about what happened with my mother and me and her threat to write about the case – I tell myself that I would never actually hurt her. Of course, I felt angry down there on the crystal path, angry enough to pick up that rock. But it was more a sensation of doing something to hurt myself rather than inflict any damage on her. Like she said, I was a victim. I knew all about suffering, and living with the consequences of a murder; a crime like that poisoned you forever. And as a result, I would never subject another family to the same horrors that I'd endured. Like other victims had said, surviving a crime was almost like a life sentence in itself, a sense of being punished for something you had not committed.

I realize then that I've lost her. I listen for her footsteps but all I can hear are the whispers of the shaman in the wind and the revving of a car in the distance. She must have slipped away, down a side path or through the series of terraces that lead back to the village. If she's taken that route there's a risk that her bare legs could get torn to shreds by the cacti. As I stand there I tell myself it's best to let her go. Who will believe her anyway? She's the one who has been drinking, perhaps taken other drugs, while I've only had one glass of wine. Perhaps she'll sleep in her car or bed down at Desert Shoots; when she wakes up she'll be too ashamed of her own behaviour to think about mine.

But then I hear her voice.

'Mia.'

I turn around and see her blonde head silhouetted against the night sky like some kind of white goddess.

Suddenly, I'm the one who feels afraid. But I can't let her sense my fear. 'Anna, thank goodness you're okay. I was worried about you for a moment.'

'Worried about me?' she laughs. 'That's odd, coming from you. Only a few minutes ago it looked as though you wanted to brain me.'

'No, I wanted to explain. You see—'

'Save me the explanation. I saw what you did back there. I know what you're like.'

'You've got it all wrong—'

'And soon Rich will hear all about it too. He's pitied you for too long, all this victim crap you spout. All those horrors from the past – how he had to feel sorry for you. How you forced him to look after you. After what I tell him, he's going to see you in a new light.'

'Anna—'

195

'And you can stop that bleating. The self-pity won't wash with me.'

'If you just let me explain—'

'I can see you for who you are.'

She takes a step towards me. There's anger in her eyes now. And a sense that she's on the side of right. Her blonde hair is rising and falling in the night breeze.

'No wonder you got too much for Rich, no wonder he felt he had no choice but to leave you.'

'What are you talking about? He said he was leaving you – not me.'

'It's not only the fact that I'm younger, more beautiful,' she continues as if she hasn't heard me. There is a note of triumph in her voice. I'm reminded of the way she smiled at me down by the crystal path, as if she'd always known she was going to win. 'I don't have to carry around all that . . . baggage from the past. It's left you warped, twisted.'

'No, it's not like that. Anna, you've got to—'

'I don't have to do anything.'

'I didn't mean it like that.' I'm finding it hard to get the words out again. My head feels in a fug, even though I only had a glass of cava. I feel a tightening of my throat. 'Look, we should both get some sleep. This isn't going to get us anywhere.'

As I move to walk past her, she grabs my shoulder.

'What the hell are you playing at?'

'You think you're so special, don't you? Surviving against the odds. Watching your mother die. Being buried alive. But you're no different to the rest of us.'

'I never said I was,' I say as I try to push past her.

She tightens her grip so I can't move. I feel the pressure in my head begin to build. 'Take your hands off me.'

196

'Do you want to hurt me? You do, don't you? I can see it in your eyes.'

'Don't be so stupid.'

'Maybe there is a story to be written here, after all.' There's a taunting quality to her voice, as if she wants me to attack her. 'Perhaps the story I need to write is about how the attack, the murder of your mother, your experience at the hands of that killer – whoever he is or was – has turned you into a psycho.'

As I try to free myself from her grip, she moves her hands from my shoulder to my right arm which she then tries to twist. The instinct to fight back kicks in. I take a breath and use my elbow to hit her in the chest.

'Fuck,' she cries as she falls forwards, clasping her breasts.

I run past her, towards the road, relieved that I'm away from her. As I'm running I'm vaguely aware of a shadow on the edge of my peripheral vision. I stop, but I can't see anyone. I continue towards the empty road. Just as I realize that I must be approaching the spot in the old olive grove where Blanca's mother's body lies, I hear footsteps, running towards me.

I turn around. A tornado of fury is fast approaching me. It's Anna. Her eyes are stretched wide and she looks possessed.

'For God's sake, Anna. It's late. You're upset. We both are.'

'You still don't get it, do you? Did you really think I'd leave here, this valley – because of you? Why should I leave a place I love?'

She sweeps back her hair and takes a deep breath as if she knows she's going to say something important, something that will destroy me.

'You're the one not suited to it. You have to have a certain

197

temperament to thrive here. That's what I said to Rich when we met at his mother's funeral.'

I can't take in the words. 'I'm sorry. What did you just say?'

'That you have to be able to appreciate the wildness of the place. It's too much for some people.'

'No – what you said about Rich's mother's funeral?'

'Oh yes, that's where we met – Rich and I,' she says, in a tone of false naivety. 'Didn't you know that?'

Her words hit me like a kick to the solar plexus. I can't speak.

'I suppose it was instant attraction. We got talking and couldn't keep away from one another. That night I led him down to the river, where we fucked all night.'

'You mean – you mean, you didn't meet in February, the day after we . . . we arrived here?'

'Of course not. He's been planning this for months. That's why he came back here to Val Verde, don't you see?' She pauses, her triumph complete. Her voice is low now, exultant. 'He came back to be with me.'

The shock takes the strength from my legs. As my arm reaches out to steady myself against the stone wall, it comes to rest on a loose rock similar to the one I held in my hands down by the crystal path.

'You must have been so stupid to think he'd stay with you.'

I think back to our time in London, and how he persuaded me to make the move from England. It would be a new beginning for us, he said. We would be doing our bit to help protect the environment, save the world. The green dream could be our reality.

I understand now that he'd used the death of Emily

198

Thomas, my pupil who killed herself because of her anxieties surrounding the climate change emergency, as a way of manipulating me into agreeing to come out here. When all the time he wanted to return to Val Verde in order to carry on his affair with a woman he'd met at his mum's funeral.

The sudden realization makes me feel sick.

I've read about people being overwhelmed with anger, like a kind of red mist that descends upon them. But that's not how it is for me now. It's more a shroud of darkness, reminding me of that time in the earth. My throat feels like it's filling up with loam again. Once more, I can't breathe. My fingers begin to close around the sharp edges of the rock. I'm not going to be buried alive again.

36

RICH

I stagger away from my vomit, clutch onto an old olive tree and close my eyes. I try to take a few deeper breaths. I know I need to calm down. I think about whether I should go back to the ceremony, to try to explain to the shaman why I left. But I realize I'm in no fit state to talk.

As I open my eyes, the bark begins to move. It's as if I can see into the cellular structure of the wood, its inner workings, complete with cytoplasm, nuclei and mitochondria. I try to recall some of the basic processes of life. There's order in the universe. Everything has a place. There are rules. Strata. Laws of biology, chemistry, physics. And yet since coming back to Val Verde everything seems to have degenerated into chaos, like I've fallen off the edge of a map.

I don't know where I am any more, or what I want. I was happy back in London, living with Mia. It's Anna who's changed all of that. She's the one who's ruined everything for me – for us. She'd told me that she was happy with a one-night stand. So why had she decided to return to Val Verde? It was almost like she'd drugged me. She'd made me lie to Mia. She had made me betray her. It had all been her fault.

If only she was out of the picture. If only we could start again, Mia and I. Would she take me back? There was a small chance, but only if she knew that Anna had gone and was not coming back. But how to get rid of her?

More dark water gushes out of my mouth, spreading itself across the dry ground. I see the plants around me – the wild thyme, the white oleanders – withering and dying, killed by a spill of my own toxic waste. What was it my mother used to say to me? Everything I touch dies.

As I raise my head, wipe my lips of the foul-tasting liquid, I'm vaguely aware of someone nearby.

I think I recognize them.

37

MIA

We're in the olive grove, looking for the remains of Blanca's mother. Diego, one of the archaeologists, has just found a body. But it's not that of Esperanza or anyone else killed during the Spanish Civil War.

This person is not long dead, he says. Blanca is asking what he's seen, whether it's Esperanza he's found. I take her bony hands in mine and tell her it's not her mother. Diego is shouting to the other volunteers to phone the police. The dig will have to be shut down. He doesn't know what the fuck is happening. Like him, I've seen the blood in the matted hair, the brain matter spilled out onto the dry earth. He's talking about murder. Diego asks me whether I'm all right. He says I look like I've seen a ghost. Memories of the night before crowd my mind, but I try to push them away.

Blanca tries to get out of her chair, but I gently restrain

her. Diego tells her this isn't her mother. That she's safe underground. He promises that he will find her.

'But we'll have to wait until the police have been and investigated,' he adds. 'There's another body nearby – in a shallow grave.'

I don't like the sound of the words. I associate them with myself. The light seems to be fading, as if dark clouds are shadowing the sky, obscuring the sun. The range of my vision is narrowing, like I'm experiencing a solar eclipse. I feel a heaviness on my chest, as though something or someone is sitting on me. I can't breathe, again. I'm back there, in the earth.

'Mia, you've had a shock,' says Diego.

From his cooler bag he takes out his water bottle, one of the things he was trying to place in the shade when he came across the makeshift grave.

'Here, drink this,' he says.

I take a sip of water. He walks over to a young female assistant who has been on the phone.

'Did you get through to them? The police?' he asks.

'Yes, they're on the way,' she says. 'They say don't touch anything.'

'I suppose they don't realize the skills we have as archaeologists,' he says. 'We're used to dealing with the dead.' The comment is supposed to lighten the mood a little, but it falls flat.

I leave Blanca's side and make my way, ever so slowly, over to the grave. Nobody witnesses what I'm doing. Just as well, otherwise they would think that I was some kind of ghoul. But I have to see it for myself again. I just can't believe it.

I caught a glimpse of the body a few moments ago, but I

must have been mistaken. My current anxieties – the way my mind has been working overtime – have warped my perception. It can't be true.

I edge my way through the buckets filled with dry earth, the trenches demarcated by little flags, past the wheelbarrows and discarded tools, towards the big olive tree. I look up to make sure no one is watching me, but as I do so I see Blanca's dark eyes fixed on me. I shake my head, a warning for her not to alert the others, and turn into the shade of the tree, below which sits the shallow grave. The sun is not so hot here.

The first thing I see is an arm, curled in an unnatural position and rising from the earth like the discarded skin of a snake. I step closer and peer down, forcing myself to look at the rest of the body not covered by the soil. There's a clump of hair smeared with a sticky redness. A part of the face has been smashed in, disguising some of the features. There's a section of the skull that seems to be missing altogether, inside of which . . .

I turn my head away. I can't bear to look any more. I wasn't imagining any of it, even in my very worst nightmares. This is all too real.

A memory from the night before flashes into my mind again. I was up here. By this spot, near this tree. I had a rock in my hand. And I wanted to use it on Anna.

The woman who is lying dead, half buried in the ground.

38

RICH

I don't know where I am when I open my eyes. My head feels like it's splintering into a million tiny pieces. My mouth tastes like I've spent the night licking the inside of a sewer. I think I'm going to be sick. I wrench myself upwards and see – what the fuck? – that I'm inside a car. I blink, but I see a steering wheel, a gearbox, a European road map. I push open the door. The sunlight blinds me and I fall out and down onto the ground. As I dry-retch onto the earth, fragments of the night before come back to me. The ceremony. The chanting. The shaman. The taste of the foul liquid. Those horrible visions. The insects. The snakes. A black velvet curtain. My mother.

'You're still alive, then?'

I look up and see Hans, holding out a cup of black coffee. He's standing outside his camper van, where I must have spent the night.

'Sorry?' I clear my throat and cough like I'm about to bring up my lungs.

'You were really out of it last night.'

'Was I?'

'Yeah, I was really worried about you. Must have been the mix of everything – booze, the weed, the ayahuasca.'

I remember getting up, my stomach cramping, stumbling around, being sick. I recall holding a tree, seeing the very insides of it, and then I saw someone I thought I knew.

'It was far out, didn't you think?' says Hans, taking a sip of coffee. 'I had the most beautiful experience, so spiritual.' He sighs as he casts his mind back to the ceremony. 'But you shouldn't have gone off like that. The shaman wasn't happy with you, but I told him it was your first time . . . and that you were going through some serious shit. Relationship stuff.'

'Thanks.' As I rub my palms across my eyes I'm aware that there are plasters stuck across the backs of my hands. I blink again as I try to recall how I got back to his van. 'Listen – how did I end up here? In your van, I mean.'

'You can't remember?'

As I shake my head, I feel another wave of nausea hit me.

'I don't know how long you'd been away from the circle, as I didn't know you'd left, to be honest. It was only when the sun was coming up that I opened my eyes. I looked for you, but when I couldn't find you I asked Jesús what had happened. He told me that, in the middle of the ritual, you got up – he'd tried to restrain you, but you pushed him off. He wanted to go after you, but of course he couldn't leave the other members of the group. Anyway, early this morning I came to look for you and found you near that old olive grove by the road.'

I realize then I'm only wearing a pair of pants and a vest top.

'What . . . what happened to my clothes?'

'Sorry – I had to strip you when you got back here.' He laughs. 'Don't worry, I didn't try anything on with you.'

I can't even raise a laugh. 'No, it's not that, it's just I—'

'They're over there, in a pile behind the van. I don't know whether they're salvageable.'

I feel a sense of foreboding begin to shadow its way over me. 'What – what do you mean?'

'You really can't remember?'

'No, sorry.'

I stand up and, feeling like I have all the coordination and balance of a man in space, stumble round the van, until I see a pile of clothes. They're sitting in a tangle on the ground and they don't look like mine. The jeans are stained with something dark and . . . and what colour shirt was I wearing last night? I'm sure it was blue. Whatever it was, I'm sure it didn't look like this.

'Hans – are you sure those are my clothes?'

''Course they are, mate. Who else would they belong to? But I really had to sponge you down and patch you up before you went to sleep.'

'S-sponge me down?' I don't want to ask the next question. 'Why?'

'You were covered in blood, Rich. Mostly from your hands, I think. You were cut up quite badly. Don't you remember any of it?'

When I shake my head again, he continues. 'You must have fallen onto some rocks, some crystal, I think. When I got you back here, I bathed your hands in a bowl of water. And I had a few strips of plaster I used to cover your wounds.'

As he talks I blank out his words. I can only think about last night. I remember having some dark thoughts. About my mother, of course. About Mia. About Anna. I recall standing by the tree and seeing someone. A woman.

'. . . You were talking some weird shit, though, Rich,' Hans continues.

I begin to listen to him again, conscious that my heart is racing.

'But it's best if you forget it. Put last night behind you. I should have told you that your first time with ayahuasca can be a bit – well, a bit unpredictable, shall we say?'

I feel my temper rising. 'No, I want to know.' I realize I am speaking too harshly. 'Sorry.' I try to smile, but I feel it fading on my face. 'I'd like you to tell me.'

'Something about . . . I don't know.' He drains his coffee cup and starts to prepare a roll-up.

I want to snap at him again, tell him to just spit it out. Stop being so laid-back. But I bite my tongue – literally. As my teeth clamp down on the sides of my tongue, the sharp pain helps me cope with the agony of waiting. I have to watch him as he licks the paper, takes out the tobacco, rolls up the cigarette and then searches for a lighter or some matches. Just as I'm about to shout, 'Just tell me what the fuck I said!' he lights the cigarette, takes a deep inhale, and starts to speak.

'You kept mumbling about how you saw her – you didn't give a name,' he says, blowing a few smoke rings. 'She shouldn't have been there, you said. Something about how she . . . how she deserved to die.'

39

MIA

I don't know what to do, what to think. I'm in the house, waiting for the police to arrive. There's no sign of Rich, which worries me. Where did he spend the night? I presume that after the ayahuasca ceremony he crashed with Hans, in his camper van. Should I try to ring his mobile and tell him about Anna? Or should I let him have a few hours of blissful not-knowing before breaking the terrible news to him? I realize as I think this that I must still care about him, even after everything. Of course I do. But I also know deep down that I can never live with him again.

I'm relieved I never told Rich about my pregnancy. I'm still uncertain about what to do, even whether to keep it. Although I'd longed for a child, wouldn't having his baby serve as a constant reminder of what a shit Rich had been and how badly he'd treated me? And what would happen if I had a son – would he grow up to be like his father?

What's wrong with me? Why am I thinking about the problems with my relationship at a time like this? The discovery of Anna's body in the olive grove seems so unreal I still can't take it in, even after seeing it with my own eyes. I picture her head smashed in, the splatter of blood, the mushy spill of brains on the ground.

Just then there's a knock at the door.

I had a shower earlier, but I check myself again in the mirror to make sure I'm looking okay. No doubt the police will want to ask me about what I saw this morning and about my movements last night, and I want to be presentable. I remember the shadowy figures of the police from when I was six: their hushed tones; their black uniforms; the seemingly endless presentation of photo-fits – slivers of noses, chins, foreheads, mouths – all laid out before me like a sinister children's puzzle; the way the officers looked at me with a mixture of sadness and astonishment, almost as if I were a walking miracle. 'To survive something like that, it doesn't bear thinking about,' I heard one of the policemen say to a female colleague. 'God knows, how it's going to affect her, the poor girl.'

I push the whispers from the past to the back of my mind and open the door, not to the Spanish police but to Freya.

'I've just heard the news,' she says. 'Can I come in?'

'Yes, of course. I'm waiting for the *Guardia Civil.*'

I lead Freya into the kitchen and we sit at the table. As I make a pot of fresh mint tea, I catch her looking at me in an odd way, almost as if she's examining me for traces of – what? – guilt?

'So you were up there, with Blanca and the archaeologists when . . . when you found her?'

I nod my head.

'You know I wasn't her greatest fan – after, well, after everything that went on – but no one would have wanted her . . .' My words trail off. 'To see her like that, in the ground. It was . . .'

'I can imagine. Do you know how . . . ?'

I have an idea – it looks as though her head was smashed in with something, like a rock – but I don't say any of this. 'No – I suppose that's a matter for the police.'

I catch her glancing at me again. Is it my imagination or do her eyes betray an expectation that she might see traces of blood on my skin, on my clothes?

'You don't . . . you don't think *I* did it, do you?'

She laughs nervously. 'Of course not – whatever gave you that idea?'

'Ignore me – I didn't have much sleep last night.'

'Hardly a surprise after what happened at the party,' she says, taking a sip of mint tea. 'Have you seen Rich since then?'

'No. Why? Do you think there's something wrong?'

'Not at all . . . But he didn't sleep here last night?'

'I assumed, after what happened at the party, that he would spend the night with . . .'

'With Anna?'

'No!' I snap. 'Sorry – no, with Hans or Bill or someone in the village.'

The image of Anna in that grave comes back to me. Perhaps it will never leave me. Another image, another memory, this time from years back, flashes into my mind. I'm on the ground. My head is hurting. I brush my hands through my hair and I feel a stickiness on my fingers. I bring my fingers in front of my eyes and see them covered with fresh blood. The man

211

who killed my mother, Iain Hastings, had used a rock to try to knock me out, after which he dumped me in a shallow grave next to her body.

I think of Anna up there in the olive grove.

She died in the same way.

But that has to be a coincidence. There's obviously nothing linking the two deaths. Hastings hanged himself in prison, while he was awaiting trial. This death, the murder of Anna, seemed – what? – more like a crime of passion or jealousy.

Just then there's another knock at the door.

'That must be the police,' I say, hardly able to get the words out.

'I better be going,' says Freya. 'But Mia, just call round if you need me, if you need to talk.'

'Thanks – yes, I will.'

'I'll let myself out – I'll go out through the garden. I need to check the flow of the water in the irrigation line anyway.'

'See you later.'

I open the door to two male uniformed officers, one young, tall and good-looking, the other older, shorter and well past his prime. After the formal introductions – their surnames are Estacio and Alameda, and they both speak English – I lead them into the house. I offer them coffee, water – which I pour for myself – but they politely refuse. Their faces are stern, serious and more than a little suspicious. Estacio begins by asking the questions, while Alameda's fat fingers grip a pencil as he prepares to take notes. I offer them seats at the dining table and they choose to sit opposite me; I feel as though I'm being interviewed inside a police station rather than in my home.

'It's just a few initial questions to begin with, to see how the land lies, so to speak,' says Estacio. 'I've already spoken to Diego Lopez about his discovery and also to Señora Blanca Rodríguez García too. But can you tell me what you saw this morning?'

I take a deep breath and outline the course of that morning's events, filling them in on how I've been helping Blanca with her mission to find her mother's remains. Estacio nods and listens, Alameda scratches away on his pad. I stand up, thinking everything has come to a natural conclusion and the policemen will thank me and take their leave, but Estacio asks me to sit down again.

'We're not quite finished here, I'm afraid, Miss Banner.' He shifts in his seat and leans towards me. He's studying me in the same way Freya had just before they arrived. 'You held a party here, at your house, yesterday, that's right?'

'Yes – it was to revive the old custom of the Val Verde fiesta.'

'And you had a good time?'

'I think people seemed to enjoy it, yes.'

'The house is now registered under the name of Richard Ellis, that's your boyfriend, yes?'

'That's right. But he's not here at the moment.'

'No, we gather that, Miss Banner. Do you have any idea where he might be?'

'I think he . . . he said he was going to sleep over at a friend's house,' I lie.

'And which friend might that be?'

'He could be at any number of friends' places. You see—'

'I know about the argument that you had at the party yesterday, Miss Banner. I know what was said and who said it. I also know that the dead woman – Anna Fleming – was also at the party, even though she may not have been invited.'

I fall silent and look down at my hands. I realize that there's still dirt under my fingernails. I want to sit on my hands, hide them out of view, but I feel self-conscious, as if Estacio and his sidekick are watching my every move. And so I slowly just let them drop to my sides, hoping they haven't noticed the odd way I'm behaving.

'Are you nervous, Miss Banner?'

Shit.

'No – well, apart from witnessing the discovery of a dead body, and the fact that I'm now being interviewed by two policemen.'

Estacio fixes me with his dark, penetrating eyes. 'There's no need to be nervous – if you tell us the truth.'

'Of course – of course I'm telling you the truth.'

'So – at the party – can you outline what happened, between you, your boyfriend, Richard Ellis and the dead girl, Anna Fleming?'

I sigh. 'Do we really have to go into all of this?'

He doesn't respond but continues to stare at me as if I have no choice but to answer his question.

'Very well, I'm guessing you probably know all of this anyway. Anna turned up, uninvited as you say. That was a bit of a shock. Also, I discovered that Rich had been seeing Anna – that she was living in a flat down by the coast. She came to the party, there was a bit of a scene. She stormed off, I think Rich followed her and that's . . . that's the last I saw of both of them.'

'Are you sure about that?'

I feel my heart racing. The sun is blazing down on the house and I can feel myself sweating. I take a sip of water. I wonder if they know about the ayahuasca ceremony: I don't

214

think the drug's illegal in Spain, but I still don't want to drop Rich in it.

'Yes, Anna seemed like she'd been drinking a lot before she'd arrived at the party. Perhaps she hit her head up by the road and . . .'

I realize the stupidity of my own words.

Estacio shakes his head. 'And what – she somehow dug her own shallow grave? Covered herself in earth?' He stands up and begins to walk around the kitchen, looking for – what? – signs of disturbance, evidence? He goes to the sink, opens and shuts the cutlery door. He bends down and checks the tiles on the floor. He stands and examines the contents of our shelves, picking up first a vase and then a large pottery cockerel.

'I don't know what you're looking for, but—'

'You seem to know how Anna Fleming was killed,' he says, placing the cockerel back down on the surface. 'You said that she could have hit her head.'

'Well – yes, after seeing her . . .'

'You're right. Her skull was smashed in with what seems like a heavy piece of rock or crystal.'

I'm beginning to feel sick. I remember seeing her there in the olive grove. Those awful words she said to me. About how she wanted to write a story about me. The knowledge that Rich had made me leave London because he'd already met Anna. At his mother's funeral. I recall the feel of that rock in my hand. 'Yes, it was awful to—'

'Awful to?'

'To see her like that! In the ground. Dead. Anna wasn't my favourite person – of course she wasn't – but I didn't want this to happen to her.'

215

'You're sure about that?'

I can feel myself losing control. 'What are you saying? Do you want to arrest me?'

'Calm yourself, Miss Banner,' says Estacio, raising his hands in an attempt to reduce the tension in the air. 'We're only here to ask you a few questions. One of the people we've spoken to talks of a specific altercation between you and Miss Fleming. Over a camera. Can you enlighten us to what occurred?'

Shit. I take another deep breath. 'It was a stupid misunderstanding.'

'A misunderstanding? About what?' asks Estacio.

God – is it really less than a day since we hosted the party? The events of yesterday seem like they occurred weeks back. Is that down to some kind of defence mechanism, one of those remnants of primitive Neanderthal life that exists in order to help us survive?

'It all happened so quickly,' I begin, 'but when Anna arrived she started to take some photographs of me. Obviously, I wondered what she was doing and so I – I asked her to stop. She didn't, she carried on pointing that camera at me. I made a clumsy attempt to grab the camera.'

'Why did she take the photographs of you?'

'I – I'm not sure,' I lie. 'I think it was some kind of sick joke.'

The men don't look impressed by my answer. What else do they know?

His questioning takes another turn. 'Was Richard Ellis in the habit of hurting people?'

'No, not at all.'

'He never hurt you?'

'No!'

216

'But you're in the process of . . . separating from him?'

'Yes, I suppose I am, I don't know, but—'

'Do you think he felt like hurting Anna Fleming?'

'I don't think so – I presume that at one point he was infatuated with her.'

'But he could have done so, if he'd wanted?'

'Well yes, like—' I'm about to say, 'like all of us,' but I think better of it. After all, how much strength would it take to knock someone out with a sudden blow from a rock? After that first swipe across the temples stunned them, it was only a matter of repetition – the showering of blow after blow, the continued force of stone on skull – that would result in their death.

Luckily, Estacio doesn't follow up my garbled half-sentence. Instead, he asks about whether Rich attended the ayahuasca ceremony. I'm not sure, I lie. Does he have a problem with drugs? Do I know Hans Huber, who lives in the camper van? The question and answer session has left me feeling exhausted. Estacio recognizes my sudden tiredness – either that or he's bored by my responses, because he taps Alameda on the shoulder and tells him it's time to go.

'Please get in touch with me if you have anything more to say, or if you're in contact with Richard Ellis.' He passes me his card, with his email and telephone numbers. 'And, Miss Banner, thank you again for your answers, and your . . . honesty.'

As he says this, the pause before the word and his shift in tone suggest that he suspects something. That I haven't been honest with him at all.

40

RICH

I'm lying on the bed in the beach apartment, surrounded by Anna's things, her smell lingering in the air. I can't believe she's gone. Anna. Dead. In a shallow grave up by the olive grove.

Where I'd been last night.

It was Bill who told me. He spotted me and Hans as he was walking along to his car. I knew something was wrong before he spoke. His normal jovial manner had disappeared, replaced by a solemnity I had never seen on him before.

'You haven't heard the . . . ?'

'Sorry?'

'About – Anna.'

'Anna? What do you mean?'

'She's been found, near the road.'

'Is she all right?'

He looked at me as if it pained him to say the words,

almost as if he were blaming me for having to say them out loud. 'She's dead, Rich.' He paused and added, 'And there's talk of murder.'

Hans's blissed-out expression – he'd been reminiscing about his ayahuasca trip – immediately turned sour. Suspicion poisoned his face and he looked at me with a stranger's eyes, as if I'd suddenly become a different person. A person capable of killing.

'D-do you know what happened?'

'No, but the police are on their way.'

'The police?'

'They're going to speak to Mia. She was there when they found the body this morning.'

I felt I could only communicate in simple sentences, like a child. Had the drug fucked up my brain or was this how shock worked? '*Mia?*'

'Apparently, Anna's body was found near the site where the archaeologists were digging, looking for the remains of Blanca's mother.'

I saw Hans's eyes resting on my scratched and reddened hands. I looked down at the strips of bandages. Bill followed my gaze.

'Did you hurt yourself?'

'I think – I think I must have fallen. Last night. After the ayahuasca thing, I—'

I felt my body go into some kind of overdrive. Adrenaline began to pump through my veins, masking the effects of my hangover. It was like the feeling I got before a fight or martial arts display. The basic instinct to survive.

'I – I've got to go.'

Bill blinked as if a cloud of dust had blown into his face. 'But what about the p—'

'Just say I've . . . I don't know. Say I've—' Fuck. What could I say? I thought of the pile of clothes, dirty and bloodied. What would the police think if they saw them? Where had Hans put them? 'Say – I've gone to the medical centre. I – I'm not feeling well after . . .' Would they arrest me if they knew about the ayahuasca?

I realized I didn't have time to go back to the house. And I didn't want to see Mia. Shit. The car keys for the Saab; I remembered taking them, together with a few things from the house. But where were they now? I patted my borrowed shorts. Nothing. They had to be in the pocket of my jeans.

'Thanks, thanks for telling me, Bill – we'll catch up later, yeah?'

Bill cast another look of concern in my direction, then he nodded and walked towards his car. I waited for him to drive off – a time that seemed like an eternity, as he sat in the driver's seat, checking his phone, messing about with something on the dashboard, getting out and bending down to look at his front tyre – before he eventually started his engine and disappeared up the twisty road in the direction of San Mateo.

'Shit,' said Hans.

I didn't speak. I felt his eyes lingering on me again. What had he seen? What did he know? For that matter, what did I know?

A few snatches of memory flashed through my mind. Images from the drug trip. I remembered running from that circle of hell beneath Devil's Head. I suppose I must have thought that if I put some distance between me and the physical space of the ceremony I would be able to lessen the awful effects of the drug. I had been full of poison, possessed by something

220

– a desire to hurt someone, to kill. I recalled being up by the old olive grove. There was a tree. I saw someone I knew, a woman.

Then I thought of that pile of dirty and bloodied clothes. My hands full of cuts.

I tried to speak, but my voice cracked. 'When— when you found me . . . where did— where did you put . . . my clothes, my jeans?'

'I said you were in a terrible state. Rich, is—'

'I'm— I'm just going to take off for a while. Nothing to worry about.'

'Look, do you want me to cover for you?'

'Cover for me? For what?'

'I don't know – but it's obvious something bad went on up there. I mean, I find you in a state, near where it happened, your clothes are covered in blood and dirt, your hands are cut up and—'

'But—'

'You could plead – what, temporary insanity or some shit like that. I could tell the police that the drug—'

'Shut the fuck up, Hans.'

'I was just trying to think of something to help—'

'Sorry,' I said, lowering my voice as I realized I shouldn't piss him off, 'but – but there's no problem. I haven't done anything.' I raise my hands to my head and press my palms against my temples. 'I'm just going to drive into town to get something for this headache. Okay?'

'Okay.'

I made my way around the van and saw my clothes sitting in a pile like the bloodied, dirtied cast-off skins of several snakes. Another memory of the writhing mass invaded my consciousness again. The rank smell of blood, warmed by the sun, caught the back of my throat. I steadied myself by the side of the van as a wave of nausea rose within me again. I turned my head away as I searched for the keys in the damp pockets of my jeans. I felt a sharp edge inside. Thank fuck they were still here. I fished them out, and noticed that my fingers were stained red.

I realized I couldn't leave the clothes here in case the police came calling. It would be – evidence. Shit. The word made it sound less a surreal nightmare and more a concrete reality. I bundled up the bloody clothes and, trying not to draw attention to myself, walked as slowly as I could towards my car, then opened the boot and shoved the clothes inside an old shopping bag. I knew I was probably in no fit state to drive, but I couldn't stand a moment longer in Val Verde. I needed to get away.

Luckily, I'd done the journey to the coast to see Anna so many times that it felt as though the car was driving itself.

I still couldn't take in the reality of her death. Her *murder*.

Surely it must be some kind of mistake, I told myself. It would turn out to be some other girl, someone who looked like her, another blonde passing through the village. But Bill had been adamant. The police were on their way. They wanted to talk to Mia. And of course, I knew they would want to talk to me.

In my head, I kept going over the same questions. How would the police react if I told them that patches of my memory of the previous night had melted away? That I'd taken a fashionable South American drug that had left me – what? Hallucinating? Deranged? Unable to remember whether I'd killed Anna or not?

From the boot of the Saab I took out the plastic bag

containing my clothes, let myself into the beach apartment and crawled onto the bed. I stayed there for what seemed like hours, curled up in a foetal position, taking in Anna's musky smell from the unwashed bedsheets. Memories of our time together flooded through me. The first touch of her. The time down by the riverbed. The taste of her. I felt myself beginning to get hard, but then shame killed that instinct. I felt so guilty I had to use a pillow to drown out my cries. I shouted her name into the soft down, felt the tears sting my face. As I lay there I knew that at some point I would have to face up to the consequences of my actions.

But what exactly had I done?

41

MIA

It should be a perfect summer's evening. Together with Freya, I'm sitting with Payton and Bill on their terrace, drinking homemade lemonade, while the three of them are knocking back the rosé. The sun has gone down and the fierce heat of the day has abated. A soft breeze whispers across the valley.

We're desperately pretending everything is normal. We're trying to distract ourselves from the messy, horrible business, wracking our brains for something to talk about: the problems with the ram pump (it could do with a service), the lack of summer rainfall, the heat (whether it's been hotter or cooler this year than previous ones), the varying quality of different grape varieties and who's going to bother making wine, and the vines' constant need for sulphur baths (traditionally applied by using an old sock).

Anything but murder.

Freya moves the conversation on by talking about her disappointing tomato crop. 'Although I've managed to salvage a few, I've had a problem with blight. They look okay, but inside it's like they're . . . dead.' She comes to an abrupt halt.

We know Freya's only talking about tomatoes, but it's a reminder of what's happened to Anna.

We fall silent, until finally Payton says, 'I'm sorry – I know we're all trying our best to take our mind off what happened, but I just can't stop thinking about it. That girl, lying in that ground, up there.' She turns to me. 'I know you had your issues with her, Mia – and frankly, who can blame you? – but she didn't deserve this.'

Everyone looks at me for a response. I'm not sure what to say. 'Nobody deserves . . . that,' is the best I can manage. I take another sip of lemonade.

'Do you think they'll get to the bottom of it?' asks Freya.

'I would have thought so,' says Bill. 'I'm sure they've got their theories already. It's just a matter of finding the evidence.'

'The evidence?' I ask.

'All that stuff you see on the TV shows,' he replies. 'You know, the fibres. The blood trail. DNA. But if you ask me, they probably suspect someone already.'

'But how? Why do—'

'We all saw what happened at the fiesta yesterday. The nasty little scene that played itself out in your garden.'

I shift in my seat. I feel sweat blistering on my upper lip. I raise my glass and press it against the side of my cheek, but it does nothing to cool me down.

Payton must sense my discomfort because she says, 'Bill, let's not talk about that, it's not fair on Mia.'

'What? I'm just saying out loud what everyone's thinking.'

'And what's that, Bill?' asks Freya, trying to come to my defence.

He takes a deep breath. 'Do you mind, Mia?'

'No – no, of course not,' I mumble, even though I've no idea what Bill is about to say.

'Okay then, here's my theory. Anna, clearly drunk, gate-crashes the party and everyone saw what happened then.'

I can feel my heart racing. My skin is burning.

'It was a classic case of a woman scorned. Anna couldn't have Rich so she lashed out, hoping to fuck up everything in Rich's orbit. I suppose Rich must have been so furious with her that he followed her and, during the course of an argument, lost his temper. What do the French call it – a *crime passionnel*? Committed in the midst of an uncontrollable rage. And this morning, when I saw Rich, he was looking really shifty, behaving very strangely indeed.'

'Honestly, Bill. You don't half talk a load of bullshit sometimes,' says Payton. 'It was obviously a stranger – it had to be, don't you think, Mia?'

I'm mute, unable to utter a word.

'Anyway, all this talk is getting us nowhere,' says Payton, picking up on my distress. 'I think it's time to change the subject. Now, anyone else for a top-up?'

Just then there's a knock at the door. Someone – a man – is calling in Spanish from below. Payton, already on her way to get the wine, tells us she'll go and find out what's happening. The voice from below echoes up the stairs. It's a voice that I vaguely recognize. I stand up and follow Payton down the steps and into the house.

Payton is in the middle of protesting, but then she stops herself. I realize who she's talking to – it's Estacio, the policeman who questioned me earlier. He's looking past Payton and at me. He's holding a piece of paper. He apologizes for disturbing us. He's pleased he's found me, he says. One of the neighbours told him that I would be here. Although his speech is polite and measured, his eyes are hard, determined. He wishes he could have left this until the next day. But it's too important to wait.

'What is it?' I ask.

I don't want to know the answer.

He holds out his slip of paper, a gesture that seems to imply I understand what's going on. He must read my blank expression because he adds, 'I'm sorry, Miss Banner, but we need to look around *La Casa de la Luz*.'

I still can't take it in.

'We've got a warrant – a warrant to search your home.'

The words are like a grenade, sending shockwaves around the house. Payton starts shouting, telling the police that she's going to call her lawyer. Freya, who heard the commotion, says this is unacceptable and demands to know what kind of evidence they have. Bill, emboldened and red-faced from too much rosé, blusters about the room, echoing both women's opinions but not adding much to the argument.

'I understand how this has come as a shock to you, but you've got to understand the seriousness of the situation,' says Estacio. 'I have men waiting outside your house.'

Payton asks to see the warrant, and she studies it with a suspicious eye before handing it back with contempt. 'You may have the proper piece of paper, but that doesn't mean you're in the right,' she says. 'I mean, does she seem like the kind of person who could have done this?'

Estacio refuses to comment. Instead, he gestures to the door. 'Miss Banner?'

'Payton, Bill – it's okay, honestly,' I say, before turning to Estacio. 'You're very welcome to search the house – but I can tell you there's nothing there.'

'In that case, you've got nothing to worry about.'

I smile weakly and follow him out of the house. At the door, Bill continues to talk about the crime of passion and the leniency showed by various authorities in different countries in the past.

'Do you know that in France, prior to 1975, if a man found his wife in bed with another chap he'd effectively get away with murder?'

As I step out into the velvet night, I'm relieved not to have to hear his pompous voice.

Estacio switches on his torch and says, 'I can lead the way.' His tone is that of a gentleman guiding his sweetheart down a darkened path, not a policeman about to search the house of a suspect. He continues down the *camino*, past a couple of volunteers standing outside Desert Shoots. As one of them takes a drag on a cigarette, the burning light illuminates her face. Surely that can't be fear in her eyes? What has she to be scared of? The presence of the police? Then I realize perhaps she's scared of me.

Outside the house there's a cluster of uniformed men. What on earth do they hope to find inside?

Estacio addresses his men in Spanish, asking them to be careful of the owners' possessions and to treat the house as if it were their own. 'Again – I'm sorry about this intrusion, Miss Banner, but the quicker we start, the quicker all of this will be over. It's purely a procedural matter.'

I lead them inside, and as I turn on the lights the men scuttle off into every corner of the house like black beetles desperate to take shelter in the shadows. Estacio asks if I could answer a few more questions. I lead him back to the dining table, where we'd sat earlier on. Initially, he doesn't say anything, but studies me as if I were a specimen under glass. The effect makes me even more nervous. I think back to last night, up there by the olive tree. What does he know? Did someone see me? Have the police found something on or near Anna that links me to her?

Finally, he breaks his silence. 'You still haven't heard from Richard Ellis?'

'No, I haven't. Apparently, he told Bill – who saw him this morning – that he was heading for the medical centre in town.'

'I heard that too, but I've since established that it was a lie.'

'Excuse me?'

'I have a friend who works there and I asked them to call me if Richard Ellis or . . . you turned up there.'

'Me?'

Estacio takes out an iPhone and, using his thumb, scans through it until he finds what he's looking for.

He talks in a low voice, almost a whisper. 'You see, I know about your history, Miss Banner—' He looks up from his phone, radiating sympathy. Are his feelings real or is this just an act, a ploy to get me to open up?

'—about what happened to your mother . . .'

I can't speak. I want to disappear.

'. . . and about what happened to you . . . as a girl.'

Will I ever be able to escape the past?

'We have very close contacts with the police in Britain and

they were able to provide me with all the information about both Iain Hastings and you. The details came through via email this afternoon.'

I feel as though I'm slipping back into that dark earth.

'I've read your files and what strikes me as very strange is the similarity between the two crimes.'

I finally find my voice. 'What – what do you mean?'

'I'm not talking about what happened to your mother – that must have been awful for you to witness.' He looks back down at his phone. 'But the way you were attacked. You were hit over the head and left in that shallow grave. Now, twenty-nine years later, we have another crime in which a young woman you know – Anna Fleming – is attacked, hit over the head and also left in a shallow grave. You do see my point?'

'B-but it must just be a coincidence. It – it can't have anything to do with me.' As I say the words I'm willing them to be true.

'Perhaps not. But you must understand the difficulty I'm in, Miss Banner? We need to rule this out before we take the investigation any further.'

'Okay.'

'I know this must be difficult for you to talk about – and I have every sympathy with you and what you went through – but if I could just ask you a few questions?'

I can't believe what I'm about to ask. 'Do I . . . do I need a lawyer?'

'Do you feel you need one, Miss Banner?'

At that moment, I feel an overwhelming longing for Rich to walk through the door. He'd know what to say. He'd tell Estacio and his men what to do. He'd always protected me.

Until the moment he'd met Anna.

I think again about what she told me in the olive grove. How they'd met. How Rich had changed his life – both our lives – on the basis of that meeting. We were both here because of her.

It was all because of her.

I feel the anger rising inside me again. I need to keep calm.

'Miss Banner, are you all right?'

'Sorry?'

'I know this is all very distressing for you, I understand that. But you can see where I'm going with this, can't you?'

'I don't, I'm afraid. I can't see any connection between the two things.'

'Let's hope you're right. Let's hope it's just a coincidence.' He looks down at his phone again. 'I see that the man who did this to your mother, to you – was Iain Hastings. He died in prison, awaiting trial.'

'That's right. So you see—'

Just then there's a call from one of Estacio's men. He's saying something in Spanish. He's got a terrible accent and I have to attune my ear to understand. He's found something. In the studio. No, that can't be right. I've misunderstood. There's shouting. More men talking over one another. I try to listen, but I must be wrong.

Estacio looks at me with uncertainty and suspicion before he pushes himself up and rushes over to the circle of policemen. He tells them to stand back, to show him what they've found. One of the men in uniform, his face bright with pride, is holding something out in a transparent evidence bag.

I stand up to go and see for myself. As I do so, I feel my immediate reality slipping away from me. It's like the world around me is melting, everything is tipping on its side. I hold onto something – a chair, the wall, a policeman, I'm not sure what – to prevent myself from falling.

The officer says something under his breath to Estacio, as he passes the evidence bag to him.

'Miss Banner, do you know what this is?' he asks, holding up the bag.

I shake my head, fearful that this slight movement will unsettle my mind even further.

It belonged to the dead girl. It's Anna's camera.

42

RICH

I'm holding an old T-shirt of Anna's, one that she used to sleep in. I push my face deep into its creases, and I can almost taste her smell.

As I breathe her in, images from our time together pass through my mind. That first sight of her at Marianne's funeral. Our time by the river. When we said goodbye that day I thought I'd never see her again. But then Anna had materialized in my life again like a spectre and our affair started in earnest. If only I'd told her I didn't want anything more to do with her. If only I'd made a clean break earlier on. If only I'd never taken part in that stupid ayahuasca ceremony. What then? Would Anna still be alive now?

The thought of what I could have done turns my blood to acid. The sweat that breaks out on my forehead, my armpits, my back, feels so poisonous it could eat away through my skin.

Think, Rich. Fucking think.

I close my eyes and cast my mind back to the moment I was by the tree, in the olive grove. I recall thinking that I could see into the living heart of the olive tree. It was like the miracle of life opening its secrets for me. I had a glimpse of the tree's cells, its beating heart. Now, I realize this was nothing more than a hallucination, a warping of my brain brought on by the drug. Even if I could recollect anything about what happened after this, how could I trust myself? Were my 'memories' just the by-product of a chemical reaction, the result of ingesting dimethyltryptamine and monoamine oxidase inhibitors?

Yet I had to try.

Remember what you did. Remember what you saw.

I'm there, by the tree. I can feel its rough bark. I open my eyes, see the crystal in the earth glinting in the moonlight. Then a figure walks into view. It's a woman, a woman I recognize. I see her back, her hair, the curve of her neck. She disappears behind another tree and I lose sight of her. Quietly, I step away from the tree and begin to move towards her to get a better look at her. As I walk, the ground seems to be melting away from me, the rocks turning to lava under my feet. *Ignore this, this is obviously not real. It's just another hallucination.* I touch the branch of a tree, which turns into the hand of a skeleton. Its fingers clasp themselves around my wrist. *Nothing more than a figment of my stimulated imagination, another vision.*

The woman stops by an old, broken-down wall, its rocks tumbling down onto the ground. Even though she still has her back to me, I can tell she's focusing on something in front of her. There's an air of concentration about her.

Determination. I take shelter behind a large tree and watch her. Her right hand drops down to the wall. Her fingers run over the sharp edges of a rock. The moonlight dances off the surface of the quartz. She turns her head so that I can see her profile. Of course, I recognize her. I've lived with that face for years.

Mia.

43

MIA

A colleague hands Estacio a pair of gloves, which he slips on. He takes the camera out of the evidence bag and using his thumb he activates the digital screen. The camera trills – a happy, silly sound that seems inappropriate in the context of what's happening – and he concentrates as he begins to scroll through the images. Occasionally, he glances up at me to gauge my reaction. But I don't know what to think or how I should look.

'I-I've got no idea h-how that camera got there,' I say, stumbling over my words. 'Are you sure that's where your men found it? In the studio? I just don't understand . . . Unless Rich could have . . .' My voice trails off.

'Richard could have done what?'

'Nothing.'

Estacio's thumb stops as he gazes intently at the camera. He presses various buttons, and his brow creases as he studies what he's seeing. He moves the images forwards, backwards, forwards again, enlarging, focusing in, narrowing his eyes as he takes in every detail. He stops again, swallows hard. Is it my imagination or does his skin turn a shade lighter?

'Miss Banner, can I ask you: last night did you see or come in contact with Anna Fleming?'

Again I'm lost for words.

'Last night . . . did you go anywhere near the olive grove, where Anna Fleming's body was found?'

'I'm not sure. I went for a walk and I suppose I could—'

'I think it's about time you dropped the facade, Miss Banner.'

'Excuse me?'

'You've had my sympathy – and to an extent, you still do. What happened to your mother was horrible, as was what happened to you as a child. But if I'm going to help you, you're going to have to help me explain something.'

'What?'

He turns the camera to face me. He tells me not to touch it. I should simply look at the screen and describe what I see. My eyes focus on the small digital monitor. It takes me only an instant to understand what I'm looking at. It's a photograph of Anna, her limbs twisted, her face lifeless, her skin covered in blood. The flash has made the colours – the red of the blood, the brown of the earth, the whiteness of the brain matter – more garish and unreal. She's lying on the ground, not yet buried in that shallow grave.

'I – I don't understand what—'

'It's a simple enough request, Miss Banner. I'm asking you to describe what you see. You can do that for me, can't you?'

'But—'

'Tell me what you see.'

He pushes the camera further towards me. I turn my head away so I don't have to look.

'Miss Banner, please just answer my question.'

'It's not a question, it's a—'

He twists the camera back so it's facing him again. 'Very well, since you seem incapable or unwilling to do what I ask, I will describe what I see myself.' He takes a deep breath. 'The first few images are of yourself taken at your party, talking to guests, walking through your garden. Nothing dramatic there. But then there are these images of you lunging towards the victim, Anna Fleming. As you can see, your face is contorted with – with what looks like anger and hatred. I'm right in saying that, at the party, you tried to grab the camera from her?'

'Yes, but—'

He quickly moves the display forwards. 'The next images taken on the camera – after those of you at the party – are those of Miss Fleming, deceased. I've no idea how long after the moment of death these photographs were taken, but it's probably only a matter of minutes. The ground around her is not yet steeped in her blood. The brain matter is still spilling out of her head, as you can see here.' A gloved finger hovers over a section of the screen. 'It looks as though she's been attacked with a heavy object or a rock.' He looks up from the camera. 'Did you do this, Miss Banner?'

'Of course not – what . . . ?'

'After all, you've got a motive. You were so jealous of this younger woman taking your boyfriend from you that you were driven to kill her. Is that what happened?'

'No, it wasn't—'

'It's understandable, after all. There are so many witnesses

238

to that argument at your party yesterday. You were furious with Anna for turning up, that she had the audacity to come into your home. When she left you must have been burning with fury, a fury that had to find an outlet. What happened – did you spot her later that night on your walk? Did you follow her, in order to continue that argument? Maybe you didn't intend for this to happen? But the situation got out of control and—'

'But I—'

'You couldn't stop yourself.'

'I've told you that—'

'You took a rock, a piece of crystal, and smashed it into her skull. You hated her and wanted her dead. Tell me the truth, Miss Banner.'

44

RICH

As the drug continues to drain out of my system, my fragmented mind begins to fit itself together again. Memories coalesce like spots of mercury forging together. I tell myself that I had nothing to do with Anna's death. Of course I didn't. After all, I'd ended the affair, made a clean break. I could never have done that to her.

But then why are the clothes I'd been wearing covered in blood and dirt? Why are my hands cut? Despite forcing myself to try to remember, I can't answer that.

I have to think. Be logical. Rational. I'm a scientist, after all. A man of due process. Of evidence, rules.

If I didn't kill Anna then it must have been the only other person I'd seen up there by the olive grove.

Mia.

I can't believe it, yet there's no other explanation. I see Mia up by the olive grove. She's driven by jealousy, a jealousy

I'd underestimated. Her hatred for Anna must have been all-consuming.

Mia is following Anna, watching her. She's standing in a patch of shadow, behind a tree, biding her time, waiting for the right moment. She steals up on her, quietly. She knows that Anna is the worse for wear after the drink, and perhaps she's also taken something else; I know from what she's told me in the past she was fond of MDMA. Mia reaches out for a rock, one of many lying around on the abandoned dry land, and cradles it in her hand. She watches as Anna sits on a broken wall and closes her eyes. She takes a deep breath as she steadies herself behind her. Anna senses something, turns her head, but it's too late. Mia strikes her across the temple. Anna's hand rises up to her forehead. She touches blood. She stands up to try to protect herself, but Mia rains blow after blow down hard upon her skull.

Mia. Quiet, respectable, *nice* Mia. Mia, the woman I'd loved. *She'd* done this.

And all because of me.

I suppose after that argument at the party Mia must have flipped. She was infuriated by Anna's presence at the fiesta, by the sight of her taking those photos. But what had happened after I'd left her? Had she gone out for a walk and spotted Anna? And what was Anna doing up there by the olive grove? Had they continued to argue? And if so, what had they said?

Mia seems so calm on the surface, but as I know, there's something that runs underneath, like a stream of dark water that wreathes its way under a bucolic landscape. She'd witnessed death at close quarters, and if she'd been left there in that wood for much longer she would have died herself. I've often

241

wondered what that experience had done to her. I'd assumed that it had made her more empathetic – she was always on the side of the underdog, the marginalized, the forgotten. But what if . . . what if it had left another mark too?

45

MIA

I arrive back at *La Casa de la Luz*, completely exhausted, like someone has drilled into my bone marrow and sucked out every last red blood cell from my body.

Estacio and his colleagues had taken me to the police station for questioning. In an airless interview room he ran through the same list of questions he'd asked at the house and I repeated the same litany of answers, but this time at least I was able to respond without his constant interruption. This was, in part, thanks to Gloria Romero, a flame-haired take-no-shit lawyer friend of Payton's who had driven up from Almería and who sat with me during the interview. Whenever Estacio tried to talk over me, she would shoot him a look that had the power to turn him to stone.

Yes, I'd survived an horrific attack in which my mother had been murdered. No, that had not made me into a killer. Yes, I had been angry that Anna Fleming had taken my boyfriend, Richard Ellis, away from me. No, I had not murdered her. Yes, I did recognize the digital camera found in the studio as belonging to Anna. No, I hadn't a clue about how it had got there and neither had I taken any images of her soon after her death.

At the end of the interview, Gloria insisted that I should be released. It was obvious that Estacio's only real lead was Anna's camera. She argued why would an intelligent woman – a former teacher – be so stupid as to stash such a damning piece of evidence on her own property? If I had killed Anna Fleming, then surely I would have gone to some trouble to destroy – or at least hide – the camera? The police had to admit that they had nothing else to link me to the crime. There were no witnesses of my presence near the murder scene. She could guarantee there would be no forensics. And more to the point, she maintained, everyone knew that I was involved with the exhumation of Esperanza García. Why would I want to bury the body of Anna Fleming only a few feet from the supposed grave site, which would be uncovered by the team of archaeologists from the ARMH? None of it made any sense.

He could arrest me or let me go.

After a lot of forced whispers between Estacio and Gloria, and subsequent heated exchanges between them in the corridor, it was decided that I could go back to Val Verde. But I was told I couldn't under any circumstances leave the area and that they would call me back for more questioning at a later date.

'It's all bullshit,' said Gloria, when the policeman left the room. 'I've known Estacio since university – he's always been the same. Desperate to make his name. Resents the fact he's

been sent here to what he regards as a backwater. He's
ambitious and recognizes this as the high-profile case it is. But
I'm not going to let you get fucked over in the process.'

'You're not?'

'Of course not. But you've got to be completely honest with
me, okay?'

I nodded, but I couldn't bring myself to tell her the truth:
that I *had* been up there by the olive grove. I had seen Anna,
in what could have been the last minutes of her life. My
motive for killing her was a strong one: I hated her because
she'd stolen my boyfriend. I'd discovered that she'd met Rich
at his mother's funeral. And I'd learnt that the reason we'd
both come out here was not to live a better, greener life – to
do something to help save the planet – but something much
more sordid: because Rich wanted to be closer to Anna.

I didn't tell Gloria any of this. Not only because it would
be tantamount to having 'Murderer' tattooed across my forehead but because I had a pretty good idea of who killed Anna.

It had to be Rich.

I knew that by pointing the finger of guilt at the real
perpetrator, I could clear my name. I would be free of the
police. I could bring the whole thing to an end. And I could
return to London. So what's stopping me from revealing
everything I suspect?

I suppose I must feel some kind of loyalty to him. He'd
kept his word: he'd protected me. But I wondered whether
his instinct to look after me had extended to another level.
Had he found out about my pregnancy? I thought I'd made
sure that I'd disposed of the test kit in a rubbish bag, which
I'd taken to the communal dumpster in the car park. But
could he have seen me buying the kit from the pharmacy in

town? Had he found it somehow? Had his attitude towards children changed?

Had he done this . . . *for me?*

I realize the idea sounds absurd, but before I do or say anything I need to talk to Rich.

'You're sure you'll be okay?' asks Gloria, as she stands by the door of the house. The light from the moon casts strange shadows onto the *camino*. 'I spoke to Payton and she told me to make sure you got home safely.'

'Of course, I'll be fine.'

'You've got my number – just call me if you need anything.'

'Okay – and thanks again for everything tonight. You were great.'

'Estacio knows he can't mess with me. And you did well in there – it can't have been easy, to see your mother murdered . . . and to survive yourself. You're a strong woman, Mia. Don't forget that.'

I let myself in and walk through the silent courtyard. There are no lights on inside the house. I take out my phone. It's two-thirty. I'm too agitated to sleep and so I pour myself a large glass of red wine in an effort to unwind. For a moment, I think about whether it will damage the baby. Fuck it. It's not a baby yet. And it's only one glass of wine. I take it with me outside to the terrace and breathe in the balmy night air. Estacio's questions echo through my mind, fragments of sentences worming their way deep into my brain.

Describe what you see on the camera. Images of the deceased. Brain matter spilling out of her head. Hit with a heavy object or rock. Jealous of a younger woman. Driven to kill. Witnesses to the argument at the party. Furious with Anna. Burning with fury. A rock. Smashed into her skull. You

246

*hated her and wanted her dead. Now she's lying in a shallow
grave.*

I'm back in the ground myself. The taste of soil in my
mouth. I feel the pressure of the earth on my chest. I can't
move. I can't let myself go down the spiral again. I know
where it takes me. I take a big gulp of wine, washing the
gustatory memory away.

I think back to what Gloria said to the police in my defence,
about how it didn't make any sense for me to bury Anna in
a shallow grave near the site where the archaeologists were
going to dig. By extension, if Rich did this, why did he leave
Anna's body there? I know he wasn't that keen on my work
with Blanca. Initially, he tried to deter me from helping her
find her mother's body, for what he thought were very good
reasons. Perhaps he didn't know the spot where Esperanza
had been buried? Was it just a coincidence that he left Anna's
body there? Or was he trying to signal something to me? Was
this some kind of message?

A *token*?

The idea sickens me and I have to take another sip of wine
to swallow down the bile rising from my stomach. Just then
I hear something. I turn my head and stare into the half-light,
past the olive trees, their tiny leaves turned to silver by the
moon. I see a shadow and then two eyes moving near ground
level. I take a step forward and hear a hiss. It's only one of
the village cats.

But then, just as I breathe a sigh of relief and start to walk
back towards the house, I see him. Rich. He's standing by the
door, his form darkened, his expression unknowable.

I feel my voice catch in my throat. 'R-Rich. Fuck. It's you.'

'Sorry, did I scare you?'

His voice sounds odd, artificial, like he's acting. But I'm not sure which role he's supposed to be playing.

I'm so angry with him I can't speak. If I open my mouth, I'm frightened of what I'll say, what he might do to me. I'm also conscious that, if things get heated, people may be able to hear our conversation from the *camino*.

'Let's go inside,' I suggest. 'It's easier to talk there.'

The skin around his eyes looks red, almost raw. His face looks unwashed. I've never seen him look worse. But it's not just the physical aspect that shocks me; there's something about his expression, his *energy*, that unnerves me.

Despite my rage, his appearance shocks me into saying, 'Oh my God, Rich – are you okay?'

'Pretty broken up, to be honest.'

'So – you heard the news? About—?'

'About Anna? Yes, I did.'

'It seems so unreal. I can't seem to take it in.'

'Really?' There's a cruel edge to his voice now, almost mocking. 'I would have thought you more than anyone would have been able to understand.'

This throws me. 'What – because of what happened to me, you mean? Because I . . . ? Or—'

'I see you've got a drink – you probably need it after everything you've been through. I could do with one of those. Yes, some red wine, I think.' He fetches a glass from the cupboard and pours what's left of the bottle into it.

'You've heard that I was questioned by the police?'

'That must have been difficult for you,' he says. 'And what did they conclude, the police?'

'Thank God Payton found this hot-shot female lawyer from Almería who was able to drop everything and get over here.

I don't know what would have happened if she hadn't been there to defend me against—'

'Against what? Charges of murder?'

His eyes harden. Fuck. Is he still high after last night?

'Look, I know this isn't easy for you, and I'd understand it if—'

As his voice rises in volume, it begins to crack. 'Under-understand what, exactly?'

'If . . . if you felt you'd acted in a way that you later regretted.'

'What the fuck are you talking about, Mia?' he shouts. 'Shouldn't you be talking about your own regrets? About what *you* did?'

My fear intensifies. I shouldn't be here with him. It's not safe. I need to get away. I take a step backwards and feel the edge of the kitchen work surface digging into the bottom of my spine.

'I'm not so easily fooled by you. I know what you're up to. What you've done.'

'What – what do you mean?'

His words echo Anna's last night. 'Always playing the victim card, trying to be so brave, so *strong*.' His tone is harsh and sarcastic. 'And I suppose it's a great disguise. No one would ever think you were capable of such a thing, after what you'd been through.'

He slowly walks towards me and stops, staring into my eyes with a terrifying power. I flinch backwards, my hands running along the top of the work surface to find something – anything – that I might be able to use. But surely it's not going to come to that, is it? I realize he could crush me – kill me – with a single blow. If he's capable of killing Anna then he's . . .

'Rich, I don't know what you're talking about.'

'For God's sake, Mia – you can drop the act. It's me you're talking to.'

'What do you—'

'I saw you, Mia. Up by the olive grove.'

'What?'

'You were there. Last night. Up by Devil's Head. Near where her body was found.'

46

RICH

Her blue eyes stare out of her pale face as innocent as a waxwork doll. But like those dolls, there's something uncanny about her. Something unreal. She's pretending to be scared of me now. But I can see it's all an act. I'm not going to be fooled by her. I suspect I know what lies beneath her facade.

'I d-don't know what you're talking about.'

'I saw you, Mia. You were there, near the place where Anna . . .' My voice is breaking.

Her hands are scrabbling behind her back. Is she trying to find a knife to use on me? I could grab hold of an arm and twist it behind her. I visualize the relevant equation. Pressure applied against certain resistance. Result: impact fracture. But I stop myself. Instead, I just take her wrists and hold her tight.

'You've got to face up to the truth about what you did,' I say, in as calm a voice as I can manage. 'That you killed Anna.'

'Rich, you can't—'

'You were so jealous of her.' I apply a little more pressure. 'Is that what this is all about?'

'Okay – okay. Listen, Rich. You're right. I was there last night, by the olive grove. But – I didn't kill her. You've got to believe me. God, I wanted to. And I was very nearly tempted. I even – even . . .'

I press down on her delicate bones, certain that this should do the trick. 'What?'

She takes a sharp intake of breath and stretches open her mouth.

'Rich – stop. You're hurting me.'

I loosen my grip on her a little. 'Don't try anything on.'

She nods. But then her hand claws for her pocket. I'm too quick for her. I wrench her phone out and push it into the back pocket of my jeans.

'So let's try again, shall we? Tell me what happened.'

'Okay – I-I had a rock in my hand ready to do it. After what she told me up there, by the olive grove. I felt I had every right to scare her and—'

I can feel the anger pulsing through her. So I was right. There had been some kind of argument. 'What did she tell you?'

'Anna – she knew all about me. About what happened to my mother, to me.' She's spitting out the words now. 'She said she wanted to do a story – not just write about Iain Hastings, but . . . about me.'

'I thought I'd—'

'And – and she told me all about how you'd met. At your mother's fucking funeral. How could you do that to me, Rich? How could you lie to me like that?'

The shame of hearing this forces me to release her and she falls back towards the kitchen units, grabbing hold of the edge of the worktop just in time to prevent her from collapsing on the floor.

'Leaving London and coming here – going off grid – doing our bit to help save the world. It was all fake, Rich. It was all bullshit!' Her face is creased in pain and fury, her normally pale skin now bright red. 'And to use Emily's suicide like that – to manipulate me into coming here, when you planned it all together. How could you be so cruel?'

'What?'

'You heard what I said. She – Anna – told me everything.'

I can hardly get the words out. 'What . . . what did she tell you exactly?'

'Don't make me spell out it for you again. I'm not that much of a victim. Even though both of you seem to think I'm some kind of pathetic, fucked-up masochist.' She uses her hand to wipe away the tears. 'Why didn't you just finish with me in London? Why drag me to this place if all you wanted to do was—'

Shit. 'Is that what Anna told you? Fuck. No wonder you're so angry. But you've got to believe me when I say that that's not true.' I take a deep breath. 'Yes, I met Anna at Marianne's funeral. Yes, we . . . we slept together.' I hold up my hands as if to acknowledge my sins. 'And I'm not at all proud of that, of my behaviour, of my actions. But . . . but I thought it was a one-off. Anna told me she was going to travel around Spain and I assumed I'd never see her again. Until she turned up that day on Payton and Bill's terrace. And you know what happened then.'

She looks at me as if she's intent on resisting my words.

'When we left London I did so with a real desire to make a difference, even in our small way. I didn't plan any of it like you said. I thought Emily's death was a tragedy, but perhaps it was a spur to help us move forwards to live a different, greener kind of life . . . Mia, you've got to believe me. God, I wish – I wish I'd never met Anna.'

She takes a moment to process what I've just told her. She fills a glass with water and takes a few small sips.

'But why – why would Anna lie about that?' She addresses the question to herself as much as to me, as if she's trying to piece together a difficult puzzle. 'I mean, she told me the truth about your flat. About how you'd carried on seeing one another behind my back. About how you really met – at your mother's funeral. About how you'd told her – about my mother, about what happened to me.'

Each sentence fills me with shame. 'I—'

'Why throw one lie into the mix?'

'I don't know – because she wanted to get some kind of revenge on you? After all, I'd made it plain I never wanted to see her again.'

She purses her lips and looks at me with deep suspicion. 'It makes me wonder what else she was going to tell me. Is there something else you don't want me to know?'

'What?'

'What else are you hiding, Rich?'

'I don't know what the fuck you're talking about.'

'It all makes sense now,' she says, backing away. 'Fuck. Why didn't I tell the police what I thought? Shit. All this time, I was protecting you, thinking it must have been some kind of accident—'

'*What?*'

'Something you did when you were off your head on a weird drug.'

'Mia?'

'But what if you'd planned it all along? You talked about how you wanted her to disappear off the face of the earth.' Her eyes look haunted, fearful. 'It was that day when you'd gone to get water. Anna came here, to the house, and started to take photographs of me. When I told you, that's when you said that if she ever turned up here again, you'd . . . you'd deal with her.'

'I know, but I didn't mean that I would—'

She's backed herself into a corner of the kitchen now. She's looking at me as if I'm a monster. 'And what was the thing with the camera?'

I genuinely don't have a clue what's she talking about. 'The camera?'

'Why did you leave it here? Anna's camera. The police have taken it away. They found it – in the studio.'

I don't understand what she's saying.

'And – and the worst thing,' she adds. 'Those photographs. Why did you take them? Of Anna's body . . . after her death.'

I feel sick. My vision swims in front of me, as if everything is melting away.

47

MIA

Rich collapses into a chair, as if the air has been sucked out of him. His eyes look dead, unseeing. He begins to mumble something under his breath, snatches and fragments of memories that make no sense. Is it my words, the after-effects of that South American drug, or his guilt over the murder of Anna that have pushed him over the edge? I'm not sure what to say, what to do. A voice inside my head tells me to run, to get as far away from him as possible. *If he's killed once, he could kill again.* I know how strong he is. I remember him telling me that he could snuff someone's life out with his bare hands. But I think back to the Rich I knew, the one I loved, the one I'd met at that Eighties' theme party dressed in that George Michael wig. I can't leave him like this. I need to find out what happened.

I'm careful over my choice of words, conscious that if I say the wrong thing he could react badly.

I try to make my voice as soothing as possible, the kind of tone employed by the legion of therapists I've listened to over the years. I make myself another coffee and I pour some more water into two glasses and pass one to him. 'Rich – Rich.' He begins to stir, and looks at me with tears in his eyes. 'What do you remember about last night? Do you remember anything at all? About what happened?'

His face crumples and suddenly he looks like a lost little boy. 'Some of it . . . but not all.' Tears fall down his face and his hands are shaking. 'There's – there's great swathes I can't remember.'

I take a deep breath, reach out and enclose his hands in mine. I notice they're scratched and covered in bandages. Could they be injuries he received during his attack on Anna?

'What happened to your hands?'

He looks down and whispers, 'I don't remember.'

If he saw me up by the olive grove then he must have left the ceremony early, but I need him to realize this. 'Surely the person who was in charge last night – I don't know what you call them, a guru? A shaman? They'll be able to tell the police that you were there.'

'That's – that's just the problem. I left.'

'What do you mean?'

His voice rises in anger, for once not directed at me but at himself. 'Fuck!' He bangs his fist on the table, which causes the water to spill out of both our glasses. I stand up, tell him I'm going to get a cloth, but he forces me to stay, his hands gripping mine with a clamp-like strength.

'You need to calm down, Rich. Tell me what you can remember.'

As he releases me his hands fly up to his head and he presses hard onto his temples. 'Shit. Shit. Shit. Shit.'

'Rich, you're scaring me now. What is it?'

His voice cracks and breaks as he speaks, a bubble of spit foaming at the corner of his mouth. 'I saw – I saw you – up there by the olive grove. That's why I thought that . . . But after that I don't remember anything.'

He pushes himself up from the table, spilling yet more water. He looks down at his hands. 'This morning I – I had to be patched up by Hans. My hands were a mess, torn up. And . . .'

His body starts to shake, as if it's being hit by wave after wave of shock, like he's resistant to vomiting up something from deep within him.

'Rich, tell me. You know you can trust me.' As I say the words, I'm not sure I mean them. 'Perhaps we can show that, because you weren't in your right mind, it's a case of diminished responsibility—'

He begins to look around the room, staring into pockets of emptiness with a frightening intensity, almost as if he can see things that aren't there. I need to get some help. But there's no landline in the house and Rich still has my phone.

'Rich, I need you to give me my phone back.'

His hand automatically moves to his back pocket to check it's still there.

'I don't know what happened to you last night, but I think whatever you took, or the combination of the drink with the ayahuasca—'

His eyes have a manic quality that is frightening.

'You need a doctor or at least let me take you to the medical centre to get checked over by a nurse. Rich – I need my phone.'

I hold out my hand, hoping the gesture will do the trick, but he turns away from me. My eyes study the pocket in the back of his jeans. Could I jump up and grab it? But even if I did, he would force the phone from my hands. He'd be so angry he could hurt me. Really hurt me.

'You'll call the police,' he snaps. 'You'll tell them that I did it. That I killed Anna.'

'No, of course not.' I try the smooth, therapy voice again. 'You're confused. You're feeling—'

'Don't tell me what I'm feeling.'

'I didn't mean it like that.' I'm going to have to try a different strategy. It's a gamble, one I could soon regret. I take another deep breath and steel myself for what's to come. 'Just that – Rich, can't you see, you've got to face up to it. It's hard for you to hear, I know that, but you're behaving like . . .'

'What?'

'Like you're guilty. Like you did it.'

Rich turns back to me and stares at me with the look of someone realizing their water has been spiked with poison. His face expresses a myriad of emotions: hatred, anger, disappointment, regret, and finally, a touch of lost love. He says nothing, but through his tears he tries to smile. But the smile is false, crooked. He looks shattered, broken, as if he's trying to hold together a personality that is splintering, disintegrating.

'Thank you, Mia,' he says, softly, gently. He nods his head as if he's agreeing with something only heard in his own interior world. 'Thank you for everything. I mean it. You deserved something better. Someone better than me.'

'Rich, I—'

I don't complete the sentence because he slowly turns away from me and disappears into the night.

48

RICH

I can't bear to look at Mia a moment longer. I feel as though I'm falling, falling and flailing through dark air to a destination unknown. I kid myself it's the after-effects of the drug, but I know the real source. It's not anything I ingested, not the result of an ayahuasca hangover, but something already within me. Where do I start? The list is endless: the fuck-ups I made with Mia, my involvement with Anna, the lies I told, the secrets I shared.

I stumble out of the house and into the darkness. As I step out onto the *camino*, I see a shadow in a doorway, but assume it's one of the volunteers from the eco-charity. That or another hallucination, another leftover from last night.

I play the conversation with Mia over and over in my head, whispering segments to myself as I run down the *camino*. What Mia said sounded unreal, as if I was still trapped in that horrible drug trip. The police came round.

They took her in for questioning. They'd found Anna's camera in the studio. On the camera were images of Anna's body taken after her death. And what was that shit Anna had told her about how I'd manipulated the whole scenario, bringing Mia out here to Spain with the intention of picking up the affair where I left off? Why the hell had she lied like that? I feel the anger seethe inside me again, flowing through my body like red-hot lava.

Why can't I remember what happened? I have to think. Even though I don't feel it, I tell myself that I'm a man of logic, science. I try to line up what I know. Anna is dead. She was murdered. Mia was there at the olive grove: I saw her and she admitted it. But is she guilty? If Mia murdered Anna, why would she have chosen to bury the body near the site of the exhumation? That doesn't make sense. But then if Mia's innocent, as she claims, then . . . then it must have been me. After all, my hands were all cut up. Hans had found me unconscious, my clothes all covered in blood – a detail I'd decided to keep from Mia. Did the fact that I'd chosen not to share that with her prove my guilt?

Fuck.

The possibility that I could have killed Anna makes me feel like retching again. I swallow down the taste of bile, get into the Saab and take a few deep breaths. I need to pull myself together. I retrieve Mia's phone from my back pocket and throw it onto the passenger seat. I drive up the twisty road towards Devil's Head. I need to see where it happened for myself. After checking that there aren't any police, I pull in and cut the engine. When the light from the interior fades I let my eyes adjust to the darkness. The moon is still bright, although there's a little more cloud than last night, the night of the . . . murder. Perhaps seeing the place where Anna died will help me process it all – it might even force me to remember.

I use the torch on my phone to light my way. The area around the olive tree is marked with tape. I shine the torch onto the ground. There's the shallow grave where Anna's body was found. The thought of her in the earth kicks the strength out of me and I fall to my knees. It's then that a memory – or the memory of an emotion – comes back to me.

I'm here, last night. And I'm feeling angry. Angry with a woman. I want to do her harm. I'm in a forest. I see a child with her mother. I realize with a sickening feeling that it's Mia and her mum. Over the years I've heard and read so much about the case that I've reconstructed the events of that awful day for myself. I've played them back in my mind many times, filling out certain details, brightening the monochrome landscape with colours. But why had this come back to me last night?

I try to apply logic to an illogical situation, but it's like trying to measure oxygen with a ruler. The normal laws don't apply. Everything I remember is slippery.

I think of some of the other things I'd visualized during those hallucinatory hours. The opening of that velvet curtain, revealing the spectre of Marianne. My feelings towards my mother were far from simple. The clutch of emotions I felt for Mia were complex too; in addition to the vestiges of love, there was a great deal of guilt and anger. And what of Anna? That was hardly straightforward either.

Had I combined elements of the emotions I'd felt for all three of them and – what? A psychotherapist might say that I'd projected my feelings for each of these women onto one of them, a woman who happened to stumble into my path as I was experiencing a series of wild hallucinations. Unfortunately, that woman happened to be Anna. She'd taken the full force of my fury. And now she is dead.

49

MIA

Payton, Bill and Freya are with me inside the house, drinking endless cups of coffee. I've just finished telling them about what happened the night before when Payton's phone rings.

'Are you sure?' she asks. 'Really?'

'What is it?' I ask.

I watch Payton as she frowns and then, as colour fades from her face, I feel something twist in the pit of my stomach: the physical manifestation of impending bad news.

She lifts her hand in an effort to quieten me. 'Sorry, Gloria, it's a bad line – and I've got Mia here with me, yes. I'm at her house.' She goes quiet. 'Are you certain?' Silence again. 'Okay – yes, I'll let her know.'

Payton cuts the connection and blinks, unsure about what to say.

'Tell me what?'

'I don't know whether to believe it, but . . .'

'Payton!'

'It's Rich – he's at the police station. Apparently, he turned up there early this morning.'

'Thank God. Is he all right?' During the night, I'd played out our conversation over and over in my head. I couldn't sleep, of course; each time I drifted off, terrible visions jolted me back to consciousness: Rich smashing Anna's head in with a rock, Rich throwing himself off Devil's Head, Rich crashing his car into one of the deep ravines.

'Yes – well, I think so. But it appears that he's handed himself in. Gloria says he's confessed to—'

'I told you so – didn't I say that Rich—'

'Oh, do shut up, Bill,' says Payton. 'He seems to be convinced that it was him who killed Anna. Gloria said that he's confessed to being there, up by the olive grove, the night Anna was murdered. He's saying he can't remember actually doing it, but he must have as there's no other explanation. Neither has he any memory of taking any photographs of Anna with her camera – or bringing it back to the house. There are probably extenuating circumstances – diminished responsibility, due to the state he was in, the ayahuasca, but—'

'That can't be right,' says Freya, a hand flying up to her flushed cheek. 'No, it can't be – not Rich.'

'I have to go to him,' I say. 'He will—'

'Gloria told me that it would be best if you stayed here. She's going to get another lawyer onto it. One of her friends from the city.'

'But—'

Payton's voice strengthens and rises. 'Mia, listen to me.

Gloria said that you could be an important witness. And after what you've told us about what happened last night, I don't think you should see him. You know that, right?'

'But somebody needs to go and check that—'

'I'm sure we can work something out,' says Payton.

'Listen,' says Freya. 'I can always stay here with Mia if you and Bill need to go.'

'Would you? That's kind, Freya. And Mia – I'll call you when I hear any more news.'

I tell her that I don't have my phone – Rich took it with him when he left. Freya has a spare one, she says – it's not a smartphone, but at least I can use it if I need to make or receive calls. She'll go and fetch it right away. I say goodbye to them and realize how empty and quiet the house seems. How long will I continue living here? I suppose I'll have to stay to see what happens with Rich and the police. If Rich has confessed then I wonder whether there will even be a need for a trial. Will I be allowed to leave the country? I make a mental note to ask Gloria these questions when I speak to her later.

I suppose I should feel a sense of relief. The nightmare is over. The police won't regard me as a suspect any longer. But any sense of consolation is skewed by a terrible sadness. Our new life together – our dream of a *better* life – was nothing but a sham. I have been deceived by Rich on so many levels, not just sexually and emotionally but something more fundamental: on a human level too. He is violent, a murderer, even if he was out of his mind when he killed Anna.

Thank God I never told him I'm expecting his child. I'll have to get rid of it now, won't I? Surely, I don't have a choice? The truth is, I'm still not certain about what I will do. What

266

will happen if I can't conceive again? I've heard about such cases. But how could I live with the child knowing that its father is a murderer?

I make myself a coffee and take it outside to one of the chairs on the terrace. As I sit there my thoughts move away from Rich and the murder of Anna. I have to face up to the truth. I need to start looking after myself. I need to make plans for my future. Alone.

Just then I hear Freya return. I go inside and greet her. She has the spare phone with her, but it will need charging, she says. It's an old Nokia, something she brought with her from England. When she showed it to the young people at the charity, they couldn't believe it, she says, as she plugs the charger into the wall: they thought it was ancient. What, like something from the ark, she'd asked. Even that phrase – *something from the ark* – made them laugh out loud.

'Now, I'm going to rustle up some lunch,' she says. 'You look like you haven't eaten properly in days.'

I offer to help, but she tells me to go back to what I was doing before. I need to relax, she insists. She's found some aubergines, peppers and tomatoes and she's going to make a ratatouille. I tell her I'm so grateful – not just for the offer of lunch but also for lightening the mood.

I go back outside onto the terrace, move my chair into the shade and force myself to relax, just as Freya suggested. Lunch won't be for a while. I tell myself not to think about the dirt, being in the ground, the sight of Anna in that shallow grave, the memory of her up there in the olive grove, the moonlight on her blonde hair, the cruelty of her words, the feel of the crystal rock in my hand. I take some deep breaths and try to let all of this, if not go completely from my mind, then at least retreat to some place where I can manage it better. That's what I learnt to do all those years ago. Survival is about compartmentalization. Not allowing one thing to define you.

I am more than a child who saw her mother murdered.

I am more than that little girl who was left to die in a makeshift grave.

I try all the tricks that I've found have helped me over the years. Visualizing myself surrounded by white light. Thinking of myself in a happy place: by the seaside with my mother, the water lapping at my toes, the feel of the soft sand under my feet; baking cakes with her, the smell of the butter and sugar so rich I can almost taste it. But today none of these techniques are helping. Each attempt brings me back to that day when I saw my mother die, the day when I was half-buried. And then I'm led back to the same question: why was Anna left there, in that shallow grave?

Rich was certainly a great listener. He'd had to put up with me talking about what had happened to me as a child. He'd read the same newspaper cuttings about what Iain Hastings had done to my mother and what that monster had done to me. Was this buried deep in Rich's unconscious somewhere? He'd seen me up there by the olive grove. In his drug-induced frenzy had he mistaken Anna for me? Was it me he'd really wanted to kill? But then I remember his last words to me last night before he left the house, when he told me that I deserved something – *someone* – better than him. Had that been a guarded confession of sorts?

My thoughts are disturbed by the sound of a phone ringing. I only hear snippets of the conversation and Freya saying that yes, she will tell me. She comes out to say the food is ready, but it's probably a bit too hot to serve lunch outside and she suggests we have it indoors. She hopes I don't mind as she's set the dining table already.

'At the moment, any decision that I don't have to make myself is a bonus, even the small ones,' I say. 'So that sounds good to me. Did I hear a phone?'

'It was Payton, checking you were okay.'

'Did she have something to tell me?'

'Oh, it was nothing. Just that she's at the police station and she says she's got everything under control. She's waiting for the other lawyer to turn up.'

She smiles and leads the way into the kitchen. The room is full of the delicious smells of cooking: onions, garlic, tomatoes; she's even warmed some bread and uncorked a bottle of red wine.

'I thought you could do with a proper meal,' she says. 'And I don't know about you, but I could do with a drink. I've been saving this bottle for ages. Someone told me it's supposed to be a good one.'

I didn't notice her carrying the bottle when she came in, but perhaps it had been inside the duffel bag she brought with her, which now sits on the floor by the dining table. She's laid the table perfectly, complete with white napkins and a jug of water, and she's even gone to the trouble of putting a few wild flowers – bright yellow cotton lavender, hot red hottentot fig – in a small vase. She tells me to take a seat and a few moments later she presents me with a bowl of steaming rata-touille. The simple sound of the wine being poured into a glass makes me relax. I raise the glass to my lips, careful to only take a sip or two. As I start to eat the stew, which seems heavy on the garlic, I realize just how hungry I am. This is exactly what I need.

'This is so kind of you, Freya. After . . . after everything that's happened.'

'It's the least I can do,' she says, sweeping back a tendril of hair from her face.

We continue to spoon the ratatouille into our mouths, until finally Freya breaks the silence.

'I can't get it into my head that Rich is the one responsible.'

'It's hard for me too. But I suppose he wasn't in his right mind. And if he has confessed to the police, what other explanation could there be?'

'I still don't believe it. Sorry, I know you had your problems, but he doesn't strike me as the kind of person to do . . . *that*.'

I've only had a couple of sips of wine, but I'm beginning to feel a little light-headed. Perhaps it's the pregnancy.

'Do any of us really know anyone else?' I quip. The comment is supposed to be a throwaway statement, but it seems Freya has taken it to heart. She's looking serious, a little upset, as if I've insulted her in some way. 'Sorry, I didn't mean to – I hope nothing's wrong?'

'No, nothing's wrong.' She tries to smile, but it's strained. 'How's the food?'

'Lovely,' I say. I decide not to comment on the amount of garlic she's added in case it makes her more distressed. She seems such a sensitive soul and it's obvious that the news of Anna's murder and Rich's confession has really shocked her. And after all, she's the one trying to be nice to me.

We move on to chatting about life in the village, some of the other people at the eco-charity, and what she's been growing in the garden.

'Everything you ate came from there – even the tomatoes which I managed to rescue from the disastrous harvest struck

270

down by blight,' she says. She's smiling again now. 'Please, have some more.' She scoops up another dollop of the stew and serves it into my bowl. 'So what's going to happen to Blanca and her search for her mother?'

'It's awful, I feel so sorry for her. I don't know how long the archaeologists will have to wait before they can start digging again. I suppose until the police give them the authority to begin.' I put my fork down and take a sip of wine. 'It's such a shame. It's the one thing that's keeping Blanca alive. In fact, I must call her today to see how she's doing, just to make sure she's okay.'

'Do you remember that time when we went round to her house?' she says, smiling at the memory.

My mouth feels dry and so I take a drink of water. 'I hope you didn't mind that I dragged you in there. It was like stepping back in time, wasn't it?'

'It was amazing, I really enjoyed it. What an extraordinary woman. I admire her spirit, how she refused to let the past just slip away. She held onto it with the strength of a murderer determined not to let their victim escape.'

I think it's a strange choice of words, but I don't comment. 'Yes, she's kept her mother's spirit alive all these years.' I put my fork down and gulp some more water.

'Are you all right, Mia?'

'Y-yes, just feeling a little . . . funny in the head. It's prob-ably the wine. I'm . . . I'm not used to drinking at lunchtime.'

'Blanca knew there was something wrong with you that day, do you remember?'

'Sorry?'

'It was almost as if she had second sight – she said she'd inherited it from her grandmother. She could see into your soul. And I believe her. I know I have a scientific training, a logical brain, but I still think some people can foretell the future. What do you think?'

'I don't know. I think a lot of the time it's . . . it's just the benefit of hindsight.'

My mind goes back to that day in Blanca's house, when she talked about her mission to dig up her mother's bones, before she started to behave oddly and say a series of strange things. At the time I thought she was having some kind of fit or nervous attack.

'She told you not to believe him,' says Freya. 'She said not to trust him, that he was betraying you. And she was right. She knew that Rich was seeing Anna behind your back.'

Despite the fact she's only telling me everything I already know, her words make me feel uneasy.

'Thank you so much for making lunch. It really was very—'

'Blanca went on to talk about her grandmother, do you remember? She'd been betrayed by her husband too. She took the sheets – her best sheets, given to her on her wedding day – and made them into a noose, which she used to hang herself.' She looks up at the ceiling. 'From these very beams.'

Even though my head feels foggy from too much wine, I try to recall that conversation. I remember translating from Spanish to English, but I'm sure that at some point I stopped because I felt uncomfortable relating certain details to Freya.

'But—'

'Blanca's grandmother killed herself in this house. Apparently, it was a choice between that or throwing herself off Devil's Head, but the poor thing had a fear of heights. And so, she chose to die at home.'

There's something wrong. My dry mouth tastes even more

bitter. It's hard for me to form the words, but I manage to whisper, 'You couldn't have understood all of that, everything that was said between us. She was talking in Spanish.'

'*No te dije la verdad*,' she says in a perfect Spanish accent. *I didn't tell you the truth.*

'What?'

'I can speak Spanish, of course I can – I did it at school. And when I knew you were coming here and I'd got the job at Desert Shoots, I did an intensive top-up course.'

'But – but why did you—'

'Why did I lie?' She looks askance at me as if I've fallen short of her expectations. 'Really, Mia. I would have thought a bright girl like you would have put two and two together by now.'

'I don't understand what y—'

I can feel my vision is blurring, as though what I see before me is dissolving into a strange, shimmering mirage. I concentrate on Freya's features, desperately trying to get a fix on her face, which with each second threatens to melt away.

There's something – *someone* – else lurking beneath her skin. A trace or a shadow. A memory or an image I've desperately tried to forget. An impression.

I narrow my eyes in an effort to will it back into focus, but just as I think I'm nearly there, my vision clouds and the suggestion disappears.

'You really don't know, do you?' she asks, surprised by my stupidity. 'I suppose you were only a small girl when it happened. How old were you? Just six years old?'

My throat constricts. Instantly, I'm underground again. The heaviness of the earth is pressing down on me. I feel paralysed, unable to speak, unable to move.

'But you saw it all, you were a witness. Even at six, you should have been able to tell the difference. That man who murdered your mother – and who nearly killed you – that wasn't the man who was arrested for the crimes.'

I remember sitting down with a nice woman – a police artist – who helped me reconstruct the features of the man I'd seen. She took me through the process slowly, and ever so carefully, using a series of charts, photographs and cardboard cut-outs to select the colour and style of the man's hair (mousy brown), the shape of his face (round), the colour of his eyes (brown), the shade of his skin (sallow), the condition of his hands and nails (stubby fingers, dirty cuticles) until we'd built up a rough picture of the attacker. I was less sure about the man's height – metres and centimetres meant little to me at that age – but I knew the man was a few inches taller than my mother.

I want to say something of what is going through my mind, but I can't speak.

Freya's talking more quickly now, driven by the intensity of her emotions. 'That man who was arrested – that man who died by his own hand, while awaiting trial – that man didn't do it. Man! He was a boy, only eighteen years old. I know he would never have done anything like that. He had his issues, of course he did, but he was too gentle, too kind. He wouldn't hurt a fly, never mind kill a woman and try to kill her child.' She gazes at me with something approaching sympathy. 'I feel sorry for you, in a way. But you should never have said that it was him.'

I can only manage to rasp out one word, but even that leaves my throat raw. '*Him?*'

'Iain. Iain Hastings,' she says, as if it's the most natural thing in the world.

Inside I'm screaming, but I can't seem to react; there's something wrong with my brain. Is this what it feels like to have some kind of locked-in syndrome?

Perhaps she mistakes my inability to talk for indifference because her face is getting redder, angrier.

'My brother.'

The kaleidoscope of fragmented features reorders itself on and under Freya's face. I'm sure I can see him now, there beneath Freya's skin. The similarly shaped face. The same colour eyes. The same slightly sallow skin tone. I realize that my memory of Iain Hastings' face comes not so much from the day of the murder itself but from the reproduction of it in the newspaper articles I'd read.

I thought I'd recognized Freya when I first saw her that day at Payton and Bill's house, but I assumed it was her type that I'd come across before; another well-heeled bohemian who had decided to leave London in search of an alternative kind of life. The realization that Freya is Iain Hastings' sister sends my already splintered mind into free fall. Traces of memories form themselves into some kind of weird collage.

I try to recall our time together in Val Verde. That first meeting at Payton and Bill's house when I made that scene in the pantry. There was something I noticed then, as she came to help me. As she told me that she'd suffered from panic attacks – she advised me to take some deep breaths – I stepped away from her because she smelt of the earth. I didn't think anything of it at the time – she was the gardener at the eco-charity, after all, *of course* she would smell of the ground. But now I realize that my subconscious was trying to tell me something. To warn me. I associated her with him. The one who had put me there, in that shallow grave.

But she'd always been so kind. She'd been a friendly face, offering to help with the garden, giving us seedlings. I remember that conversation with her that day when Rich and Guy had been talking about the solar cooker and I had wandered down to the Desert Shoots house. She'd come in from the terraces and had talked to me about the therapeutic effects of gardening, of planting a seed and watching it grow. What were her words? 'You just have to accept that some things will take a long time to come to fruition.'

She starts to hum a song. I'm sure I've heard it before, not just on the radio or TV. Yes, it was here, in this valley.

> *When will we meet again, sweetheart,*
> *When will we meet again?*
> *When the autumn leaves that fall from the trees*
> *Are green and spring up again.*

The name of the folk song comes back to me: 'The Unquiet Grave' sung by Joan Baez. Freya must have been singing about her dead brother.

I try to open my mouth to talk. I need to explain. I didn't put him in jail. I can't even remember what I said to the police. I was only six years old, for God's sake. What makes her so certain that her brother was innocent anyway? I feel my lips moving, quivering, like a fish wrenched out of water. But no words come out.

'It's a shame you can't talk, but that's one of the side effects of the plant. You know it grows wild in Spain, but you have a lovely specimen outside, here in your own garden. It goes by various names – *datura*, moonflower, devil's trumpets – and it has these white trumpet flowers, quite exotic-looking.' She talks as if she's giving a public lecture in a village hall or at a gardening show. 'But of course, it's deadly. *Datura* does have rather a bitter taste, but you probably thought I'd added a bit too much garlic to the stew.'

I can feel my eyes stretching wide with terror. My hand goes down to my stomach. What about the baby? Is it too late to make myself sick?

'Don't worry, I haven't given you a fatal dose.' She stops herself to take a closer look at me, almost studying me as if I'm one of her specimen plants. 'Do you remember that day when I found you upstairs in my house? I almost thought, for a moment, that you'd been rifling through my things and discovered who I really was – I have a file hidden away in my bedroom about my brother and the whole case, proving his innocence. But luckily you weren't there looking for that – it was evidence about the affair between Rich and Anna that you were after. You were consumed with jealousy. I suppose it was then that I began to think about the specifics of the plan.'

What does she want from me? It's not safe to be here, near her. I think back to the newspaper cuttings. Iain Hastings did have family. A mother and a father. A sister, yes. But I'm sure she wasn't called Freya. What was her name?

'And if you're wondering about how I found you here, it was Rich's tweet about leaving London. He mentioned coming to live in Europe's only semi-desert, to settle in a lush valley which was also the base of an eco-charity, Desert Shoots. A few clicks and I had you. But I've been watching you for a long time, Mia Banner – or should I say Gibson?'

It's a long time since I heard anyone use my real surname. I know I mustn't tell her that I'm pregnant. My mother died with a child inside her. I realize I will do anything to keep my baby safe.

'I got your address from the electoral register and moved just a few streets away. Sometimes, I'd watch you walking to school. As I followed you through the streets of Hackney, I fantasized about what I would do to you. Once I got so close – I stood behind you on a busy road – I think I could smell your body lotion – dewberry, wasn't it?'

I almost find myself nodding, until the horrific reality kicks in.

'I could have pushed you under a passing lorry and although I was tempted, I knew that wasn't right,' she continues. 'The death would be too easy and it would be reported as an accident. One day, I think it was lunchtime, I remember following you from the school while you chatted to a pretty girl with dark hair. It was clear you were fond of her. You smiled at her as you parted ways – you said you were going to have lunch in a local café. I felt I was going to explode. I had to get rid of the feelings of hatred towards you that were building up inside me. I was so consumed with anger that I shadowed the young girl with dark hair. When we reached a junction busy with traffic and crowded with people, I simply came up behind her and, while nobody was looking, gave her a gentle push. She fell forwards into the road and disappeared under the wheels of a bus. Almost immediately I felt better.' She smiles at the memory. 'Fresher, lighter, happier.'

The news that she was the one responsible for Emily Thomas's death almost stops my heart. Each word is like a small dagger pushed deep inside me. So Emily didn't kill herself because of her worries surrounding climate change, after all. And I had been wrong to blame myself for her death. All those moments when I questioned myself whether I'd said something to trigger her suicide. Those times in the middle of the night when I woke up wracked with feelings of guilt.

'When I learned that you were coming to Spain, I couldn't just let you disappear. There was a job going at Desert Shoots as a gardener – the pay was lousy, but I think the charity was grateful to have someone with my experience and enthusiasm. I gave up my job at the university to start a new life out here. It was a sacrifice, of course, but it was the least I could do for my brother. I didn't have a plan to begin with, apart from an idea that you had to suffer like my brother had suffered. All I knew was that I had to keep you close, so that when the opportunity arose I could act quickly. And when I heard Blanca talking about how her grandmother had killed herself here, in this house, well . . . you can imagine. And then when I learned about Anna, the situation was just too perfect. It was almost as if the stars had been aligned, like God – or Gaia – was looking down on me.'

She sounds insane, she *is* insane. She killed Emily Thomas, a girl who had a bright future ahead of her. But if she's related to that man – the man who killed my mother – she could do anything. Even if she says he was innocent, which I don't believe for one second. But then another thought hits me. She's *especially* dangerous if she thinks he's innocent.

I push myself up. The world around me is tipping on its side, like I'm on one of those rides at the fairground. I hold onto the table and try to focus. I need to get to the phone. It's over by the counter, charging. I stagger across the kitchen, grasping for anything that will give me some support. The edge of the table, the back of a chair, the flat surface of a wall which seems to be melting like ice cream. I try to take some deeper breaths, but my breathing seems to be slowing down, shallower. I can see Freya on the edge of my peripheral vision – she's just standing there, a look of amusement in her eyes, watching me.

Finally, I make it over to the counter. I reach out and take the phone in my hands. I press on the power button, but nothing happens. I hold my finger down. I let go. I press again, harder. Still nothing. I check the adaptor is in the plug. But the screen of the phone remains dark.

'You won't get anywhere with that old thing – it hasn't worked in years,' she says.

She walks over towards me and I flinch as if she's going to strike me.

'Don't worry, I'm not going to hurt you. You're going to do most of the work yourself.'

I support myself by the counter to stop myself from falling to the ground.

'You see, I've brought some other things with me.'

She picks up her duffel bag and extracts a pair of clean gardening gloves, which she puts on. She looks as though she could be readying herself for an afternoon on one of the vegetable terraces. She smiles in quiet satisfaction as she uses both of her hands to pull out a sealed, transparent plastic bag containing a large piece of crystal rock. Its surface is speckled with a dark red smear and on some of the more jagged edges there are strands of blonde hair.

'Everyone saw you the afternoon of the party, how you grabbed Anna's camera from her,' she says. 'You really hated her, didn't you? Enough to follow her up the crystal path to that olive grove. Oh yes, I saw you all right. I was there. I was following you, listening, and I know what you nearly did.

How you took a piece of rock – similar to this one – into your hand with the intention of smashing it over her head. And who could blame you after what she did – after what she said? It was unforgivable for Rich to share that information about your past with her. That – coming on top of the betrayal – was more than enough motive for murder.'

I look at the door, but it seems like a million miles away. I try to move my feet, but they feel like they belong to someone else.

'When I saw you with the rock, you gave me the idea of how to do it, how to kill her. Now – where's the best place to put this?' she asks herself as she takes the rock out of the plastic bag. The crystal glints in the summer sun, but the light also catches something else. Something that could be a piece of bloodied skull. 'It has to look as though you'd hidden it somewhere, obviously. I'll put it somewhere after you've gone, don't worry. And did you like my trick with the camera? After I killed Anna, I used her camera to take some photos of her dead body.'

I remember how, just before the police arrived at *La Casa de la Luz*, Freya left the house via the garden. She told me she had to go down to the river to check the flow of the water in the irrigation line.

'I hid the camera in the studio, but of course I could have sneaked into the house at any point – everyone leaves their doors open here.'

That's what Rich said the first night we arrived here. He said the village would be safe. Not like London, where my night-time ritual had involved a thorough checking of the locks on the door and windows. He said he would protect me. But he had failed. That failure was not just his, though. It was mine. It was my past that had come out of the

281

shadows. It was the horrors of my own early life which had been resurrected. Now that spectre is living, breathing and standing in front of me.

Freya is taking something else out of her bag now. A line of rope, which she loops around her arm. She looks up at the vaulted ceiling and studies the beams.

'Eucalyptus, I think,' she says. 'Plenty strong enough. And there's not much to you. By the way, if you're wondering why you can't move or talk, that's all down to the *datura*. You know I'm an expert on the medicinal properties of plants, right?'

I vaguely remember her talking to me about herbs and plants and their health benefits, but I think my mind had been elsewhere at the time.

'Anyway, *datura* has a number of physical effects on the body, so don't be surprised if you experience an abnormal heartbeat, dizziness, increased sweating, nausea, muscle cramps or spasms or whatever. But it's the mental effects that interest me more. In addition to confusion, delirium, depersonalization and feelings of paranoia, *datura* also brings about a state of high suggestibility.'

She unwinds the rope and runs her rough hands over it. She goes to get a chair and positions it beneath the beams.

'You know what I'm going to ask you to do, don't you?' she whispers.

I can almost feel myself nodding.

'And if you don't do it quite as willingly as I'd like, with the state you're in it won't be hard for me to make it look as though you've chosen to hang yourself. If the pathologists do test your blood, I'm going to leave some *datura* seeds in the pestle and mortar. Next to your suicide note, of course. They will assume you took something to ease you into death.'

She looks at me and laughs to herself, the kind of amused little laugh people make if they've done something stupid like put a carton of milk in the oven or a packet of teabags into the fridge.

'This morning, when I heard that Rich had confessed, I thought everything had been ruined. It wouldn't be right if he was the one who took the blame for Anna's death.' Then her face turns serious again. 'It has to be you. You have to die like my brother died. You have to take your life just as Iain took his life. If I'm questioned, I'll tell the police that you must have become fixated on how Blanca's grandmother died here, in this house.'

She goes over to the table and picks up a scrap of notepaper. She grabs a pen and walks towards me, then takes hold of my shoulders and guides me back to the table. She clears away the things.

'Don't worry – by the time the police arrive, I'll have wiped everything down. I'll tell Payton that I left you sleeping. That you seemed fine. After all, we know how those who commit suicide can be so good at pretending. Keeping up appearances and all that. Putting on a good show.' She places the paper in front of me but keeps hold of the pen. 'Your handwriting is likely to be a bit shaky, so why don't I help you with this? I think it's best we keep it short and to the point, don't you?' She wraps my fingers around the pen, no doubt to make sure my fingerprints are all over it, lifts my hand above the paper and then begins to write. Although I try to resist, there's nothing I can do. I feel like I'm a puppet and Freya is controlling my strings.

'*I couldn't forgive Anna for what she did, what she said. Not just for taking Rich away, but for telling me how they met. But now I can't live with what I've done. Sorry – Mia.*'

283

The scratchy handwriting bears only a faint resemblance to my own, but as Freya said, my state of mind is hardly conducive to neat calligraphy. She takes the pen from my hand. 'Once the police find this – and your body – Rich will tell them what the note means. They will understand that his confession was meaningless. After all, Rich has no memory of committing the crime – because he didn't. Although he'll be released from custody, I'm sure he'll continue to beat himself up about it all – he'll realize the part he played in driving you to kill Anna. But it will be you, Mia, who will be always known as a murderer. Just like my brother.'

She moves a chair underneath the beams, glancing up and down between floor and ceiling until she has the right spot. Quickly, expertly, as if she's done this a hundred times before, she fashions a noose. She climbs onto the chair and ties the rope around the beam, making sure it's secure. If I wasn't a prisoner in my own body I would either make a run for it or knock the chair away from her, so that she might hurt herself, but I still can't move. What can I do? I realize I'm helpless. I may not be buried in the ground but I feel as if I am. The air presses heavily on me. My lungs feel as though they are about to collapse. I'm slipping away. Will no one come to my rescue?

Freya looks around the room with banal satisfaction, as if she's pleased with the way she's cleaned the place. 'Okay, let's get this over with.'

She comes to stand behind me. I feel her touch me, a hand on each shoulder. She guides me slowly, as if I were a lost child. It seems to me as though I'm taking baby steps, shuffling along the floor as if this is one of my first attempts at walking. 'That's right, you're nearly there.'

We come to a stop by the chair. I look up at the line of rope attached to the beam. She takes hold of my arm and helps me step onto the chair. 'Your conscience is telling you that you're doing the right thing. After what you did to Anna, you can't carry on, you can't live with yourself.' I hold onto her arm. 'You took that rock and smashed it over her head – you killed her, Mia. How does it make you feel that you snuffed someone's life out, just as someone snatched your mother's life away all those years back? There's no going back for you now, is there? Here, let me help. Bend down and lower your head a little.'

She slips the noose around my neck and checks the rope.

'That's right, you're doing beautifully, Mia.' She stands back and looks at me with appreciation, as if the noose she's fitted around my neck were an exquisite string of pearls. 'Yes, just perfect.'

She smiles and moves forwards again to grip the edge of the chair. 'Don't be alarmed, don't try to fight. I promise you, it's for the best.'

She raises her right leg and kicks the chair away from me. The noise of it clattering to the floor startles me and suddenly, I'm back in my body again. How did I let this happen? Why didn't I fight back? I don't have any time to think as the noose tightens around my neck.

My fingers fly up to the rope, clawing away as the knot begins to squeeze the life out of me. I strike out in a desperate attempt to find something to hold onto, flailing, swinging around in the air. I feel like I'm a bird in a cage, fluttering wildly, conscious of the ineffectiveness of my actions. I'm aware of a guttural noise coming from deep within my throat. My face feels bloated, as if every last drop of blood is rushing to my head. I know what's coming. I know what's happening.

I'm going to die.

50

RICH

I jolt awake with a shock, my neck hurting, my mouth dry. I don't know where I am.

Then the horror of it all comes back to me.

I'm in a cell in San Mateo.

I've lost all sense of time: the police took away my phone – and the one belonging to Mia – and there are no windows here. I don't know whether it's night or day.

Memories begin to flood into my brain like drops of poison. The hallucinogenic nightmare of the ayahuasca ceremony. The sight of Mia up there in the olive grove. The news about Anna's murder. My torn hands. My bloodied, dirtied clothes. That horrible conversation with Mia. My confession to the police.

Estacio had informed me that a lawyer was on the way to see me, but I didn't see any point in waiting for them. And so I told him everything I could remember. How I must have killed Anna. How the drug must have warped my mind into thinking that she was someone else. I couldn't remember anything about taking photographs of Anna's body. Nor could I recall hiding her camera in the studio. However, I did tell him where he could find the clothes I'd worn on the night of the attack – I gave him the address of the flat in La Isleta; no doubt he'd be able to pick up traces of Anna's DNA on them. The police have also taken various swabs from me, evidence which I'm sure will settle the case.

I'm just hoping that my honesty – and the fact that I committed the crime while under the influence of a mind-altering drug – might go in my favour. Mia had mentioned diminished responsibility – does that defence, or its equivalent, exist here in Spain? I suppose I can ask the lawyer this question when he or she arrives.

Honesty is the one thing that I owe Mia too. I've let her down, badly. I've failed her on so many levels. She made me feel wanted, not so much in a sexual way; she made me feel good about myself because she allowed me to look after her. I protected her.

My mind goes back to the first time we met. It was at a drunken student party, hosted by my friend Joe. I'd taken the trouble to dress up like George Michael in his Wham! days, complete with fake tan and curly wig. Everyone thought that Joe had forgotten to pass on the message to me that it wasn't going to be fancy dress. When I stepped into the room – to find every other guest in normal clothes – the laughter exploded around me. I was made to feel the fool. I remember blushing so hard it felt as though my face was burning. But it hadn't been a mistake: I'd planned the whole thing.

Joe – who'd heard it from his girlfriend, Sophie – had told

me all about Mia and what had happened to her mother. Sophie, Mia's best friend at uni, had also informed Joe about how Mia had a thing for the underdog.

I'd watched her from the periphery of our little group, but she never seemed to notice me. I doubt she even knew my name. It was like I was invisible. And so I hatched a plan to get seen, to get *pitied*. The embarrassing incident would serve as a natural icebreaker. I'd sworn Joe to secrecy – who readily agreed. After all, both Joe and Sophie had something to lose: he didn't want his girlfriend to find out that he'd told me about Mia's past, while Sophie had promised Mia that she would never tell a soul about the murder of her mother.

I thought the whole thing was a bit of harmless fun. I always meant to tell Mia, but in those early days the moment never seemed right. And when Mia sat me down to tell me all about Iain Hastings and her mother's murder – and how that monster had buried her alive in a shallow grave – it felt wrong to reveal my silly prank. After leaving uni, we both lost touch with Joe and Sophie – after they split up, he went to work in America, and she became a volunteer in South America. And so there were no recriminations or reprisals.

Morphing from underdog to protector wasn't that hard. Once I'd got her attention it was just a case of constant reassurance, telling her that I would always look after her. I told her I was already an expert in martial arts, even though that wasn't true. However, I did take it up and soon I got my black belt. She told me that she loved the feel of my strong arms around her. She even asked me if I could kill someone. I hoped I'd given her the impression that it would be as easy as breaking a biscuit in two.

Well, now I have.

Maybe deep down Mia is happy I killed Anna. Perhaps I can tell her that I did it for her.

I'm suddenly struck by an overwhelming urge to speak to her, to hold her in my arms. The absence of her hurts like the loss of a limb or a piece of my heart cut from me. I want to whisper in her ear how sorry I am. I should never have accused her of killing Anna.

I wonder what she's doing now. I say her name quietly to myself. If only I could have my time with her again. How different everything would be. Will she wait for me while I'm in prison? When I come out I won't make the same mistakes again. This time I will really protect her. I'll never let her out of my sight, I'll watch her every move.

Then it comes to me. What could be more attractive to Mia than someone sent to prison? I would be a real underdog then. She'd be bound to feel sorry for me. Perhaps she'd even visit me. Then I could start to rebuild our relationship, and I could begin the transformation all over again.

I can feel my spirits lifting. I see myself travelling through a long, dark tunnel, at the end of which is a beacon of light.

The noise of the cell door opening brings me back to the present. A guard ushers in Estacio, the police officer who took down my confession. He looks me over with a world-weary eye, and it takes him a moment or so to speak. I'm fully prepared for what he has to tell me.

'Mr Ellis – you're free to go.'

I don't understand what he's saying to me. I can feel the skin on my forehead creasing, my eyes hardening.

'What?'

'I said that you're free to leave here.'

'But – I told you what happened. What I did. That I – I killed Anna.'

'You confessed to the crime, Mr Ellis. That's not the same thing as actually committing it.'

'But my hands – they were all cut up.'

'We have a witness – Jesús Huaman Rojas – who saw you trip and fall over some rock, cutting your hands and knees. As you know, the crystal is very sharp and—'

'But my clothes? You found them, right?'

'Yes, indeed. Thank you for directing us to the flat in La Isleta. We sent them off—'

'But they were covered in blood. What about the DNA samples? Surely you've—'

Estacio's phone buzzes in his pocket, but he ignores it. 'That's just it. My colleagues in the laboratory have assured me that there are no traces of Miss Fleming's blood on your jeans. Neither is there a speck of her blood on your shirt. Yes, it was spattered with blood, but that blood . . . was your own.'

51

MIA

I don't want to die. I don't want my baby to die.

I feel the emptiness stretch beneath me like a deep ocean. I thrash about as if I'm drowning. The rope cuts into my neck. My throat is closing, my eyes bulging. My tongue seems like it's swollen to twice its normal size, filling my mouth, blocking any last trace of air from entering my body. My head feels like it's so full of blood it's going to explode. Any moment now the world will begin to slip away and I will lose consciousness.

I hear a noise. I open my eyes and through a veil of tears I see a streak of colour and the blur of sudden movement. There's a scuffle of feet, the sound of raised voices. I can't believe it. There's someone here to help me, to rescue me. Everything I hear is muffled – like I'm listening to a conversation under water – but I can make out what they're saying.

It's a male voice. 'What the—?'

'I just came in from the garden side and found her. I was just trying to find a way to get her down,' says Freya.

Someone runs over to me. I feel them take me in my arms. But I still can't breathe.

'Mia. I've got you.' It's Rich. 'Quick – a knife! Freya, you need to find a knife – a sharp one. We need to cut her down.'

I want to tell him he can't trust her. That's she's the one who has done this to me. That she poisoned me with something. That she told me to step onto the chair. That she placed this noose around my neck. That she was trying to kill me. That she's Iain Hastings' sister. But I can't speak. Instead, when I open my mouth, all I can do is groan.

I hear footsteps and the rattle of the cutlery drawer. I see the glint of a blade reflected in the afternoon sunshine.

There's panic in Freya's voice. 'Rich – I thought you were being held at the police station? That you'd—'

'I'm fine – we need to save Mia,' he shouts. 'How long has she been like this?'

Freya remains silent as Rich continues to hold me, supporting the weight of my body, reducing the drag of gravity that threatens to pull me towards death.

'Freya – what the fuck! Why are you just standing there? What's wrong with you?'

I can feel his grip on me falter. I know Rich is strong, but how long can he continue to hold me like this?

'Give me the knife – Freya!'

The noose begins to tighten around my neck again.

There's a desperation in his voice. 'Why are you stepping away? Freya, please – you've got to help.'

I feel Rich's cheek against mine. He begins to whisper that he's sorry.

292

'Mia, I'm going to have to let you go, only for a moment or so,' he says. 'But trust me – I'm not going to let you die.'

He tries to support me as he bends down and rights the chair, but the noose tightens with each small movement. I begin to choke again. But then he guides my feet onto the chair. He tells me to try to stay still while he gets the knife. But my body is so weak that I can't stand up. I'm like a rag doll whose stuffing has been knocked out of her. I know that if I allow myself to drop too far the strangulation will start again. I manage to right myself for a second and take in a few gasps of air.

'Give me the knife!' screams Rich. I notice that his hands are covered in plasters, which are now stained red with what looks like his own blood. 'I need to cut her down.'

I see Freya take another step back. 'How do I . . . how do I know whether you're going to use the knife to cut her down? You might want to hurt her – or me. How do I know that you didn't do this?'

'What?'

'You might want to use the knife to kill her.'

'Are you out of your fucking mind?'

'Everyone has been saying it was you who killed Anna. Is that how you hurt your hands, during the attack on her?'

I want to scream and tell him that she's trying to trick him. He needs to know that it was Freya who murdered Anna. That she's dangerous. My fingers try to loosen the rope a little, but it still grips me like a medieval neck brace. As he takes a step towards her, she raises the knife.

'Get back – get away from me!' she says.

'Freya, I'm not going to hurt you – you must know that.' He tries to soften his voice in an effort to placate her. 'But we need to get Mia down from there. Look at her – she's nearly half-dead. If you're not going to give me that knife I'll get another one for myself. I know there's another one in—'

As Rich takes another step towards the drawer, Freya whips the knife out in a semi-circular sweep to prevent him from passing her. There's a change in Rich's face, an acknowledgement that he's not dealing with a woman who is simply afraid of him but one who wants to do him active harm. He takes a step back and catches sight of my suicide note. As he picks it up and scans it, he looks confused and, for a moment, gazes at me with horror as if I am the one responsible for Anna's death after all. But then his expression changes, and he assesses Freya with cold logic.

I feel my legs melting beneath me again. I'm not sure how long I'll be able to stand. And if I slip, the noose will begin to squeeze every last breath out of me again.

'Why won't you let me help her?' shouts Rich in frustration.

'Step back,' she says, raising the knife to the level of her face.

'Did Mia write that note?'

'Don't come any closer.'

Rich moves like the martial arts expert he is, quickly but with precision. He gives the impression he's going to lunge towards her but corrects himself and curves his body in the opposite direction. Freya stabs the air with the knife, but misjudges and misses, a split second of opportunity that Rich uses to his advantage. He grabs her wrist and pins it behind her back. She tries to struggle free, but he pushes her up against the kitchen unit and intensifies the pressure.

'What the f—'

'Drop the knife.'

'How do I know that—'

'Just drop it. Now!'

'You're hurting me.'

Rich takes hold of her head and smashes it down onto the work surface with a force that surprises me. As she falls to the floor, she drops the knife. Rich grabs it and stumbles over to me.

'I'm sorry – I'm so sorry, Mia,' he says.

He brings another chair and places it against mine. He bends over as he pauses for breath, then eases himself up onto the chair, using my body as a support.

'Stay still – that's right. Just another moment.'

He reaches up and begins to cut into the rope. As he does so, the noose tightens a little more around my throat, but a few seconds later I feel the tension loosen and I'm falling. Rich is forced to drop the knife as he takes hold of me and gently guides me down to the ground. His hands claw at my neck as he slips his fingers under the knot and frees me from the grip of the noose. The skin on my neck is stinging so badly it's as if I've been burned.

'There – you're free,' he says.

As I begin to cough – a great hacking cough that threatens to bring up my lungs – I feel the tears streaming down my face. I'm alive. I just hope my baby is too.

'What happened?' He takes a look at me and registers my fragility. 'Let me get you some water.' He passes Freya, who is still slumped on the floor.

I want to tell him everything – how Freya killed Anna, and how she was going to frame me for the crime – but I still can't speak.

He returns with a glass of water. I take a couple of small,

delicate sips. The water trickles down my throat like acid, but it begins to ease the coughing, and soon I begin to breathe normally.

'I-I didn't . . .' Speaking is like the slow draw of sandpaper across the back of my throat. 'It was her.'

'How – why?'

I shake my head. It's impossible for me to speak at length. It would take too many words to explain the dark tendrils that bind Freya and me together. I want to tell him about the poison – the *datura* – in the food. She said she hadn't given me a fatal dose, but how could I trust her? I want to tell him about what she made me do, but the muteness seals me off from him. I want to tell him that I'm pregnant, that I want to keep the baby, despite everything that's happened, but the idea of talking seems alien. Instead, it's Rich who begins to talk, about his regrets, his love for me, his need to be honest, and how the police released him because they could find no evidence linking him to Anna's murder.

'The blood that they found on my clothes wasn't Anna's – it was mine,' he says. 'They also took a statement from Jesús, the shaman who oversaw the ayahuasca ceremony, who said he saw me trip over and hurt myself. Apparently, he tried to help me, but I pushed him away and I went and slept by the side of the road. I suppose I must have put two and two together and made seven or something and so I confessed. Listen, I'm sorry I accused you of . . . of hurting Anna. But my head was so fucked up. I promise from now on, everything's going to be okay. We'll move back to London and I'm going to look after you and . . .'

Through my tears I see Freya easing herself up. I try to warn Rich, but I still can't speak. She's walking towards us and she's got something in her hand. I rasp something out, but it's just an unintelligible noise. He's so wrapped up talking about our future together that he can't see the look of panic and fear in my eyes. I reach out for him, but it's too late. As he turns his head, Freya strikes him with the heavy marble mortar. He looks startled, before his eyes close and he crashes down onto the floor.

She continues to walk towards me. I shuffle backwards on the ground like some kind of creature from the sea floor. I spot the knife lying over by the upturned chair. But Freya sees it too. As I make an awkward lunge towards it, she stamps on my outstretched hand. The pain forces my fingers into a claw. She grabs the knife and, as she moves towards me, her eyes seem to glitter as if she's possessed. But, instead of continuing in my direction, she turns back to Rich, prostrate and bleeding on the ground.

'Why did you have to go and complicate things?' she asks. Her tone is that of a mother talking to a child who has messed up his homework or brought back the wrong gym kit from school.

What's she going to do?

'You see, Mia – now I've got to make it look as though you killed him too. The police will piece together the evidence and think that you must have been possessed by a jealous rage that forced you to kill first Anna and then Rich. Once I've stabbed him, I'll place the knife in your hands to make sure your fingerprints are all over the murder weapon. And then you can take your own life.' She looks over at her duffel bag. 'Oh yes, I've got plenty of rope. It won't take me a minute.'

Despite everything Rich has done, I cannot let her kill him. And there's no way I will allow her to put another noose around my neck. I don't know whether it's the rush of adrenaline through my system or the experience of near death which has somehow lessened the effects of the *datura*, but the effect is like I've been shocked back to my senses: my body may have been weakened, but my mind feels sharp. Razor sharp. A fragment of that old Lorca quote comes back to me:

. . . *the dead are more alive than the dead of any other place in the world.*

I'm back in the ground again. In the dark. I've seen my mother murdered. I've been left to die in the dirt. I feel the fury I felt at the time and the fury I've felt burning over the years meld together and begin to rise within me.

I lie still, corpse-like, but I'm aware of what Freya is doing. It's like I'm watching her from above, almost from some spot on the ceiling.

She's standing over Rich, no doubt deciding where to strike: a stab to the heart or stomach, or a slash of the blade across the throat? She moves the knife from one gloved hand to the other and back again. Her fingers grip its base. She takes a step nearer and bends over Rich's body. She kneels down and raises the knife high in the air.

I try to wiggle my fingers and move them towards the edge of the rope. I want to grab it, wrap it tightly around my hands and strangle her to death. I see myself as her mirror image, a shadow in revolt. But then I realize I still can't move. I'm still paralysed.

Just as she's about to bring the knife down, just as she's about to strike, Rich shifts to one side, his lithe body moving like a snake. The movement unsteadies Freya and in that instant he rises up and grabs her hands. He presses down with such force that he cracks her bones, and wrenches the knife

298

from her fingers. She screams in agony and frustration. He is pure rage now, possessed by a kind of blood fury.

His voice splits the air. 'You're going to die for what you did to Anna – what you tried to do to Mia.'

Freya tries to speak but the onset of terror cuts off her words. 'But I—'

'You thought you'd knocked me out, when all you'd done was stun me. I lay there waiting for your next action, to see whether you'd actually try to kill me. Well, now it's your turn to suffer.'

He brings the knife up to her throat and presses the tip of the blade on her skin. A bead of blood glistens on her skin like a sinister jewel. With one cut she'd be dead. We could say – and it would be true to some extent – that Rich was acting in self-defence. After all, Freya had tried to kill me, she'd hit Rich over the head and was about to stab him to death. In fact, only a few moments ago, I would have murdered her myself, if I'd been physically able to do it. But now?

I think back to my mother, to that time when Iain Hastings had snuffed out her life and nearly ended my own. Time split into two parts: before and after the attack. I know that if we do this – if I allow this to happen – nothing will ever be the same again.

If Rich slits her throat, and Freya dies, what will my future look like? I see nothing but a seemingly infinite stretch of blackness, as dark and lonely as that shallow grave. The revelation comes to me as clear and hard as a piece of crystal.

I try to lift my hand to signal to Rich, but it lies there by my side like a dead thing.

I direct all my energy into my voice and, with all my strength, scream, 'Rich – no!'

He turns to me and freezes. He swipes her across the head, knocks her unconscious and then retrieves a length of rope, which he uses to tie her hands behind her back. As she lies there, her face almost a death mask, I study her features once more. It's then that her real name comes back to me.

Fiona.

52

RICH

I'm buoyed up by the fact that I saved Mia, and I feel as though I'm walking on air. I'll never forget the look in her eyes when I appeared in the house. She was gasping for air as the noose cut deep into her neck, her legs and arms moving like the tentacles of an octopus flung onto land. I went to grab her, to hold her, and in that moment it was as though all my sins were forgiven. I was her saviour, her protector. Of course, she was mine, too: by screaming those two words – 'Rich, no!' – she'd prevented me from killing Freya. And so we were united by an experience that would bind us together, forever.

I've been out of hospital for a few days now. Mia's still inside the soulless white cube of a building in Almería, where they've been treating her for the after-effects of *datura* poisoning and neck injuries sustained during Freya's attack. Mia had nearly died at the hands of Freya Watson, or the woman born Fiona Hastings; apparently, she changed her name by deed poll following her brother's suicide. But the doctors said they were pleased with the progress Mia was making and they were confident that she'd be discharged from hospital within the next fortnight.

I picture us together, probably not at *La Casa de la Luz*, which holds too many awful memories, but starting somewhere new. Perhaps in a city such as Seville or Malaga, or maybe even Madrid. Mia could get a job teaching at one of the prestigious English schools, and I would work as a solar power consultant. There's nothing to stop us from trying to live the green dream again. But I realize that if that's going to happen, I'm going to have to change. I'm going to have to be honest with Mia.

I rehearse the lines in my mind as I enter the hospital building. I say them to myself over and over again as I stand by the reception desk, nervously switching from foot to foot as I wait to be given the clearance to go up and see her. I'm twenty minutes early, but I can't stay away a moment longer. The stern-faced woman on the front desk puts the telephone back down and tells me, in heavily accented English, that the officer stationed outside Mia's room – 437 – says that my name's on the list of approved visitors and it's fine for me to go up. That's a good sign, I say to myself; perhaps my instincts are right, after all. I step into the lift and as it glides upwards through the modern steel and glass building, I feel my heart beating faster.

As I come out of the lift and walk down the unnaturally bright corridor towards Mia's room, I silently repeat the words to myself again, 'I need to be honest with you, Mia – totally honest.' I'm confident that I'm going to win her back, eventually. It might not be easy, I know that, and I'm prepared for some initial resistance. But the fact that I saved her must count for something, surely?

I find her room and give my name to the young *Guardia Civil* officer standing outside. He checks his iPad and nods for me to go inside. Mia's lying in bed, tubes attached to her body. She's looking pale, drawn, vulnerable. There's a ring of bandages around her neck, covering the wounds she suffered during the attack.

'I'm pleased you've come, Rich,' she says, in a voice that is weak, strained.

Her words give me hope.

'Do you want to sit down, there's something I need to say,' she adds, pushing herself up in the bed. She doesn't look at me.

I do as she says and sit in the white plastic chair by the bed.

'You must know that—'

I cut her off. 'Look at the state of you.' The sight of her, weakened, nearly broken, her eyes shadowed by dark circles, brings tears to my eyes. 'I'm so sorry, Mia. I should never have left you in that house. If I'd only been there, none of . . . none of this would have happened. What did the doctors say?'

'They're no longer worried about the *datura*. They gave me some kind of antidote, but the drugs and the sedatives have left me feeling a bit weird.'

'But you're going to be okay?'

'Yes, I'm going to be fine, but—'

'I don't think you need to worry about Freya, I mean Fiona Hastings. After she confessed, the police charged her with the murder of Anna and also the attempted murder of you. They've also been in touch with the authorities in England and she'll no doubt be charged with the murder of Emily Thomas too. It's likely that she'll spend the rest of—'

'I don't want to talk about her.' She's looking at me now, but her eyes are full of fire.

'Sorry, I shouldn't have mentioned her name. But she'll be locked up for a very long time and I doubt she'll ever—'

'Rich, I need you to listen to me. I really need to tell you that—'

'I know – and that's why – if we're going to . . . if we're going to move forward, I think I need to be completely honest with you. We need a clean slate if—'

'What do you mean?'

'I want to make another go of it.'

She looks shocked. 'After everything you—'

I jump in. 'I know I was a prick. I should never have cheated on you. I should never have lied.' I realize I'm talking too quickly, the words spilling over one another. 'But I realize now that if we're to have any chance of happiness, I need to get everything out into the open. I need to tell you – I'm sure you already know – but I need to spell it out. I – I never loved Anna. She was just an infatuation . . . a dangerous obsession. My head was all over the place. I didn't know what I was doing, but I know now that I never really loved Anna – it was just a fling, a stupid, meaningless fling.'

She stares at me as if I'm invisible.

'Just hear me out.' I take a deep breath and try to slow down. 'I had a lot of time to think when I was held at the police station. And you know I was prepared to go to prison for what I . . . what I thought I'd done.'

'But—'

304

'I'll never forgive myself for what I let happen to you. I should have been there, with you. You nearly died, Mia. And I want to make sure nothing like this ever happens to you again. You know I'll always look after you, protect you.'

'Rich—'

'I've decided I've got to be honest with you – we've got to be honest with one another.' I take her clammy hand, but it just lies in my palm like a dead fish. I'm convinced what I'm about to say is the right thing to do. She'll respect me for it. 'Do you remember how we met?'

'What's that got to do with—'

'Just hear me out. It was at that cheesy Eighties' theme party. I came as George Michael in his Wham! days.' I laugh at the memory. 'And you took pity on me because I was the only one there in fancy dress.'

'I don't—'

If I don't say it now, I'll never say it. 'I planned the whole thing. You see, Sophie told Joe all about you – about your mum, about your past.'

She's gone as rigid as a marble statue. Like something you see in a museum.

'And I thought it would be a good way to break the ice between us.' The words come too quickly again. Is there a manic edge to my voice? 'You see, I'd always fancied you, but you never seemed to notice me, even though I was always hanging around. But I think it did the trick. Because we got on so well, right from the first moment, and then—'

What's wrong with her? Why is she looking at me like this?

'And I told you that I would protect you. I even took up martial arts because of you.'

Her voice is so cold it could freeze the air. 'You mean you didn't – you didn't know how to do that before you met me?'

'I wanted to protect you. So you'd never come to any harm again. After what happened to you as a girl, after what you saw happen to your mother, you needed someone who would—'

'Get out.'

The words threaten to choke me just like that piece of rope that nearly killed her.

'You don't mean that—'

'I said – get the fuck out.'

'That poison's still in your body. You're still in shock after—'

She raises her voice. 'If you don't leave, I'll shout for the officer outside and—'

'Mia.'

The words hiss out of her, 'I never want to see you again.'

I squeeze her hand a little harder, just to show her how much I love her. 'But we've got a wonderful future ahead of us. We could have children—'

Her face is full of hate now. It must be the drugs in her system.

'I allowed you to visit me so I could tell you that it's over. I wanted today to be the last time I ever saw you.'

I apply a little more pressure. 'You don't mean that, you can't possibly . . .'

She tries to move away from me, but there's nowhere for her to go. She's in bed, wired up to various machines. It's the best place for her, for now. But I'll soon get her out of here. She needs to be cared for.

By me.

53

MIA

As I wrench my hand away, I see Rich for what he really is: a delusional obsessive. The hatred I feel for him now is pure, glacial. I smile with the knowledge that I've kept from him. I'm going to have his child. When I came round in the hospital that's the first thing I asked. Was my baby still alive? The hot tears spilled down my face when they told me that yes, it was fine, I was going to be a mother. I'm determined the child will be nothing like Rich. I will give it all the love he never had. Rich will never know about his son or daughter.

And to think that I used to trust him, that once I'd loved him. I think back to that first meeting. The way he blushed when everyone laughed at him for walking into the party dressed like an uncool George Michael. The way he seemed to understand me. The way he listened to me when, later in our relationship, I told him all about what Iain Hastings had done to me and my mother. It had been bad enough discovering, through Anna, about how he'd betrayed me. Even though I'd believed him when he told me that he never brought me to Spain with the intention of taking up with Anna again, hearing this latest revelation confirms that our life together has been nothing but a sham.

At that Eighties' party, he'd already known about my past. He'd manipulated me like some kind of living doll.

I take a deep breath and try to say the words without emotion. I make sure I stare him straight in the eyes. 'Can't you understand – I never want to see you again.'

'But – I saved you. If it hadn't been for me, Freya – Fiona – would have killed you.'

'I know, and I'm grateful, but I can't be beholden to you forever for that.'

'Grateful? Is that all you've got to say? That you're fucking grateful?'

As I flinch away from him, he tries to rein in his temper. 'I'm sorry, Mia – I shouldn't have said that. I know you're still in a delicate condition, you're still recuperating. You're not in your right mind.'

I draw myself up as best I can in my bed. 'I've never felt more certain of anything in my life.' I clear my throat again. 'I've made some plans and you're not part of them.'

Lying in this hospital bed, wired up to various tubes, I've done nothing but think about the future and what I want from it. I've had to stop myself from revisiting that awful day at *La Casa de la Luz* and what Freya, or Fiona, nearly did to me. I've had to banish the sound of her soft voice coaxing me onto that chair. I've had to erase the feeling of the rope cutting into my neck, the pressure behind my eyes as the blood rushed to my head.

I learned as a girl – after my mother's murder and the attempt on my own life – that I had to concentrate on what was coming, not what had gone before. Now, it's time to go forwards again. That's the only way to survive. After making sure that Blanca has secured her mother's remains – I can't let her down, not after everything that's happened – I'll go back to London and rent my own place, ready for the birth. Rich will never know that I have a child. After the baby is born, I'll get another job, at a different school. I'll never contact him again. To begin with, I may not thrive, but I know I'll be fine. *We'll* be fine. I'm determined that I will look back on my time living off grid in this wild place in southern Spain not just with sadness but with a sense of having learnt something. About life. About myself.

I feel the need to explain myself to Rich, for one last time.

'The problem is that you never stopped seeing me as the girl left to die in that shallow grave.' I take another deep breath. 'But the reality is, I'm no longer a victim, Rich. I only thought I was. And I let you treat me as one. I don't need you any more. In fact, I know I'll be better off without you.'

As he stands from the chair, it seems as though my candour is finally working. I've no idea what he's thinking because his face is expressionless.

'Oh, by the way,' he says in a casual manner, 'do you remember that both Anna and Freya Watson – or rather Fiona Hastings – thought Iain Hastings was innocent?'

I wince when I hear her name again. I don't want to think about her, about what she did to me.

'Well, I've got proof now that they were right. It wasn't him – it wasn't Iain Hastings who killed your mother, who left you to die,' he continues. 'I looked at the evidence compiled by Anna, who as you know wanted to do a story about it. And it seems as though it was one huge fuck-up on many levels. A few years back, Freya – Fiona – tried to appeal to have the case reopened, but it was dismissed. It seems that's when she started to . . . to plot her revenge.'

I turn my head to one side in an effort not to hear.

'Hastings was a vulnerable young man – I suppose today we'd say he was on the autistic spectrum. One of the main pieces of evidence that suggests this was a miscarriage of justice is the testimony from the policewoman who was involved in the original honey trap operation, an operation that secured a confession from Hastings. But that confession would never have stood up in court – it was inadmissible. The policewoman says Iain Hastings should never have been arrested. But that's not all. It seems as though the description you gave of the man you saw was altered by a corrupt officer so that it was a match with Hastings. I suppose the police must have been desperate to try to close the case. But they got the wrong man.'

He pauses as he examines the effect his cruel words are having on me. I can't allow myself to be convinced by him – surely he's lashing out because he's unable to accept it's over. But what if he's telling the truth?

I can feel my face crumbling, the tears welling in my eyes. I do everything I can to stop them from falling. I don't want to give him the pleasure of watching me cry.

'You know what that means, don't you?' he whispers. He pauses, enjoying watching my pain. 'It means that the killer is still out there, and he's waiting for you.'

He walks across the hospital room, but stops by the door and turns. His face looks odd, twisted, and there's a glint of something approaching satisfaction in his eyes.

'You'll always need me to protect you,' he says. 'You'll never be safe unless I'm with you, right by your side.'

Acknowledgements

Like Mia and Rich I moved from London to live in an eco-village in Almería, in south-east Spain. Unlike them, my six-year stay in a beautiful Andalucían valley did not involve murder. My first thanks must go to my many friends there: you know who you are. Next an apology for taking this paradise and using it as a setting for a psychological thriller. While many of the details of life in this Spanish eco-village are authentic, Val Verde is a figment of my dark imagination, as is the nearby town of San Mateo.

During the research for *Murder Grove* I consulted a number of books, and for those interested in learning more about the province of Almería and Spanish culture, I'd recommend *South From Granada* by Gerald Brenan; *Ghosts of Spain: Travels Through a Country's Hidden Past* by Giles Tremlett; *The Spanish Civil War* by Paul Preston; *Federico García Lorca* by Ian Gibson; and *Flamingos In The Desert: Exploring Almería* by Kevin Borman. For those interested in the work of the Association for the Recovery of Historical Memory (ARMH), check out their website: memoriahistorica.org.es. I'd also recommend the fascinating Storyville documentary, *Facing Franco's Crimes: The Silence of Others*.

At Aitken Alexander I'd like to say a huge thank you to my agent and friend, Clare Alexander, as well as Lesley Thorne, Lisa Baker, Laura Otal, Jazz Adamson, Anna Hall, Amy St Johnson and Joaquim Fernandes.

At HarperCollins I'd like to acknowledge the input of my fabulous editor and fellow author Phoebe Morgan, who saw the potential in an early draft of *Murder Grove* and made it a hundred times better. I'd also like to thank Julia Wisdom, Kimberley Young, Jaime Witcomb, Sophie Churcher, Lizz Burrell, Ann Bissell, copy editor Sarah Bance, and the designer of the fabulous cover, Claire Ward.

Thanks too to Ana Castillo, who read the book in manuscript form and corrected my rusty Spanish, and to consultant psychiatrist Dr Susan Shaw. And as always the biggest thank you goes to Marcus Field, with whom I lived in the Spanish eco-village and who came out alive.

Five strangers.
One horrific event.
What did they see?

When disgraced journalist Jen Hunter witnesses a horrific murder-suicide on Hampstead Heath one February alongside four strangers, she is compelled to find out what really happened that day. They all saw Daniel kill his girlfriend, Vicky – but can they trust their own memories?

Jen's best friend, Bex, is worried about her. She knows Jen hasn't always been the most stable of women. She knows about the lies. She knows why Jen lost her job at the paper.

As the lives of the Parliament Hill witnesses begin to unravel, one thing becomes clear: there is more to what happened that day on the heath.

And Jen needs to find out the truth – even at a cost.

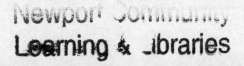